LOOKS LIKE RAIN

JOHN AND ROBIN DICKSON SERIES IN TEXAS MUSIC
*Sponsored by the Center for Texas Music History,
Texas State University*
Jason Mellard, General Editor

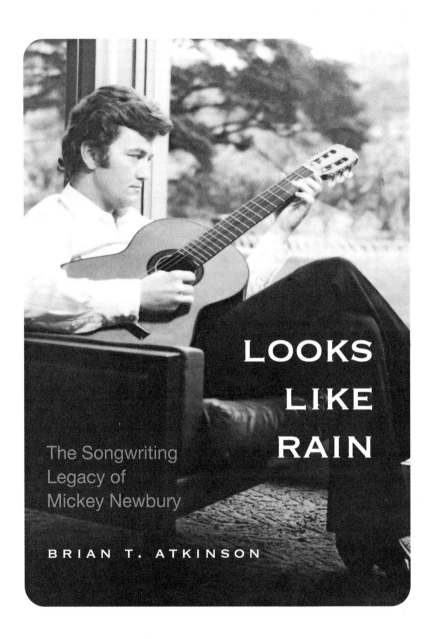

LOOKS
LIKE
RAIN

The Songwriting
Legacy of
Mickey Newbury

BRIAN T. ATKINSON

TEXAS A&M UNIVERSITY PRESS • COLLEGE STATION

Library of Congress Control Number: 2020950814

ISBN-13: 978-1-62349-926-6 (cloth)
ISBN-13: 978-1-62349-927-3 (ebook)

*All photos are courtesy of the Newbury family archives
unless otherwise indicated.*

For my mother,
Ruthanne Atkinson,
who loves great singers

CONTENTS

Chorus: Heaven Help the Child

Interlude: A Song for Susan

Verse: I Came to Hear the Music

Verse: Sweet Memories

Chorus: A Long Road Home

Larry Gatlin: Mickey Newbury told me, "Larry, you don't have enough great songs yet to do an album, but you will in a year. Sing your own songs. It's gonna break your heart for three and a half minutes every night for the next forty years if you have a hit record sung by someone else." He was right. Mickey wouldn't bow to Nashville commercialism. They turned him a cold ass, and he did the same to them. I've done the same. I'm ranked fourth all-time in most number one records by a singer-songwriter written alone. Merle Haggard, Marty Robbins, and Hank Williams Jr. are ahead of me. I'm tied for fourth with Dolly Parton, but I'm not in the Nashville Songwriters Hall of Fame.[1] I've had songs recorded by Barbra Streisand, Elvis Presley, and Roy Orbison, but I didn't do it the Nashville way.

Mickey Newbury unquestionably shaped my career. My brothers and I have had an incredible career. I screwed things up with drugs and booze thirty years ago, but we own it. I ended up doing *The Tonight Show* with my brothers and sang at the Astrodome. Many people in Nashville didn't like that I did it my way. Stinky Poobury, who you'd call Mickey Newbury, is one reason. We all want to be popular but not by doing it when it doesn't touch your soul. I can't wait to read a book about Mickey Newbury. He deserves a book because people don't know about him. Mickey was an intriguing little shit, a weird little duck. God, I loved him. He was a great songwriter who championed my cause. Mickey wrote that line in "Sweet Memories": "Night after night the past slips in and gathers all my sleep." Phew. What a true wordsmith.

Don McLean: Mickey struck me as a very generous and thoughtful soul. I liked his beautiful voice, and he was very kind to me. I was shocked when I heard he had died because he seemed like a young man. I wish I had not been in such a hurry in those days. I might have gotten to know him better. Mickey deserves a biography. He deserves attention paid to his artistry.[2]

Acknowledgments

As always, very special thanks to the John and Robin Dickson Series in Texas Music, Thom Lemmons and everyone at Texas A&M University Press, and Dickson series editor Jason Mellard for making this idea a reality. Special thanks to Jenni Finlay, who serves as partner in all my crimes. Thank you to my parents, Ted and Ruthanne Atkinson, who continue offering endless encouragement. Additionally, big thanks to the *Houston Chronicle*'s Andrew Dansby and Newbury champion Jerry David DeCicca for connecting several essential dots. Ditto Jonny Fritz, Owsley Manier, Gretchen Peters, Jennifer Warnes, and all the songwriters who whispered behind my back on their own accord to open doors to interview opportunities. Importantly, Joe Ziemer's *Mickey Newbury: Crystal & Stone* (AuthorHouse, 2004) served as an endless research source.

Biggest thank you to all the singers and songwriters, players, producers, and industry veterans who offered their time to talk about Mickey Newbury. Some I wished to interview remained unavailable despite several requests, but nearly everyone jumped at the chance. A quick note about projects colliding: Jenni and I were producing *The Messenger: A Tribute to Ray Wylie Hubbard* for our Eight 30 Records as *Looks Like Rain* came together. We deliberately scheduled a few recording sessions for the album at Wayne Moss's Cinderella Sound Studio (where Mickey Newbury recorded essential early material). We were greatly pleased to discover how welcoming Wayne, Dee, and engineer Robert Lucas were. Most importantly, thank you to Susan Newbury Oakley, Chris Newbury, and all Mickey Newbury's family for their cooperation as this book came together.

Finally, thanks to my personal advisory board: Janet Berger, Ginger Bloomer, Mary Keating Bruton, Lefty and Lil (and their late great sister, Banjo Finlay), Chris Fullerton and Lindsay Preston, Mike and Michelle Grimes, Matt Harlan, David Holmes and Mary

Miken Holmes, Jennifer Menchen, Tamara Saviano, Troy Schoenfelder, Sean Tracey, and Marianna Whitney. Additionally, thanks to everyone who has supported our Squeaky String Productions, Eight 30 Records, Burgundy Red Films, Barefoot Recording, and Catfish Concerts. We're forever grateful.

1940: Mickey Newbury is born on May 19 in Houston, Texas.

1954: Newbury joins the teenage doo-wop group the Embers as a backup singer.

1956: The Embers sign a recording contract with Mercury Records.

1959: Newbury joins the air force and serves three years overseas in London, England.

1963: Newbury returns to Houston and works on shrimp boats in Galveston.

1964: Newbury performs at Houston-area folk clubs and signs a publishing deal with Nashville's Acuff-Rose.

1966: Newbury moves from Houston to Nashville.

Don Gibson and Tom Jones both record "Funny Familiar Forgotten Feelings."

Newbury befriends future outlaw country icon Kris Kristofferson.

1967: Jerry Lee Lewis records Newbury's "Just Dropped In (To See What Condition My Condition Was In)."

Roy Orbison records "Here Comes the Rain, Baby."

1968: Newbury records his debut album, *Harlequin Melodies* (RCA Victor Records).

The First Edition record "Just Dropped In (To See What Condition My Condition Was In)."

Newbury makes history when four artists top different charts with his songs.

1969: Newbury records *Looks Like Rain* (Mercury Records) at Wayne Moss's Cinderella Sound Studio.

Mickey Newbury and New Christy Minstrels singer Susan Pack are married.

The Newburys move onto their houseboat on Old Hickory Lake.

Jerry Lee Lewis records "She Even Woke Me Up to Say Good-bye."

Johnny Darrell records "Why You Been Gone So Long."

1970: Newbury debuts "An American Trilogy" at the Bitter End West in West Hollywood, California.

Ray Charles records "Sweet Memories" and "Good Morning, Dear."

1971: Newbury releases "An American Trilogy" on *Frisco Mabel Joy* (Elektra Records).

Joan Baez records "San Francisco Mabel Joy," "33rd of August," and "Angeline."

1972: Buffy Sainte-Marie cuts "Sweet Memories."

Newbury and Townes Van Zandt cowrite "Mister Can't You See."

1973: Newbury releases his third album recorded at Cinderella Sound, *Heaven Help the Child* (Elektra).

Newbury's early albums inspire Waylon Jennings, Willie Nelson, and more toward the Nashville fringe.

Jennings records "San Francisco Mabel Joy."

Newbury records *Live at Montezuma Hall* (Elektra Records).

Newbury wins the Tokyo World Song Festival with "Heaven Help the Child."

1974: The Newburys leave Nashville and move with their young son to Oregon.

1975: Newbury releases his final major label album (*Lovers*, Elektra).

1977: Waylon Jennings salutes Newbury with "Luckenbach, Texas (Back to the Basics of Love)."

Newbury begins a three-album run on Acuff-Rose's Hickory Records with *Rusty Tracks*.

1980s: Newbury is inducted into the Nashville Songwriters Hall of Fame.

John Denver records "San Francisco Mabel Joy."

Nick Cave and the Bad Seeds record "Weeping Annaleah" (retitled "Sleeping Annaleah").

B. B. King records "You've Always Got the Blues."

Newbury bookends a creatively slow decade with the albums *After All These Years* and *In a New Age*.

1990s: Newbury meets Jack Williams at Joe Gilchrist's Frank Brown Songwriters Festival at the Flora-Bama.

He releases *Nights When I Am Sane* on Winter Harvest Records (1994).

He plays his first house concert with Jack Williams in Columbia, South Carolina (1995).

He performs live throughout the country more than ever during this decade.

He founds Mountain Retreat Records.

He triumphantly performs at the Kerrville Folk Festival despite severe emphysema in 1997.

The Big Lebowski (1998) features "Just Dropped In (To See What Condition My Condition Was In)."

2000s: Newbury's creative resurgence begins with *Stories from the Silver Moon Cafe* (2000).

Newbury releases his late-career high-water mark, *A Long Road Home* (2002).

Mickey Newbury dies in Springfield, Oregon, on September 29, 2002.

LOOKS LIKE RAIN

Mickey Newbury simply sang with soul ablaze. After all, the long-time Nashville-based singer, a criminally overlooked artist during his lifetime but his generation's most successful songwriter, owned an otherworldly tenor demanding fire from deepest depths. "Mickey was as close to Roy Orbison as anyone at the time with his operatic voice," iconic songwriter Rodney Crowell says. "'San Francisco Mabel Joy' is a beautifully composed short story with a wonderful melody and unexpected twists and turns. Mickey had a real knack for high-stakes drama. He practically screams at the end of his original recording of 'San Francisco Mabel Joy.'" "Mickey no doubt had one of the best voices I've ever heard," echoes Americana all-star Steve Earle. "Larry Gatlin was emulating Mickey Newbury with the way he sang and phrased, an operatic style but with gravel in his voice."[1]

Newbury, born in Houston, Texas, on May 19, 1940, revolutionized the songwriting form. He backed every vibrant vignette ("Cortelia Clark") and sharp story song ("Heaven Help the Child") with his transcendent voice ("The Last Question (In the Dead of the Night)"). Composed lyrics with unforeseen depth ("Frisco Depot," "So Sad") and boundless ambition ("33rd of August," "The Future's Not What It Used to Be"). He made music his way ("Why You Been Gone So Long"). Period. Future outlaw country beacons—Johnny Cash, Guy Clark, Ray Wylie Hubbard, Waylon Jennings, Kris Kristofferson, Willie Nelson, Billy Joe Shaver, and Townes Van Zandt—immediately took notice and eagerly mapped his creative blueprint. They became legends.

Mickey Newbury did not.

He should have been.

Mickey Newbury should have been a legend. After all, he single-handedly birthed modern country music's most influential movement. "Texans like to remind the rest of the world how Willie Nelson, Waylon Jennings, David Allan Coe, and a few other mavericks reinvented—or destroyed—the country music formula and

gained independence from the controlling powers in Nashville,"
Texas Music magazine said in 2011. "Yet if you're looking for the
beginning of the outlaw movement—a seminal event that forever
changed the studio system and the tight production control the
money men in Nashville had maintained over writers, performers, and the sound for years—one need look no further than the
day Mickey Newbury, the man Nashville disc jockey Ralph Emery
dubbed 'the first hippie cowboy,' was released from his RCA recording deal. Things would never be the same."[2]

Newbury flipped Nashville upside down ("She Even Woke Me
Up to Say Goodbye") and turned the town around ("An American
Trilogy"). He consistently followed his muse no matter the cost
and forsook every dangling diamond the industry offered without
compromise. Case in point: "Interludes," as he called them. Newbury frequently tightly tied together concept albums with ambient
noises—birds and crickets, cars and trains, wind and rain—enhanc-
ing story lines. Somehow his decidedly unconventional and uncom-
mercial approach resonated with singers across genres. Newbury
became the only songwriter to notch hit songs on four different
charts in the same year when Kenny Rogers and the First Edition
("Just Dropped In (To See What Condition My Condition Was In)"),
Andy Williams ("Sweet Memories"), Solomon Burke ("Time Is a
Thief"), and Eddy Arnold ("Here Comes the Rain, Baby") climbed
ranks with his songs in 1968. He burned brighter than any other in
Music City for nearly a decade. Hundreds and hundreds recorded
his songs.

"Mickey was like a North Star, a fixed point of class, dignity, and
intelligence high above a sea of Nashville slime," said late singer-
songwriter Steve Young ("Seven Bridges Road," "Lonesome, On'ry
and Mean"). "My hunch is he simply didn't belong in the sorry
Nashville system. He was for real, and he told them the truth. I
doubt he thought in terms of career. He probably only thought
about the quality of the music."[3] Newbury's early high-water mark
albums—*Looks Like Rain* (Mercury Records, 1969), *Frisco Mabel
Joy* (Elektra Records, 1971), and *Heaven Help the Child* (Elektra,
1973)—alone prove the point. "There was something very special
about Mickey," says iconic folksinger Joan Baez. "He wrote end-
lessly beautiful heart-wrenching, sad scores of music."[4]

Newbury's songs overcrowded radio. Several superstars such as Engelbert Humperdinck ("Funny Familiar Forgotten Feelings"), Jerry Lee Lewis ("She Even Woke Me Up to Say Goodbye"), Buffy Sainte-Marie ("Mister, Can't You See"), Roy Orbison ("Good Morning, Dear"), and Elvis Presley ("An American Trilogy") turned his songs into hits. Ray Charles, the Everly Brothers, Jerry Reed, Nelson, Orbison, Rosanne Cash, Dottie West, Don Gibson, and dozens more made his stunning "Sweet Memories" a standard. These few examples only scratch the surface. Newbury's music soundtracked lives worldwide. "Mickey Newbury expanded the songwriting form, opening up country narrative and story-telling songs," folk and bluegrass pioneer Peter Rowan says. "He's one of the greats."[5]

Humility effortlessly charted his journey. "[Newbury] is so not taken with himself and knows what he deserves and what he would like to have happen in this life, but he's so un-self-assuming," says celebrated *Rolling Stone* writer and biographer Ben Fong-Torres early in the radio documentary *Mickey Newbury: An American Treasure*. "He seems to care more for his fans, family, fellow writers, and performers in the industry than he cares about himself. I think of him not just when his music is on but when any music is on. When music really touches you then you think about someone like Mickey, a truly singular talent and person."[5]

Additionally, Newbury served as a mentor to several aspiring songwriters. He steered Guy Clark, Kris Kristofferson, and Townes Van Zandt toward Nashville. Then they did the same for Rodney Crowell and Steve Earle. "I didn't have to go through back doors," Van Zandt once said. "I just came straight down the freeway because of Mickey. It was hard trying to explain the sound of Mickey's voice and the guitar on a good night at the same time. You can't do it. It's like from outer space. I've heard about people trying to explain a color to a blind person like Helen Keller. There's no way to do it."[6] "[Mickey Newbury] was one of the best writers we've ever had," Willie Nelson says directly, "and one of the best friends."[7] Jennings went further by cementing his legacy in the song "Luckenbach, Texas (Back to the Basics of Love)": "Between Hank Williams' pain songs and Newbury's train songs and 'Blue Eyes Cryin' in the Rain' / Out in Luckenbach, Texas, ain't nobody feeling no pain."[8]

Newbury ultimately soured with dealing business in Nashville despite his considerable success. "I would sooner be robbed by a fan than a company," he once said. "The fan may be broke and have but one choice. There is no excuse for the way the songwriter is robbed by everyone from the record company to the broadcaster by the pure bottom line: greed. I have been so disappointed in so very many people over the years who became corrupted by money and betrayed a trust. I might do that too if I were fast enough, but I'm not. Everybody sued [Newbury's publisher] Acuff-Rose over unpaid royalties: Don Gibson, John Loudermilk, Roy Orbison. Wesley Rose screwed just about everybody."[9] Music Row's unchallenged songwriting king packed up as his powers peaked and moved his wife and young child away from the city in the midseventies.

Newbury quietly continued writing timeless albums—*The Sailor* (1979), *Lulled by the Moonlight* (1996), *Stories from the Silver Moon Cafe* (2000), and his final masterwork, *A Long Road Home* (2002), among them—in rural Oregon well into his later years. They made little impact even as the notoriously reticent performer finally took to the road. However, Newbury's sway on outlaw country—and on all popular modern music, really—remains undeniable. "Mickey [was] a natural phenomenon and a songbird," Kristofferson says. "He [came] out with amazing words and music."[10] Jennings emphatically doubled down. "Somebody said, 'I don't like country music,'" he famously told anyone who would listen. "I always answer, 'Have you ever heard Mickey Newbury sing?' Because you're not American if you don't like to hear Mickey Newbury."[11]

Kris Kristofferson

We would still be writing songs if we had never made a penny. Guy Clark, Townes Van Zandt, and Mickey Newbury were in it for the love of music. The heart in the music attracted me to Nashville at the time. Everybody lived for the music if they weren't making any money, or if they were like Jack Clement, who had written and produced a lot of hits.[1] Just hanging out with Mickey Newbury was one of the biggest influences on me. I remember when Johnny Cash's television show came to Nashville. We got to meet these people like Joni Mitchell and James Taylor, who felt the same way about music. I'd go out to California, and Joni Mitchell would take me around to meet all these people who loved hearing something good almost as much as writing it themselves.[2]

I called Mickey one time in Nashville after I'd out been roaring all night. He said, "Can you make it to the hotel? If you can get here in fifteen minutes, Roger Miller's gonna fly us to Los Angeles. He wants to hear '[Me and] Bobby McGee.'" I got there as they were leaving and rode with Mickey and Roger in the scariest ride ever. Roger was driving up on the curb, but we made it to the plane in record time. We flew out to California, and we'd wait for Roger to come back every night so we could pitch him our songs. He didn't want to hear them. He went right to bed every night. Mickey and I did this for three days. We were on the way to leave the house on the third day and Roger said, "Mickey says you got a good song, 'Me and Bobby McGee.'" He had me sing it to him right there and recorded it when he got to Nashville. I think Mickey and me are singing background on Roger's record.[3]

"Freedom is just another word" seems truer the older I get. It makes me think about the time when my apartment got robbed and everything was gone. I was disowned by my family. I owed money to a hospital and I owed my wife five hundred dollars a month for child support. I thought, I'm losing my job. I hadn't any money, I hadn't anything going for me, but it was liberating. I was in the filthy Evangeline Motel like something out of *Psycho* just sitting there with this neon Jesus outside the door in the swamps outside Lafayette, Louisiana. I thought, Fuck. I'm on the bottom. Can't go any lower. I drove my car to the airport, left it there, and never went back to get it. Went to Nashville and called Mickey Newbury, and I told him I'd just got fired. He said, "Great. Johnny Cash is shooting a new TV show. Come up, and we can pitch him some songs." They cut three of my songs, and they were hits. I never had to go back to work again.[4]

Mickey meant so much to me as a songwriter. I'm sure I never would have written "Me and Bobby McGee" or "Sunday Morning Coming Down" if I had never met Mickey. I probably heard ["San Francisco Mabel Joy"] more than any human being on the planet. Newbury [was] such a resolute artist. He [was] never going to compromise his vision of what the whole picture should be. Perhaps he [was] a visitor from outer space. I learned more about songwriting from Mickey Newbury than anybody. [His] simple lyrics and simple melodies worked to break your heart. He was my hero and still is.[5]

Legendary singer-songwriter **Kris Kristofferson** has written hit songs recorded by stars such as Janis Joplin ("Me and Bobby McGee"), Johnny Cash ("Sunday Morning Coming Down"), George Jones ("Why Me, Lord?"), and Waylon Jennings ("To Beat the Devil").

VERSE: JUST DROPPED IN

ERIC TAYLOR

Mickey started the Houston songwriting community in the sixties. Houston was a writers' town. Mickey intrigued me because he could sing a story and didn't talk much in between. I was quite infatuated with what he was doing when I saw him live. We have such different songs and approaches to writing, but I was infatuated with the storytelling on "San Francisco Mabel Joy" and "Just Dropped In (To See What Condition My Condition Was In)" and the distance he put between the songs in his set. Also, his ability to cover great songs like "Shenandoah" made me cry. Mickey was not afraid to take chances with his voice. Sometimes his voice would be almost operatic. You couldn't escape him if you heard him sing live. He took you from one end of the world to the other.

My relationship with him was come and go for good and bad. He could be the nicest, sweetest guy in the world. He could also really tighten up and become mean spirited. Very rarely did I ever see him do that, but we were all that. [Being underappreciated] happens to the best of us. I don't think I'm very well recognized. Mickey and I became closer in his final years. I watched him walk out onstage, hook up his oxygen machine, and he sounded like Mickey Newbury. His legacy is he didn't give up. He sang right up until the last days. A promoter friend put Mickey in the hospital in Florida, got him out several times, and took him to the final shows. Mickey played with an oxygen tank sitting beside him and absolutely blew them away. He was a very rare man.[1]

Eric Taylor's literate songwriting helped define Texas folk music during the sixties and seventies. His albums *Shameless Love* (1981), *Eric Taylor* (1995), and *Scuffletown* (2001) were key inspirations to several Lone Star State singer-songwriters including Lyle Lovett.

JERRY NEWBURY

Mickey was overweight until he was sixteen years old, but then he slimmed up and started getting interested in music. Kenny Rogers would come over to the house. Mickey had an old Pontiac when he got started in the music business and lived in the damn car. He'd go to Nashville and sleep in the car because that's all he had. Of course, we never knew that. He came home one time and told me. I had an office supply business, so I gave him a credit card and said, "Use it when you need it." He hardly ever used it except in an occasional emergency. Then he caught his first break, made his first album, and was discovered by Acuff-Rose. They all thought he was gonna be a superstar. He showed me a contract for a million dollars once from a record label wanting him to tour, but he didn't want to tour. He didn't want anything holding him back from writing songs. He enjoyed going on the road later in life.

Mickey was dating a girl in south Houston, and she had been dating this guy in a gang. They caught Mickey out there with a friend one day and almost beat him to death. There were five or six guys. They were trying to get him to cower down, but he wasn't having it. The main guy hit him as hard as he could and knocked him down. That's when they all jumped him and nearly beat him to death. His friend said, "First time I got hit, I fell down and never moved. I got out of it pretty well." Mickey was all swollen and beat up when he came home. That's when he went into the air force.

Mickey later worked at a restaurant called the Balinese Room in Galveston [which hosted famous entertainers such as Bob Hope, the Marx Brothers, and Frank Sinatra]. The restaurant was way out on the seawall at the very end of the pier. There was gambling down there because it was so far out, and they knew they could clean everything up before anyone got down there to raid them. Mickey would walk around and sing in what sounded like a different language. I don't know how he did it. Somebody asked him what language he was singing in one time and he said, "Portuguese." Mickey was funny as hell and would keep you laughing all the time.

Townes Van Zandt used to come over to the house on weekends to play music. Mickey and Townes were real close and loved each other. I heard Townes before anybody. His music didn't appeal to me then, but now I think he's a genius. Don Williams would come over to the house and sing. I met so many people like that when we were kids before they were anything. Don Williams had that hat on the first time he came over, and that's all he ever wore onstage. I'd think, That guy and his hat, but he could sing. In fact, he credited Mickey with how he learned how to write and phrase.

Acuff-Rose gave Mickey an office when he moved to Nashville, but I don't know that he went in. I went there one time, and Mickey showed me around. Roy Orbison was there, and we talked for a while. I asked, "Hey, Roy, do you have any albums in your car?" Unfortunately, he didn't. Mickey was living on a houseboat out on Old Hickory Lake. Those guys would come to see him, ride around on the lake, and sing music. In fact, Ricky Nelson came out to the houseboat one day. Then Mickey bought a hundred-year-old log cabin. I think that's the first place he and Susan lived besides the houseboat. Kenny had introduced them, and Mickey fell in love.

Mickey stayed married to Susan until he died. She came from Oregon. I think that's why they moved there and bought a log cabin overlooking the big river. Most of their kids were born in Oregon. Mickey told me that they couldn't stay in the log cabin longer because it was too dangerous. He thought Susan or the kids might have a wreck going down that mountain. They ended up buying a little farm in Springfield. That's where he stayed until he died. I carried my mother out there many times, but Mickey was on the road all the time at that point. He ended up down at the Flora-Bama later in his career. He loved it there and had gone to school in Perdido, Florida, when he was in the air force. He would still go out on tour even after he got sick and had oxygen. I asked him one time what changed. "I just never enjoyed performing when I was younger," he said. "You should have done that thirty years before," I said. "You could've made a fortune."

People from every genre recorded his songs. Etta James, Bobby "Blue" Bland, B. B. King, Willie Nelson, Andy Williams. Mickey was really impressed with Ray Charles doing his song "Sweet Memories." Mickey loved Ray Charles. He was one of our heroes when we were in high school. You know, Mickey won the Tokyo World Song Festival in 1973. He was on the plane with the Jackson Five and saw all these people out on the tarmac as the plane started landing. He tried to find a way out the back. He thought they were all there for the Jackson Five. He got off the plane and they were all hollering, "Newbury. Newbury." Pretty cool. I'm proud of his career and how much people loved him.[2]

Jerry Newbury is Mickey Newbury's younger brother. He lives in Texas.

GEORGE ENSLE

I discovered Mickey Newbury through my guitar teacher, who also introduced me to Townes Van Zandt, Guy Clark, and the Sand Mountain Coffee House folk scene in Houston in 1962. I was taking lessons from this teacher when I was fourteen years old. He showed me Mickey's song "She Even Woke Me Up to Say Goodbye" during a lesson around 1963. Then I heard "San Francisco Mabel Joy" and "An American Trilogy." Mickey had an amazing melodic sense and was a great storyteller. I especially appreciated his storytelling.

Sand Mountain was the centerpiece for folk music in Houston. John Carrick's mother owned the coffeehouse when I started there in 1967, but I didn't really run with John. I think John was a wild character. The Jester Lounge was in the same area, but it was on the way out when Sand Mountain was coming to the fore. Guy was living upstairs from Sand Mountain with his first wife [folksinger Susan Spaw] and working on Martin guitars and Volkswagens. I got a chance to see John Lomax and Lightnin' Hopkins perform at the Jewish community center, but Sand Mountain was the place for folksingers. Don Sanders was a sardonic humorist folksinger. He gave me my first booking there.

I ran around with Eric Taylor and Vince Bell. We were a generation behind Guy and Townes, who were about six years older than us. Townes was so poetic. He blew everybody out of the water. Blaze Foley ended up in that scene, but he was pretty iconoclastic, a wrecking ball and inconsistent. Sand Mountain back then was a folk community. Townes was doing old folk songs like "Ballad of Ira Hayes" and "Old Shep." Don Sanders did Bob Dylan. Guy did Kris Kristofferson, but we mostly sang our own songs. We were burning the candles at both ends with the songwriting.

Sand Mountain was an old-school folkie place with no alcohol. Then the Old Quarter and Anderson Fair came about. Anderson Fair was just a little fifteen-by-forty-foot-long shotgun room. The Old Quarter was a hardcore place by this cop shop and a transient hotel called the De George. Guy got the character for his song "Let Him Roll" from this guy Sinbad at the De George who was an ex-merchant marine character and drank white port wine. I started opening for Mance Lipscomb at the Old Quarter and then got my own night. Billy Joe Shaver, Townes, and Guy would play there regularly. I think Mickey Newbury had already moved to Nashville by then and was pretty well established. Steve Earle and Rodney Crowell played at the Old Quarter. Rodney Crowell came in and was playing Beatles songs. We were so full of ourselves. We said, "What is this kid doing in here playing Beatles songs?"[3]

George Ensle was a regular performer on the Houston folk club circuit when he was a teenager in the sixties. He met fellow songwriters such as Guy Clark, Townes Van Zandt, and Jerry Jeff Walker performing together at venues such as the Sand Mountain Coffee House.

JOHN CARRICK

Mickey was a nice guy and a beautiful man. All the girls were crazy about him. He had that voice and style and was pretty mesmerizing. We were hippies and experimenting with different things, but he dressed more conservatively. He would wear sports coats with blue jeans, which was not so common in that circle. My mom really liked him. He was polite without being a square. Mickey showed up and occasionally played Sand Mountain, but he wasn't a regular like Guy Clark, Townes Van Zandt, and Jerry Jeff Walker. He seemed more business savvy than the rest who got famous. He was already recording demos to sell.

Sand Mountain was a stop for anyone playing on the road. Janis Joplin played there three times. We had a futuristic mural [on our back wall] painted by Larry Schacht, who later became famous as the guy who made the [poisoned] Kool-Aid in Jonestown [which cult leader Jim Jones served to his followers in a mass murder–suicide in 1978]. Larry was a Lamar High School graduate and a great blues player. Anyway, after a while time came to change that mural and a guy named Charlie Sims painted the songwriters [Clark, Newbury, Sanders, Van Zandt, and Walker] on there. I don't remember whose idea it was, but once the concept was there mom and I picked out who was gonna be on the mural. Most musicians have an egotistical side, so I'm sure they were delighted to be up there.[4]

John Carrick cofounded the iconic Houston venue Sand Mountain Coffee House with his mother, Corrine "Ma" Carrick, and his business partner Steve Gladson.

JOHN NOVA LOMAX

The two main thoroughfares in the neighborhood where Mickey Newbury grew up in Houston are Fulton Street and Irvington Street. Drive up either and you see really solid street names. Three are Frisco, Melbourne, and Joyce. I wonder if that was in Newbury's mind when he wrote "San Francisco Mabel Joy." Mickey's boyhood home is still standing in the Lindale Park neighborhood, and the home is much less nice than the next neighborhood. His was a very narrow street with ditches and nowhere to park. Lindale Park looks very suburban with ranch houses and huge yards. The Mexicans moved in after the white folks moved out. Newbury was always on the outside looking in.

Guy Clark and Townes Van Zandt used to see my grandfather [legendary ethnomusicologist] Alan Lomax sing at the Houston Folklore Society. I remember Guy telling me my grandfather would be onstage singing "Nine Pound Hammer" and slamming an ax into a chunk of wood while he was singing. "Man, I was on acid and there were these wood chips flying around everywhere," he said. "Your grandfather was up there singing 'this nine pound hammer.' It was so intense, Nova." Mickey was a different part of the same strand. Guy certainly went to those gatherings, but I don't know if Mickey ever did. The Houston Folklore Society was unique because they were exposing people to real blues in an intimate setting as opposed to just singing protest songs off records.

Mickey was like John the Baptist to the scene. Mickey and Willie Nelson were both here from 1959 to 1961. Willie wrote his best songs then, and that was right when Newbury was coming up. Mickey's such an odd figure for me as a Houston music historian to fit into everything. He was never that commercially successful like Kenny Rogers. He didn't really leave many memories behind as a gigging Houston artist, but he also seemed to have been a very proud Houstonian. He doesn't get enough credit for being the spiritual godfather to Townes, Guy, and Steve Earle.

Houston erases everything. Anderson Fair stopped accepting new talent before I became music editor at the *Houston Press*. Hayes Carll came up around Houston, and I don't think he's ever played Anderson Fair. He played shrimper bars in Bolivar [Peninsula, near Galveston]. You would think that Anderson Fair would see this guy who [Old Quarter Acoustic Cafe owner] Wrecks Bell approves, adopt him, and have him play in Houston. They never did. Anderson Fair became a supper club and sealed itself off in this cul-de-sac where they just have the same people come. They were going to shows and having sex with each other in the seventies. It became very insular and inbred and that's still the way it is. That killed the whole thing that Mickey helped start. Houston doesn't have any reputation as a music hub because nobody cares to preserve any of this shit.[5]

Longtime *Houston Press* music editor **John Nova Lomax** currently writes for *Texas Monthly*.

RAY WYLIE HUBBARD

Mickey probably influenced everybody in Texas. I played "San Francisco Mabel Joy" over and over again when it came out. The song is epic Shakespearean storytelling. "She Even Woke Me Up to Say Goodbye" also had that quality. Mickey's songs were very tragic and sad, but there was a beauty about them because they were so well written. Mickey was the master of tragic story songs. The folk circuit in the sixties was the Rubaiyat in Dallas, Castle Creek in Austin, and Sand Mountain in Houston, where the foundation was folk music and original songs. Townes Van Zandt and Guy Clark were in Houston, Michael [Martin] Murphey was in Dallas, and Allen Damron was in Austin. Willie Nelson hit right after that folk thing, so they opened up the Texas Opry House and the progressive country scare happened.

We were on our way to play the Tractor Tavern in Seattle many years later when Mickey lived in Oregon. "Mickey Newbury heard you were playing the Tractor," somebody said, "and he wants to know if you want to have a cup of coffee on the way." We got to his house in Springfield, and he had a cool little place like a cedar cabin. He had his oxygen tank and was on a funky old couch there with blankets, near a coffee table and a couple of guitars. We sat and talked for a while, and he said, "Sing me [Hubbard's song] 'The Messenger.'" I went, "Really, you know that song?" He gave me his nylon-string guitar, and I played the song for him. He said, "Man, I really dig that song. I'm getting ready to do a new record. Here's one I wrote." He played a song and then he said, "Okay, let's go outside. I need to smoke a cigarette." We went out back and he lit up. I really respect that he took the time to have a songwriter-to-songwriter moment.[6]

Ray Wylie Hubbard has transformed from court jester of seventies outlaw country in Texas into the state's most sage and sober mystical songwriter. *The Messenger: The Songwriting Legacy of Ray Wylie Hubbard* (Texas A&M University Press, 2019) tells his story.

SAM BAKER

Mickey was always part of the Texas landscape growing up. He came from the generation who were all so lyrical. Mickey had one foot more in the commercial side than Guy Clark and Townes Van Zandt, but he was the real deal, a writer who wasn't afraid. His production was interesting. I think his internal compass said, "This is the art I want to produce." He stayed pretty true to that, which could have been even harder because he was such a success as a commercial writer. I don't feel like he compromised ever. I always felt like Mickey was authentic.

He was more ambiguous as a Texas lyricist than Townes and Guy. Mickey had the voice and vernacular, but his writing was not Texas. He didn't place his songs geographically the way Townes and Guy did. He wrote the story he saw and let the chips fall where they may. Lyrics were vital. I don't think he threw away lines. He was meticulous and wasn't a writer who took shortcuts. I think people overlook him because his songs flow so nicely. Nothing really stands out as, "Yeah, I just need that line to rhyme." He was conscientious as a lyricist. I have one speed, and it's pretty slow. Mickey was different. Look at Shaver, Townes, Guy, me, even Willie. There's a distinct grittiness with Guy, Shaver, Townes, and me. You listen and wonder if it's a train wreck. Mickey had magnificent command of his voice. He was a real musician.

Listen to "Just Dropped In." Kenny Rogers and the First Edition's version and Mickey's are two completely different pieces. The song was an interesting piece for radio, but listen to Mickey's version with the strings. He does that moan in "Just Dropped In" and leans closer to Blind Willie Johnson, who was one of my heroes, too. Mickey had a certain authenticity that I deeply admire. How in the world was "Just Dropped In" a radio hit? The lyrics are so beautiful. They follow a subconscious line. Most pop songs show a pretty conscious recognition of something that's easy to grasp. Man, there is nothing easy in that song. The connecting line is an emotional, subconscious line. I think at our time in our cultural evolution people found that very valuable.

Mickey was pretty clear about his art. He wasn't afraid to do what he believed his art should be. Guy, Townes, and Willie were real artists. They all had an internal gyroscope that said, "This is what I wanna say. This is how I wanna say it." That's an artist's job. Otherwise, you're in a consumer production mode. Mickey had an internal calibration that said, "I will not rest until this is the way I want it." There was an interview with Paul Simon where he said he wished he had taken more time to rewrite his early songs with Art Garfunkel. Look, that's Paul Simon, who's another writing hero. I think Mickey always took the time. He got songs the w ay he wanted them. Mickey Newbury was always beautiful.[7]

Sam Baker writes sharp ("Say Grace") and sparse ("Juarez") songs that are as poetic as Mickey Newbury's in their lyrical economy.

HAROLD F. EGGERS JR.

I was sitting in my Acuff-Rose office in Nashville one day and could hear everybody talking. Mickey coming in felt like Elvis visiting.

There were twenty people surrounding him. I could tell people loved Mickey. Mickey was very confident, but he wasn't arrogant. I leaned over and said, "Hey, Mickey. I worked with Townes Van Zandt for years." "Let's go to your office." We talked for almost two hours. "I don't know what's wrong with this town," he said. "Townes is too good a writer." I asked Mickey if it was true that he used to sleep in his car outside the Acuff-Rose office. "Oh yeah," he said. "I did. Mr. Rose said, 'Wow. You're one of the few people who actually shows up.'"

Mickey felt he could get Townes a publishing deal because of his position in Nashville. Mr. Rose said, "Mickey, I just don't hear it." Mickey got real mad. "What do you mean, you don't hear it? You kidding?" He said Townes was a modern-day Hank Williams, who had been with Acuff-Rose. Mickey was very frustrated and went all over town trying to get Townes a deal. Everyone turned him down. Townes getting together with Jack Clement was all Mickey's work. Mickey respected Townes. Mickey won an award once and called Townes. "We both won," he said. "You're the one I've learned the most from." They had so much admiration for each other and had written a couple of songs together. Buffy Sainte-Marie had the big recording with their song "Mister Can't You See." Townes was staying with Guy and Susanna at the time.

You would hear stories about how Mickey was dangerous. He carried guns in his holster. You didn't mess with Mickey because those guns would come out. Townes used to tell me that Houston cops were the most dangerous cops in America. They'd kill you and throw you in the bayou. Mickey was soft spoken and quiet, but I'd tell Townes, "Lean forward and reach down toward his boots and see what happens." I never did because I didn't want to get shot. Townes had his own ways of letting me know who was dangerous. Mickey was.

We stopped by Mickey's farmhouse in Oregon in the later years on tour. "Hey, Townes," Mickey said. "You wanna hear something?" He played something and then they went right into a song they were making up right there. Man, you should have heard how beautiful it sounded with those two voices. I ran outside to get my recorder. "Hey," I said, "would you guys do that song again?" They both laughed. "The song flew in and flew out," Mickey said. "It ain't coming back." Townes used to always call Guy and Susanna and sing a new song when he wrote it to get their approval. He did the same with Mickey Newbury. Townes didn't reach out to anyone else about his songs.

Townes and Mickey both did Farm Aid one year. We walked into the dressing room, and Mickey and Townes joked about the old days in Houston. Then they talked about who would die first. "Hey, H," Townes said when Mickey walked out to go onstage. "He looks pretty bad. I don't think he's gonna live too long." I thought, You're saying this, Townes? I mean, let's get a mirror. They laughed about dying, but I think they both worried about each other's lives. I remember shaking hands with Mickey. He was frail. Townes was always frail.

Townes wouldn't have evolved in the music business if Mickey hadn't brought him to Nashville. Guy and Townes didn't have a clue about the music business. Mickey was the catalyst for them moving to Nashville. Townes said Mickey was treated like an ambassador when he would introduce him around town. I think that's why it bothered Mickey so much that Nashville rejected him. They had a camaraderie. Townes told me one time that he wanted to do an album with Mickey. Mickey said the same separately. Man, they would have made a hell of an album.[8]

Harold F. Eggers Jr. served as Townes Van Zandt's business partner and road manager for nearly two decades. His book *My Years with Townes Van Zandt* (2019) chronicles that time.

GUY CLARK

Townes and I wound up in Nashville because of Mickey Newbury. I was in Los Angeles, and I got a publishing deal. The publisher said, "Where do you want to live?" Susanna and I decided on Nashville because we knew Newbury. We stayed on Mickey's houseboat for three weeks when we first got here. Mickey was a giant help. I'd be in the middle of figuring out what to do about song or record contracts, and he'd hand me his Elektra Records contract and say, "Here's what mine says." I got the hang of it right quick being pretty smart and a lawyer's son. The first thing I did was rewrite Mickey's contract in my own handwriting and send it to RCA. They offered me a job instead of a record deal.

When I got my record deal with RCA, I made a whole record with the producer they assigned to me, and by the end of it I said, "Man, if you put this record out I will change my name. I will not be associated." Rodney [Crowell] heard what was happening, heard the record, and said, "Guy, this ain't you. Let me help you. We'll get another budget, go into the studio with Neil Wilburn and beg, borrow, and steal pickers and studio time until we get something you can live with."

This was not an easy decision to make. I had no power, other than to put my foot down and scream, which is what I did. Rodney, Neil Wilburn, and I stole the master tapes out of the vault at RCA, went to some studio, remixed and overdubbed some things, cut some things, and recorded some new things. There it was: *Old No. 1*. You really couldn't argue with it when we were done. They were great songs. *Playboy* magazine reviewed mine in the same issue as Willie Nelson's *Red Headed Stranger*. My review was better than his. Willie recovered.[9]

Iconic tunesmith **Guy Clark** helped define country music in the seventies with songs recorded by the Highwaymen ("Desperados Waiting for a Train"), Ricky Skaggs ("Heartbroke"), and Jerry Jeff Walker ("L. A. Freeway").

VERSE:
LOOKS LIKE
RAIN

BOBBY BARE

Mickey Newbury would sit down, grab a guitar, and sing in Bob Beckham's office at Columbine Music in Nashville. Everybody wanted to hear Mickey sing "Sweet Memories." He sure could put himself into that one. Magical. Also, he was a good-looking guy with all this good-looking hair. It was a treat to watch him sing. Songwriters like Harlan Howard and Hank Cochran couldn't play guitar very well, and they were not very good singers. Mickey Newbury could do both. Everybody was a Mickey Newbury fan. Everybody. You mention Mickey Newbury, and everybody would say, "Yeah." He was unusual, a deep songwriter who could sing his ass off and play that gut-string guitar.

I produced [Newbury's *Rusty Tracks*, Hickory Records, 1977]. The songs I produced were pretty bare. He would have all these crazy, off-the-wall ideas, and we'd do what we could. He'd come up with some ideas that were hard to implement, but we did. We put a lot of thought into it and finished the album with all the trains and music in between. We had Larry Gatlin come in to do harmonies. I think Acuff-Rose's Wesley Rose was managing him. He turned it in to Wesley, and I don't know what he did. He whacked it up by using pieces from one song and put them on another.

Mickey could sing the alphabet and make you like it. I loved "Poison Red Berries," "Sweet Memories," and "An American Trilogy." Mickey should have been a monumental [success], but he was his own worst enemy. He always needed money. Wesley Rose would get him a record deal, but Mickey always wanted money. He wouldn't compromise and do what somebody else wanted. He was pretty strange, but you had to love him. You never knew what would happen. One day he showed up with a big diamond he was trying to sell. I went out to see Mickey, Susan, and the kids in Oregon years later when I was driving through Eugene. Their house was a nice enough place out in the boonies, and Mickey was just lying around. He seemed to be all right with it.[1]

Bobby Bare has earned the distinction of being country music's finest songcatcher over the past half century. He introduced several legendary songwriters including Cowboy Jack Clement, Harlan Howard, Mickey Newbury, and Billy Joe Shaver by recording their songs.

WAYNE MOSS

Mickey Newbury and I became good friends. He wanted to use my studio Cinderella Sound and have me to produce him. I said, "You have great ideas, man. You don't need a producer. You just need a studio." He got Dennis Lindy to produce him, but it always reverted back to the way Mickey wanted anyway. He would argue. "Now, I want to run the voices through a Leslie [speaker]. I want this. I want that." You either had to do it Mickey's way or end up in a big argument. I'd seen him get into nearly knock-down, drag-out fights. If you said something wouldn't work, he'd argue with you until he got it the way he wanted it, which obviously worked very well. I didn't want to argue. I said, "Hey, man, I'll do whatever you tell me to do." Mickey had very specific ideas.

Mickey wanted crickets on one song. I said, "Let's go get some." We went to a bait shop, bought a container of crickets, and brought them back to the studio. We put a microphone in front of them, but they wouldn't chirp. He said, "Well, maybe they need to be in a dark place." I said, "Okay." I put them in my echo chamber. They still wouldn't chirp. He said, "Let me go adjust the mike." He went to the echo chamber, opened the container, and dumped the crickets all over the floor. Well, I don't use those chambers anymore. I still have crickets in there today.

Mickey wanted rain and train sounds on his albums. We took those sounds from a Mystic Moods [Orchestra] album on vinyl for background. We tried recording our own rain and thunder, but it didn't work out so well. Mickey had a lot of good ideas like running background voices through a Leslie, which has a "wah-wah-wah" Doppler effect like a tremolo when four or six voices are run through. The sound pans from left to right, a real spacey effect to add to voices. Mickey was famous for overdubbing things and turning them down real low behind his vocal, which stood way out front.

Charlie McCoy knew exactly what he wanted to do in the studio, but some young hopefuls who come through here don't have a clue. They need producers. Bob Dylan was like that. You'd say, "Bob, what do you want to do?" He'd say, "Well, what do you think?" He had to be produced. Dylan wanted input from everybody. "Do what you feel." That's what we did on [Dylan's landmark 1966 album] *Blonde on Blonde*, and that worked out pretty well for him. These weren't his visions, though. They were the visions of the musicians he hired, who were Charlie McCoy and the Escorts.

Cinderella is my two-car garage. The studio has always been a fascination for me. I picked the brains of every engineer in Nashville. "What's that microphone for? What kind of speakers are those?" I got a lot of information from Bill Vandervort and Bill Porter at RCA. The echo chambers that Mickey put the crickets in were designed after the RCA echo chamber. The guy who designed it said that if he could do it over he'd make them a third larger. So, I made mine a third larger than RCA. Some of those echoes you hear on Newbury's records are the result. You put a signal in a vocal to a speaker in one corner of the echo chamber and a microphone in the opposing corner. The chamber has no two parallel walls. So, anywhere the sound hits it bounces off.

Mickey was highly praised and got critical acclaim. Every time he put a record out he'd get an offer from another label, and he would double his price. They would pay it. He went through several labels. He was very sought after. Gretchen Peters came in here recently because she wanted to use the same studio and microphone and everything that Newbury did. Linda Ronstadt did many vocals from our bathroom. Not that it makes much difference. We used a German microphone called the U-67 Telefunken, which has a tremendous frequency response from zero to where you can't even hear it. Anything that you put into it reproduces. They're very expensive, about ten grand each.

Mickey was very famous within the music community. Your peers are your best critics. I found that to be true with [Moss's band] Area Code 615. We had a full-page ad in *Rolling Stone*. The label Polydor ended up dropping us, but we got nominated for Best Contemporary Instrumental Group of the Year against Henry Mancini and Blood, Sweat and Tears, who won that year. We still got a Grammy nomination [for their self-titled debut in 1969] even though the label didn't have enough faith in us to do a third album. The same was true with Newbury within the business. I guess the Elvis cut of "An American Trilogy" was the biggest thing he had going for him. I was tickled with "American Trilogy" when we were recording the song, but I didn't know how far it was gonna go depending on music industry politics. Elvis did the song almost note for note like Mickey did on his record. Mickey was very influential. I enjoyed every minute recording with him.[2]

Legendary session player and engineer **Wayne Moss** recorded with Joan Baez, Bob Dylan, Waylon Jennings, Roy Orbison, Dolly Parton, Linda Ronstadt, and several others before founding Cinderella Sound outside Nashville in Madison, Tennessee, more than a half century ago.

CHARLIE MCCOY

Mickey had some crazy ideas about sound effects when we did *Looks Like Rain* at Cinderella. He was thinking way outside the box and put crickets out in the echo chamber. I'd known Mickey because he'd come to a session I was playing where an artist was doing his song. I met a lot of writers that way. I was very impressed with his songs. He had a different approach than the standard Nashville songwriters. I knew Johnny Darrell's version of Mickey's "Why You Been Gone So Long" and then heard "Sweet Memories." Such a great song. I was drawn to the melody and the way it was put together. The lyrics were great.

I did the bulk of my fourteen albums for Monument Records at Cinderella. I have forty-two solo albums, and many songs were done there, too. In fact, I helped them build the studio. We had a rock band in the sixties, and Wayne Moss said, "You know what? We ought to build a studio and have a publishing company." All the guys in the band chipped in and we helped him put it together. I was there for the first note ever recorded there. Wayne and I go way back, and we're still great friends. Now, I've wintered in Florida the past twenty-one years, so I'm not in Nashville now, but we return on April 1 and I have a session booked at Cinderella on April 3. I do what I want there. [Engineer] Robert [Lucas] and I work well together, and they have that Flickinger [recording] board that always sounds great.

I loved Newbury's vocals because he had so much emotion. We'd become pretty good friends by the time we recorded *Looks Like Rain*. I'd see him around town all the time. His songs were fresh and different from Nashville then, and he had some great musical ideas. As a studio musician for fifty-eight years, we're taught that the producer and the artist are always right. Some people come in with ideas that are crazy, but Mickey's were great. One day someone had left the door open to an echo chamber before I went in to overdub harmonica. I'm hearing this noise in the background every time I play. It sounded like a woman screaming. I said, "Wayne, there's something in the echo chamber. Do you hear what I hear?" He said, "No, what is it?" I started to play and stopped real quick. He said, "Oh my gosh, something's in the echo chamber." There was a kitten in there. The volume was so high. The kitten was crying for mercy every time I played harmonica.

I didn't hang out much because I was busy when we did *Looks Like Rain*. That was my peak as a session player. I was doing three hundred–plus sessions a year, but I'd see Mickey at events. He was often at one of the restaurants down on Music Row where the session guys hung out. I was fortunate to be working all the time. It was a blessing to work with such great artists and play on great records. The floodgates really opened after I was bandleader for the sessions on Dylan's *Blonde on Blonde*. A whole lot more musicians got to work because Dylan did that album in Nashville. There was such a demand for the original Nashville A-team guys so there was plenty of need for new people to come in, more singers and more engineers. We called it the Dylan Explosion.

We have [legendary drummer] Kenny Buttrey's drum set in the back room at Cinderella. He played those drums on Dylan's *Blonde on Blonde*, *John Wesley Harding*, *Nashville Skyline*, and *Self Portrait*. When Dylan's producer Bob Johnston got the job with Columbia Records and moved to New York, he said, "If you ever come to New York, I'll get you Broadway tickets." So, I was going to New York and called him and said, "Okay, I'm in town. How about my tickets?" He said, "No problem. By the way, I'm recording Bob Dylan this afternoon. I wish you'd come by and meet him." "Okay." I went over and met Dylan. He said, "Hey, I'm getting ready to do another song. Why don't you grab that guitar over there and play on it." The song was "Desolation Row" from *Highway 61 Revisited.*

There was no comparison between Dylan and Newbury in the studio. Dylan didn't know the answer to "hello." Mickey was a great communicator. He was one of us southern boys. Dylan was out in space somewhere. I was session leader, so I'm the middleman between the artist, the producer, the musicians, and the engineer. Dylan would play the song. I'd walk over and say, "Bob, what if we did this or do that?" His answer was like a recording. "I don't know, man, what do you think?" Finally, I went to Bob Johnston and said, "I'm telling him what we're doing, and he's not giving me any feedback. I'm gonna quit asking. Maybe he'll speak up if we do something he doesn't like." Bob said, "Yeah, I think that's the right thing to do." Mickey came in with great creative ideas. They were like night and day.[3]

Grammy Award–winning session player **Charlie McCoy** has performed on recordings by Johnny Cash, Bob Dylan, Elvis Presley, Waylon Jennings, Loretta Lynn, and several others.

NORBERT PUTNAM

I saw this kid from Houston at Acuff-Rose one day. He had a big leather bag like doctors would use to make house calls with song lyrics inside. I thought his name was interesting: Mickey Newbury. Mickey was a handsome guy, almost movie star quality with a beautifully sculpted face, chin, and hair. He had a great smile and great eyes. He got his guitar out and sang a song for us with such emotion that you would hardly pay attention to the lyrics. He was projecting the emotion. I would imagine in that three-hour session we might've demoed five, six new Mickey Newbury songs. I don't know if it was because of that session, but he signed a deal with Acuff-Rose. We probably did five demo dates with him over the next month. "Just Dropped In (To See What Condition My Condition Was In)" made it to Kenny Rogers and First Edition.

That was the beginning of our long relationship. Mickey got a deal with RCA with Felton Jarvis, who was a producer who had come to Muscle Shoals frequently. I played bass on Mickey's first record, *Harlequin Melodies*. The great Tupper Saussy came in and wrote those over-the-top strings that you hear. Tupper was a jazz musician and classical composer. I believe "Sweet Memories" became Newbury's first standard. A standard in those days meant twenty-five or thirty people recorded it in the next five years. I would imagine there were more like fifty to seventy recordings of "Sweet Memories." Andy Williams recorded the song.

Mickey Newbury suddenly was a valuable entity in Nashville and at Acuff-Rose. He wrote the most depressing songs I've ever heard, but he was the most positive person I've ever known. Kris Kristofferson wrote, "He's a walking contradiction / Partly truth and partly fiction" [in "The Pilgrim, Chapter 33"]. He could have been writing about Mickey. Anyway, Mickey had that big doctor's satchel that must've been eight or ten inches wide. I went out to his cabin one night looking for songs. He said, "Putt, I have a bag of unfinished songs. You wanna hear one?" He reached in and pulled out a verse and a chorus of a great, great song. I said, "Mickey, when are you gonna write the last verse?" "I don't know," he said. "I'm not just gonna write something to finish the song." He reached in again and pulled out another song with a great verse and chorus. Mickey would never write unless he felt the flow. He never sat down with a rhyming dictionary. He waited until he was moved to write.

Joan Baez called me up years later and said, "I'm coming to Nashville, and I want you to lead the rhythm section [in the band in the studio]." I asked who was producing. She said Kristofferson. I had introduced Kris to Joanie the previous year, but Kris backed out when it took time to do the record. He claimed he wasn't familiar enough with the technical aspects of the control room. He talked Joan into letting me produce. One song we did was "The Night They Drove Old Dixie Down," which gave me a career as a record producer by selling a million copies. Mickey was actually there a couple of sessions because we did three of his songs on that record [*Blessed Are*, 1971]: "San Francisco Mabel Joy," "Angeline," and "33rd of August." Mickey wrote unusual songs.

Joan called me the next year when we were going in to do a second record. She said, "Call Mickey and see if he has a song for me." He said, "Putt, I know I have a song. I'll get it to you in a week or so." I didn't hear from him for a week or two. I called him. "Ah, yeah," he said, "I gotta get that down. I have a great song for her." He never mentioned the title. As we got closer to doing the record, I still hadn't heard from him. We were going to the studio the next week. So, I called him at his place out at Old Hickory Lake. He said, "I'll come down in the morning. I have a smash for Joan Baez."

He came in the office the next morning and sat down. Thank God I didn't call Joan. "Hey, Putt. You have to promise me that you won't interrupt me until I finish." Odd request. I would never interrupt Mickey Newbury. He said, "Do you promise that you will not stop me?" I said, "Okay, Mickey. I will not stop you." He gets his guitar and tunes it. He looks at me and delivers one of the greatest vocals I've ever heard Mickey Newbury do, but the first line was disturbing: "On top of Old Smokey, all covered with snow / I lost my true lover for courting too slow," the campfire song. You can see why I would want to stop him. You see, he said he had a song for Joan, but he didn't specifically say he had his song. I sat there while Mickey delivered a version of that song that was so brilliant and so wonderful. Joan called me a day later and asked, "Did Mickey ever get that song to you?" "Joanie," I said. "I'm sorry, he hasn't gotten me any new material."

Mickey and I were both represented by a lawyer in New York, David Braun [2008 Entertainment Law Initiative Service Award winner from the Grammy Foundation], who was considered one of the greatest music attorneys in America. His clientele was Barbra Streisand, Bob Dylan, George Harrison. You find people like me who are just record producers when you come on down the list. Mickey called me in the early eighties. I had just bought the Bennett House [the famed recording studio based in Franklin, Tennessee] and had just retired from music. Mickey said, "You've gotta do one more record. David Braun has taken a position of president of MCA Records, and he's always wanted you to produce me." I thought, We both lost our attorney. David called me and said, "Norbert, I want you to make the quintessential Mickey Newbury album. Just tell me how much money you need, and I'll send it."

The record was *After All These Years*. Well, I open up *Billboard* magazine and see: "David Braun has been fired from MCA Records." Oh my God. You know what a new president does when he comes in? He calls all the people who have been making product for the previous president. I received word. "Norbert, I know it's a great record you've made, but the new president isn't interested in promoting David's product," they said. "There'll be no promotion of the Mickey Newbury record." The record was released silently. I doubt that one dollar of MCA's money went toward promoting that record. Some of that was the finest record Mickey and I ever did. It broke my heart. Mickey never got a major record deal after that.

I spoke to Mickey a week before he died. A bunch of us were at a restaurant in Nashville that we would frequent. Bob Beckham said, "Mickey's on an oxygen tank." He had emphysema. "He's not gonna make it. Let's call out there and wish him well to let him know we're thinking about him." Bob dialed him up, and Mickey picked up the phone. He passed it around so we could talk to Mickey. I said the most foolish thing you could possibly say to someone in that condition. "Mickey, how are you?" Well, he's dying, okay? Mickey laughed. We all broke up. What a dumb thing to ask a man who would be gone a week later. "Putt," Mickey said, "things couldn't be better."[4]

Iconic session player **Norbert Putnam** has performed on recordings by J. J. Cale, Dan Fogelberg, Henry Mancini, Roy Orbison, Linda Ronstadt, and Tony Joe White. He made his name as one of the players from Muscle Shoals, Alabama, brought to Nashville to record with Elvis Presley in the midsixties.

DONNIE FRITTS

Everybody admired Mickey. He was so good. We all drifted in together and hooked up at Columbine Music. Tony Joe White would be there when he was in town. Mickey, Billy Swan, Kris Kristof-

ferson, and I would listen to each other's songs, a great time to be
in Nashville with all the changes taking place. Mickey and Kris
were very close. They loved each other. Kris and I went over to the
studio when Mickey was cutting *Looks Like Rain*, and it was just
magic to hear him. I thought the world of Mickey. He was one of
my songwriting heroes. He wrote some of my very favorites, beautiful songs like "San Francisco Mabel Joy" and "Sweet Memories."

We'd met when we were doing a demo session at RCA Records.
Mickey barreled in from Houston that night and looked pretty
rough. He'd been up for a while, but we got to talking. He said, "I
have a song I want y'all to hear." He'd just written "Funny Familiar Forgotten Feelings." I'll never forget it. I didn't know anything
about the guy. You had Kris writing those brilliant songs. Waylon
Jennings was starting to happen. This was 1968 and 1969. Mickey
was a good guy, man. If you listen to those songs, it was like how
Kris came in. Kris came in with a whole different attitude toward
songwriting. The songs were much deeper and there was so much
more to them than the regular country songs that were coming out
at the time. Mickey was the same way. His songs were absolutely
gorgeous.

I loved that Ray Charles cut Mickey's songs. Mickey was brilliant, and his melodies were so beautiful. He could sing so great
and could do it all, but all that matters is his songwriting and singing. He was one of the best ever. Like any great songwriter, it's the
way you put things together. You can say "I love you" a million different ways, and Mickey did. Most songs were about loving somebody. "Sweet Memories" is a beautiful song about loving somebody.
Only Mickey could have written "Funny Familiar Forgotten Feelings." He was one of the most talented guys I was ever around.

Waylon and Charlie Rich were two friends and great heroes. I
loved what they did with my songs. They're both geniuses. Those
guys can sing and play. Ray Charles cut one of my songs, which
was probably the biggest deal of my life. Ray had been my hero
since I was about twelve years old. That meant absolutely everything and was the best thing that ever happened to me as a professional songwriter. That makes it all worth it. Dobie Gray cut a
beautiful record with "We Had It All." Bobby "Blue" Bland doing
a song I wrote was huge. I just had a cut by Willie two years ago

with "Old Timer." That's one of my favorite recordings and meant a hell of a lot.

I wrote that with a great songwriter named Lenny LeBlanc. I said, "Look, there's one guy in the world that this song's perfect for. Willie." I called Willie that night and said, "Willie, I think I have you a hell of a song." "Well, let me hear it." We sent him an MP3 that night and Willie called the next afternoon and said, "You were right. I have to cut that." I've known Willie for forty years, so I could call him at his house. Having him agree with me was a big deal. Willie is one of the most famous music people in the world and one of the greatest songwriters, too. I felt weird saying that I thought I had a song for him. I know he's cut a couple of Mickey songs, but he's one of the greatest songwriters ever.

Why Mickey isn't better known is a damn good question. I can name a bunch of people who I thought were gonna be biggest stars, but they weren't for whatever reason. They did well but didn't do nowhere near what you thought. I don't know if it was Mickey holding himself back by not playing the game. Many things go into being a big star, and I don't know if Mickey was suited for that. Seems like he was almost there all the time. He was always [supposed to be a star] next year. You've got to play the game. I don't give a shit who it is. Some people around here could be huge stars, but they're not gonna be because they're not giving in to what you need to do to be a star. Mickey was in that spot. On one hand, you had one of the greatest songwriters who ever lived. On the other, he didn't have that star thing like Kris.[5]

Session player and songwriter **Donnie Fritts** has written songs recorded by Charlie Rich ("You're Gonna Love Yourself in the Morning") and Waylon Jennings ("We Had It All"). He played keyboards for Kris Kristofferson for more than four decades.

BILLY EDD WHEELER

I invited Mickey Newbury and his friend Walter to come visit in Swannanoa, North Carolina, around 1998. Mickey had lip gloss handy that he used several times a day. Walter was an expert about old things and would go to flea markets and buy stuff and sell it to restaurants to decorate their shelves and walls. "We stopped at almost every flea market along the way," Mickey said. "Walter was so amazing. He went into one with nothing to sell and came out with several thousand dollars." I asked how he did that. "Well," Mickey said, "he would walk up and say, 'I think I'd like to buy your cash register.' They'd say, 'Hell, that ain't for sale.' Then they'd show their stuff, and he'd say, 'Well, you'd take a thousand dollars for that other thing, wouldn't you?' He'd buy it, then go to another spot and convince some guy that it was worth three times what he'd paid." Mickey admired that.

My wife, Mary, and I belonged to the Biltmore Forest Country Club in Asheville. Walter was entertaining the big shots with card tricks when we were there. He did one trick when he was dealing and said, "I'm missing a card here." He looked at a guy sitting across from him and said, "Look under your foot over there." There it was. I don't know how he did that. Then we played golf. Mary and I resigned about two years later because the club had a policy to not admit Jews or blacks. That bothered our consciences. Anyway, my friendship with Mickey lasted forever. His passing really broke my heart because there was something so beautiful about his singing voice. So different than anybody else. He was like an angel. Nobody had anything like it in their list of talents. Everybody knew that "An American Trilogy" was a classic as soon as we all heard him sing it.

Mickey could bullshit like everybody else. You could engage him in any conversation. He was a bright guy and a master writer. We were in the same boat trying to get our songs published and recorded, which often happened on the golf course. For example, I would play golf with Jerry Chesnut. He was quite a bigoted guy and made no apologies, but he was a great writer. Jerry had a big, fat guy named Lamar Fike, who was Elvis's flunky and errand runner, with him. We became friends because we loved jokes. One day when we were golfing, Jerry said, "Why don't we write a song?" I had an idea about a guy who broke with a girl but when nighttime comes he misses her so bad [the 1974 Elvis Presley cut "It's Midnight"]. The first verse I'd written was so convoluted, Jerry said, "How about 'maybe it's too late / sometimes I even hate myself /

for loving you.'" I said, "Damn, that's it. Let's write." I wish I had written with Mickey. He was a great writer. We had a kinship.[6]

Billy Edd Wheeler wrote the Grammy Award–winning song "Jackson" for Johnny Cash and June Carter Cash. His songs have been performed by Judy Collins, Bobby Darin, Jefferson Airplane, Neil Young, and several others.

CHRIS GANTRY

Mickey traveled with everything he owned in the back seat when he drove up to Nashville from Texas. We'd see his Cadillac parked around town with a clothing rack in the back. Nashville was really small in 1963. You noticed everything. We were young with our eyes open. I always wondered who owned this car. Finally, he was parked out behind Cedarwood Publishing Company. I walked over. Mickey was sitting in the car smoking a cigarette, and we introduced ourselves. I had never heard his music.

Mickey came over to Buckhorn Music Publishing to talk with [songwriter and song publisher] Marijohn Wilkin. Kris Kristofferson and I both became aware of his music then. Mickey was a romantic. He was writing beautiful songs that sounded different lyrically than what was coming out of the old guard even though his songs had plaintive country melodies. I got to know Mickey real well because Kris and I soon moved over to Columbine Music where Mickey hung out. Mickey and Bob Beckham were great friends. Mickey would be there every day hanging out with Billy Swan, Tony Joe White, Shel Silverstein, Chet Atkins. They would hang out at the end of the day in the front room, drink, and carry on. Silverstein loved Mickey's music.

Mickey was the John the Baptist of revolutionary country music in the sixties. Mickey's delivery and the way he put words together were such a huge influence on Kris. There would be no Kristofferson had there not been Mickey. Mickey had one foot in both worlds. He knew old country and could play that as good as anybody else, but he was also aware of the revolution that was taking place in the whole country. The old guard didn't want to look. Took time for those guys to accept things were changing, but Mickey knew they were. He was trying new things with songs that the old guard weren't putting their heads into.

Mickey was a little older than everybody else and was really heralding the young writers. He was fascinated with Eddie Rabbitt, Billy Swan, Kris, and me. We were starting to get things recorded, but we weren't having hits yet. Mickey already had some big action with cuts but never wrote for anybody. Mickey wrote for Mickey. He didn't go in saying, "I'm gonna write this for such and such" like they do today and some did back then. The old songwriters had a pitch list and would say, "Let's write a truck-driving song for Dale Dudley. He's having a hit right now." Mickey was a hero to us. He knew how to construct the most gorgeous melodies in the simplest two or three chords. Kris picked up on what Mickey was doing and learned how to write beautiful melodies in three chords. Mickey appealed to people because it was in Nashville and the lyrics were intriguing. They were taking people into new places where most people hadn't been before.

Looks Like Rain was an iconic, cultish, timeless record when it came out. The utter simplicity blew everybody away. Mickey really stepped out and said, "I'm a totally different person. I'm a singer-songwriter and always have been. Here's some of my best work." I love to listen to that album even today. Mickey was the dean of those who came in from the coasts and changed country music forever. They were influenced by him first. He didn't write [Kristofferson's] "Me and Bobby McGee" or [Tony Joe White's] "Rainy Night in Georgia," but his writing was bordering on that place. The young guard saw that those songs were possibilities, and they took it a step further.

We were all young and impressionable, and we were all looking for our voice. We didn't know where to go, but Mickey had his voice. He wasn't consciously mentoring us, but his music, his enthusiasm, and the way he constructed story songs pushed us. He was already The Mickey Newbury when I came to Nashville. Waylon hadn't even gotten here, and when he did come he was a straight guy. Willie Nelson was a straight guy. Willie was a great songwriter, but he had no idea what great change was happening musically. Mickey got very little credit for being there because he was the change guy in the sixties even though he didn't do the Waylon or

Johnny Cash thing. His music was more subdued. Mickey was a great writer and genreless like James Taylor and Paul Simon.

Mickey [eventually became] disillusioned with the business. He was evolving in his own little wild head and didn't relate to the music in Nashville. He was never a guy who put his footprint into anything too long before it dried up. Mickey was an in-and-out guy. He'd show up, blow everybody away, and disappear. He was a musical world unto himself and had other dreams and ideas. There was only one Mickey Newbury musically. Nobody kept in touch after he moved. His presence got scarcer and scarcer even though he was producing a lot of music. Mickey didn't care about fame. He cared about strange things in his head and how he approached songs. He didn't attack stardom like Kristofferson did. He loved making the music, and he loved to disappear.[7]

Chris Gantry wrote "Dreams of the Everyday Housewife," which has been recorded by several singers including Glen Campbell, k.d. lang, and Wayne Newton. His albums include *Introspection* (1968) and *Gantry Rides Again* (2015).

BILLY SWAN

We were so stoned at Mickey Newbury's apartment one night when he made a balloon stick to the wall. I know he must've done something like rubbed it against his body to make it stick, but we thought he had really done something, like a spirit had taken over his body. Mickey had this little character that he'd get into when we were smoking pot. He'd put this blanket around him and do this small, small voice like he was a mystic. Bucky Wilkin was there. Bucky is the son of Marijohn Wilkin, who used to write for Cedarwood Music before she started her own publishing company. In fact, she published some of Kris Kristofferson's first songs. Anyway, Mickey would have fun and goof like that.

Mickey and Kris would turn people on to other writers' songs. Kris would tell people about Mickey's songs, and Mickey would talk about Kris. Mickey and I mostly hung out at Columbine Music, and I went over to that apartment a couple of times. Everyone loved Mickey. He was a great songwriter. I always remember

"Funny Familiar Forgotten Feelings" and "An American Trilogy." I
heard that one many times before he recorded that. He would sing
"Sweet Memories." Mickey absolutely had the songs. He also was a
gentleman and a great guy. Kris and I went to New York City and
spent the night with Mickey the first time he played the Bitter End.
Kris and I slept on the floor in his room. Mickey played a couple
of nights starting the next night and had a full house. He did well
everywhere he went because of his great personality. He was an
intelligent guy.

Mickey wrote for Acuff-Rose, but he would come over to Columbine in the afternoons. Mickey had already written "Just Dropped
In" and had a gold Cadillac that he bought from money he made
from the song. He'd come by with Felton Jarvis, Henry Hurt, Donnie Fritts, and Dan Penn. Spooner Oldham, Tony Joe White, Dennis Lindy, Johnny MacRae, whoever was in town and knew Bob
Beckham would be there. Every now and then people like the
actor Jack Palance would show up. You never knew who would be
in that circle in the evenings. We'd be drinking beer and talking
about songs. I remember that Cadillac sitting in the dirt parking
lot in the back of the Columbine building. They'd get in a circle and
pass the guitar. Mickey lots of times would be by himself singing
his songs. You wouldn't be talking to him for two minutes, and he'd
make you laugh. He had a great sense of humor.

Bob was happy that Mickey would come over to Columbine. In
fact, he parked his Cadillac there a few times when he first came
to town. He had that apartment, but then he bought that houseboat
and lived on it. I remember going over to Acuff-Rose one time in
the early eighties. He had already left Nashville, but he was back.
He took me all around there trying to show me something but I
had no idea what the hell he wanted to show. I don't know if he was
confused or I was. He was doing a demo at the time, and I think
he was feeling pretty good. I remember when he would get in that
mystic character he would say, "Green. Bad." That stuck with me. I
don't know if he was referring to pot, money, or what. "Green. Bad."
Why is green bad? Who knows.[8]

Billy Swan has written songs recorded by Conway Twitty, Waylon
Jennings, and Mel Tillis. He played bass guitar with Kris Kristof-

ferson before signing a record deal with Monument Records. He reached number one on the country chart with his song "I Can Help" in 1974.

BUCKY WILKIN

Mickey maintained a mystery. He had a pattern of orbiting the country: Nashville, Houston, Oregon. I don't think I ever met the people in his other lives, but I saw him around town. He had a style. Everybody wondered why he was underappreciated and not a big star. There was a group in the sixties who would get together in the back room at Tuneville Music, which was Bill Justis's publishing company, and pass the guitar with beer at happy hour. Newbury, Kristofferson, Chris Gantry, a few others were in the group. I met Mickey there. Newbury said, "If you ever get to Houston, look me down." He was brilliant with songs like "She Even Woke Me Up to Say Goodbye" and "So Sad." My favorite female singer Jennifer Warnes has a nice version of "So Sad" on her new album.

Acuff-Rose gave him everything they could as a publisher, but they didn't have what it took to make him an artist. Mickey really wanted to be an artist, but he couldn't play a song the same way twice. His creative wheels were running faster than his performing wheels. I used to get irritated trying to get him to do a song the same way twice. Maybe that held him back. I think he was resentful of his publisher and not being able to make it as an artist. Mickey was magnetic in a living room setting with eight or ten people. He would go into this trance world where he'd perform with his great voice and fabulous, dreamy songs. He was psychedelic before it was fashionable. Maybe that didn't click with country music.

I look at music as culture and personality after notes and lyrics. Mickey had his culture and personality all wrapped up and packaged, and it was recognizable, identifiable compared to country music today. Country music is in the doldrums now. There are no star writers as far as I know, which is a little depressing. Mickey was the whole package. Sitting in a room and hearing that big voice with an original song is a rare combination. Most people are singers or writers. Mickey was both, and the singing part was excel-

lent compared to Kristofferson, Johnny Cash, or Bob Dylan. Mickey
had something, but maybe he never got big enough management
to control, package, and market him.

Owsley Manier did a video on him called *Live at the Hermitage*,
a fairly simple three-camera shoot of him with just [guitarist Jack
Williams in 1994], which was wonderful. I see the guy who masked
where he was coming from—the poor side of Houston with the
Spanish and black people—and had to stand up for himself. That's
what interested me. You can hear it in his music like "In '59." He
tells his story in that song. Mickey was very private and always
on the way to somewhere else, but I know he had a nickel-plated,
pearl-handled .32-[caliber] revolver that he kept in the armrest
of his Cadillac Eldorado. He was a real good friend with Nicholas
Johnson, the man who was head of the FCC, when he got some
fame and success. Mickey shook hands with people at the top even
though he wasn't a huge star. He found some happiness.

He had a cabin on the lake north of Nashville, which was rather
stark. The cabin was like a weekend bunkhouse with inadequate
heat, air conditioning, or lighting. People would go there and hang
out with Mickey, smoke pot, take acid, and play each other songs,
a grim get-together that wasn't particularly happy, but that was
Mickey. He always had a smile, though. He didn't sing the blues in
public except through his music. I think that's to be respected. His
private life was in another state. He would drive his Cadillac down
to Houston for a couple of weeks and then drive up to Oregon for
a couple of months, then come back to Nashville. He always had
shined cowboy boots and pressed jeans and was a neat dresser.
You knew not to fool with him because he'd grown up hard. You
knew he could handle himself in a situation.

I think Mickey was generally unhappy about where his career
was going. He was mainly known for that Kenny Rogers track,
which was psychedelic country. We all loved Mickey and wished
good things for him. I can say "we" because in the late sixties and
early seventies there really was a cadre of songwriters in Nashville.
Then things got too big. Kris had a manager, and Mickey didn't.
Kris moved to Los Angeles, and Mickey didn't. Kris had power
coming in. He just had to prove his humility and sincerity. I guess
I'm saving the rest for my book, which will get into sex, drugs, and

the darker side of the music business that's always been there.

Kris has harassed me for various things. I don't know where his personality has gone. He's the kinda guy I love and hate when I'm around him, the coolest guy in the world. I've played on his demos and picked him up at the airport when he was writing for my mom. Then he'll turn around and have an attorney write me and say, "You owe us this and that from 1968." Then I have to have an attorney write them back and say, "No, this is not true." They play hardball a little too hard. I don't know where all that comes from, but I sent him a check with some reluctance once a year for his share in "One Day at a Time." That's show business. There's no reality in the music business. I may sound a little cynical, but I grew up in it. Fame just gets you a better seat at a restaurant.[9]

John Buck "Bucky" Wilkin was the founder, singer, and primary songwriter of the surf rock band Ronny & the Daytonas. The group's debut single, "G.T.O.," reached number four on the *Billboard* pop singles chart. His mother, Marijohn Wilkin, was well known as a cowriter behind Lefty Frizzell's "Long Black Veil" and cowriter with Kris Kristofferson of "One Day at a Time."

BUFFY SAINTE-MARIE

Mickey's song "Mister Can't You See" [cowritten with Townes Van Zandt and released on Newbury's debut, *Harlequin Melodies*] is so contemporary. Have you thought about the words since [Sainte-Marie recorded it on *Moonshot* in 1972]? "I can hear the rivers flowing / I can see the winds a-blowing / Since the endless marching of the time / If you don't know what I'm feeling / Take a look because I'm revealing / Everything that's now running through my mind." Sounds like the environmental political crisis that we're going through now. Mickey was writing about questionable leadership and questioning environmental insanity as brought to us by the business and political powers that be. He was right on. Somebody should redo that song because it's right on for right now.

I met Mickey when Chet Atkins invited me to Nashville around 1970. Chet loved putting songwriters and guitar players together.

He introduced me to Mickey Newbury and Kris Kristofferson, and
we all used to sit around and play our songs together. Chet thought
we should know each other. He was right. Mickey had a poet's artistry combined with a vision and common sense. His songs weren't
just about chest thumping or toe tapping. We were coming out of
songs like [Bobby Darin's 1958 hit] "Splish Splash" that were fun
but not really poetry or heartfelt brainpower. Mickey's songs were
a snapshot or movie of his life. There was always something to
them. I guess I learned "Sweet Memories" from Mickey.

It was exciting when we would [swap songs]. Mickey would play,
Kris would play, I would play, and then everybody would go home.
I didn't drink and still don't, so it never got to fun times at the bar
for me. Our conversations were concentrated about the music and
what the songs were about and who you heard lately. We were all
real young. I was twenty-two. Mickey's songs weren't as contro-
versial as my own, but they touched on things that anybody could
understand. The best folk songs from the last hundred years usually were about stuff that anybody in any generation could understand: love, war, comments about oppression, fears about the environment. We were writing about that in the sixties. We were all
about the songs.

I had already had a hit with "Universal Soldier." "Now That the
Buffalo's Gone" was becoming well known. People think "Universal Soldier" was written by Donovan [who cut the song as the title
track to his 1965 EP], but I did. I had a poetic side to my music with
love songs like "Until It's Time to Go." Elvis, Barbra Streisand, and
other people whose lives were very different from my own were
singing my songs. I had this variety going on, but Nashville was different. There are a million ways to write a song. You balance words,
content, poetry, emotion, and the whole musical side and whether
you want people to dance or listen or hang the whole thing on the
melody.

We had fun recording "Mister Can't You See." Norbert Putnam's
band was a new thing for me. I had been a one-man band traveling
around by myself until then. I had never been around musicians
who played naturally by ear like me. The musicians I had been
around for an occasional studio session that Vanguard Records
would have set up for me read music and were highly literate. I'm

not literate in music. I can write for an orchestra, but I'm dyslexic and can't read music back the next day. Norbert and his Area Code 615 band—Charlie McCoy, Billy Sanford, David Briggs, Kenny Buttrey, Kenny Pruitt—were wonderful. Norbert produced, and we ended up doing four albums together. The musical change with *Moonshot* was real significant for me.

Moonshot let me settle back and fly on the music instead of fighting with the guys. "How come you're the boss? You can't even read music." You get competitive lip. Norbert and David owned Quadrophonic Studio, so there was zero pressure. The people he hired were really his best friends. I felt totally comfortable as the songwriter and the artist with the people playing. We were all relating to the music in the same way. I was totally comfortable musically, personally stress-free because the guys loved working with Norbert. I lucked out. I was used to working with musicians in LA. We never had a bad session with Norbert. There weren't any songs we recorded that I didn't like, and that's not how it was on other albums.

Norbert was even-tempered, funny, and liked other musicians. He's a great bass player, a beautiful player no matter what they were playing. He definitely preferred rock and roll to country. I was playing some pretty different things than they would play. Norbert and I cowrote a song called "Nobody Will Know It's Real but You." He had the most beautiful melody and the song's still one of my favorite recordings of anything I've done. Norbert would play that on the piano and I'd go, "Oh, what is that? I have to write words to that." I did, which doesn't happen very often. The musical environment he created by working with his friends was relaxed and everybody was having fun. You can see all kinds of crap in studios— people drunk or nodding, angry. Everybody was eager to play, and some of those guys were playing three sessions a day. They were awake. There was coffee.

I was not a part of the cliques in folk music like Peter, Paul and Mary, Joan Baez, and Bob Dylan, who hung out during hours and after hours. I was much more a working musician on the road with a guitar and bus or airplane tickets. I had started to get into acting as well. I had already finished the first two-hour movie series that was called *The Virginian*. I had been writing songs that weren't based only on the music. Others had a real social edge. They were testing bombs. There was a war on. We were very much concerned with that, as we are today. Concern for the environment was not new. "Mister Can't You See" was right up that alley, but Mickey was a much more commercial songwriter with so many pop hits. Eartha Kitt, Taj Mahal, and I were excluded from the airwaves. I hope that Mickey didn't suffer from the same political oppression that was going on with me and the FBI files.[10]

Canadian political activist and singer **Buffy Sainte-Marie** won the Academy Award for Best Original Song for cowriting the Joe Cocker and Jennifer Warnes song "Up Where We Belong" from the film *An Officer and a Gentleman*.

Ramblin' Jack Elliott

I was on the Johnny Cash television program in Nashville in 1969. Mickey Newbury and I were both staying at the Ramada Inn. Kris Kristofferson introduced us in the hotel restaurant, and then we visited in Mickey's hotel room on a lower floor. I was playing him "912 Greens," a long, talking song that I wrote about the first trip I ever took to New Orleans. He seemed to enjoy the story. I played the first three verses and then wandered out into the hallway and played. I walked up the stairs to the ground floor and strummed along. Mickey remained in his room a little nonplussed and patiently waiting for me. I continued on down the hallway to the lobby and then back to Mickey's room. I got back in time to sing the last verse. He was amazed and amused by the gesture even though he missed most of the song because he didn't come along. Mickey was a marvelous guy. I loved his singing.

He let me drive his black Eldorado later on that very warm day, but the car had air conditioning. I drove it a few blocks around Nashville and back to the hotel, which was a nice reward for having sung him the song. We went out for some lunch after and hung out with Kris. I had just met Kris the day before that. He had taken me for a ride in his Hillman Minx. We went over to meet his manager. Some car repo guys came while we were there and repossessed his other car, which was a Volkswagen, because Kris had missed payments. He seemed pretty nonchalant about the whole deal. We got back in the Hillman Minx and drove out to Johnny Cash's place. We visited John and June out at the lake. Mickey was a marvelous guy. Nobody let me drive their Cadillac before.

Mickey and I were on the Bread and Roses concert bill with Joan Baez, her sister [Mimi Fariña], Kristofferson, and Hoyt Axton the next time we met. We all had a memorable time there. Hoyt was drunk, and people were a little dismayed by his behavior. I knew him, though. Hoyt could pull it off drunk or sober. I believe Mickey played "33rd of August" that night, but Kris was very angry with him. Kris was cussing him out and berating him because he felt people were missing out on a lot because Mickey was denying the world by not playing more gigs. Mickey didn't like to play nightclubs. Kris thought he really should get out there and let the people hear him, see him, and share his wonderful talent and beautiful songs.

The last time I saw Mickey was when I visited him and his wife, Susan, at home in a little town outside Eugene, Oregon, around 1998. He had a lovely motor home. I had never owned one at that time but was a big mobile home appreciator. I wished I had one like Mickey's. I'd never tour, either, if I did. I did get a very nice motor home years later that I did more than three hundred thousand miles in over nineteen years. That was the happiest time in my life. I didn't mind touring and playing gigs, and I loved that motor home. Mine was a Cross Country by Sportscoach. Mickey's was a GMC with front-wheel drive and two rear axles. You shouldn't drive them too much because you can't find parts if they break, but I guess Mickey didn't have any trouble with that beauty since he didn't tour too much. I feel very lucky to be one of the few people who met him.[11]

Legendary folksinger **Ramblin' Jack Elliott's** close apprenticeship with Woody Guthrie secured his place in history. Elliott wrote the popular "912 Greens" but largely made his name interpreting songs by others such as Bob Dylan's "Don't Think Twice, It's All Right."

CHORUS: HEAVEN HELP THE CHILD

"You look like Mickey Newbury," Dotty West said when we met. "I love his songwriting. You have to write songs." I'd never written a song in my life, but I was an English major and had written poetry. I was auditioning at the time for the Imperials, a gospel group who were with Elvis, but I didn't get the job. So, I started writing a few songs. I went back to Houston, wrote eight songs for Dotty, and sent them to her. She sent a plane ticket, and my wife, Janice, and I decided to move to Nashville. We pulled into Dotty's house pulling our little Mercury Capri car behind a Hertz rent truck. "Let's go see Mickey" was the first thing Dotty said. "Let's go to Mickey's boat."

We got on Hank Cochran's boat around eleven in the morning and went across the lake to Mickey's place. Mickey came strolling down the dock with a cup of coffee in his hand, a guitar over his shoulder, and a cigarette in his mouth. He climbed onto Hank's boat. "Man," he said. "You do look like me." We hit it off immediately. Mickey sat there on the boat and sang "An American Trilogy" for us for the first time anybody had heard it. He had arranged and put it together the night before in his boat.

I already had his albums *Frisco Mabel Joy*, *Looks Like Rain*, and whatever I could get my hands on when I was still living in Houston. Mickey was the one I really listened to the most. He was my first real influence. Mickey was a master craftsman, a real wordsmith with haunting songs. I loved the way he put words together. He called memories "remembrances." His internal rhymes, storytelling, and guitar playing were masterful. He wasn't Larry Carlton or Vince Gill on guitar, but he played that little boom-chuck, boom-boom-chuck riff in Drop D that gave him the full octave for an orchestral D. "San Francisco Mabel Joy" and "Cortelia Clark" were great story songs. Think about that line from "Cortelia Clark": "He was black and I was green." Holy cow. Brilliant language.

Mickey was a melancholy cat. He sang with passion and was in tune. You might be able to sing the notes, but I doubt you sing like Mickey Newbury. There's very little inflection and dynamic with ups and downs, louds and quiets, falsetto, vibrato, shading tones with most people. He added very special vibrato and changes. Mickey and I would get together and talk about Paris in the twenties and

Gertrude Stein's house and her salons with William Faulkner, John Dos Passos, Ezra Pound, James Joyce, Ernest Hemingway, all the people who hung out at her place at 27 Rue de Fleurus in the sixth arrondissement on the Left Bank in Paris.

I knew about all that as a kid in English class. Mickey, Kris, and I would talk about our favorite poet William Blake. There aren't many songwriters in Nashville talking about William Blake. Harlan Howard's frame of reference was the assembly line in Detroit. Kris and Mickey and I came from a little different angle through reading Ulysses, William Blake, William Butler Yeats, Shakespeare, John Donne. I'm not trying to exalt that—well, maybe a little bit—but it's just coming from a different place. The songs and wordplay are gonna sound different from other people when you're getting together and talking about the expats in Paris.

I write every song the best it can be written. Everything doesn't have to be "tyger, tyger, burning bright" [from Blake's poem "The Tyger"]. I don't sit down and try to write above or down to people. Take the song idea, melody, and hook, and write that song. I wrote "All the Gold in California" because I saw a 1958 Mercury station wagon with Oklahoma license plates right in front of the Hollywood Bowl. "My gosh," I said, "it's the Joad family from *Grapes of Wrath*." I said out loud, "All the gold in California is in a bank in the middle of Beverly Hills in somebody else's name." I wrote it down on a Hertz rent-a-car slip. I wouldn't have known about the Joad family going from the middle of Oklahoma to California to pick grapes if I hadn't read Steinbeck's *The Grapes of Wrath*.

Some songs are simpler than others. Some are funny, some are sad. Some are story songs. Some have two verses and a chorus and others have one verse and two choruses. You take the idea and try to do it right for that song in that moment in time. The craft is very special to me. Besides my family and the way I feel about God, my country, and my friends, songwriting is the most special. I tell people, "All the words you need are in the dictionary." I know what order they come in and so does Kris and so did my favorites: Mickey, Roger Miller, Johnny Cash, Willie Nelson.

Mickey knew straightforward language and economy are key. You say the most you can with the fewest words. You use them over and over so people will remember them and use the right ones.

Mickey wrote in "San Francisco Mabel Joy," "In place of Mabel Joy he found a merchant mad Marine." My God almighty. "Sweet Memories," "Funny Familiar Forgotten Feelings" are great songs, too. Really listen to "She Even Woke Me Up to Say Goodbye," the first song about bipolar disorder. "It's not her heart, lord, it's her mind / She didn't mean to be unkind." He's saying, "Her heart's in love with me, but she's a nutbag. She's bipolar. She can't help it." That's what I take away from it. Mickey didn't say she was manic depressive. He said that about her heart and mind. "She did things when she didn't want to." Mickey was a pretty deep cat.

Mickey wasn't better known because other people sang his hits. The listening public didn't give a shit who wrote them. They didn't know who wrote "Funny Familiar Forgotten Feelings" for Tom Jones or who wrote "Just Dropped In (To See What Condition My Condition Was In)" for Kenny Rogers. They just want to play the song. That's one reason Mickey wasn't better known, but the other is that Mickey wouldn't do it Nashville's way. He didn't bend. He wanted to sit there and play songs by himself. He didn't care about commercial success. He wanted to sit on that stool, drink coffee, smoke cigarettes, cross his legs, play that gut-string guitar, and play sad songs. That's great for a certain part of the population, but that's not gonna get you playing the Houston Astrodome. You know what Mickey thought about what others think? Fuck them.[1]

Larry Gatlin has been the lead singer and songwriter for the chart-topping Gatlin Brothers for more than forty years. He's written and recorded many hit songs including "Broken Lady," "All the Gold in California," "She Used to Be Somebody's Baby," and "Houston (Means I'm One Day Closer to You)."

ALLEN FRIZZELL

I've been married thirty-three years now. I played Mickey Newbury on my first date with my wife. She fell in love with the music. I was doing Ralph Emery's *Nashville Now* television show a couple of years after we got married, and Mickey came out to see me. I introduced him to Gayle, and he had such great manners when she met him. He was so sweet to her. She loved him even more. It was special anytime we'd get together. We got together over at my brother David's house two or three times and laughed all the time. Frizzells are real loud when we get together. Mickey would just smile and laugh. I never got into any real deep conversations with him about sad stories. We didn't have big drinking parties. We just had a good time and enjoyed being around each other. He always had a guitar and was singing new songs. We talked about our latest songs. Our whole family loved Mickey. He was down to earth. There was nothing like being around him and just the guitar. Incredible. He's my favorite writer.

Mickey was a big fan of my brother Lefty, who went about things real oddly. Mickey would ask me to tell the legendary stories about him. Merle Haggard was the same way. He wanted to hear the same Lefty stories every time I was around him. I hadn't really gotten strong into songwriting when I was around Mickey, but I loved his. Man, I would love to be able to spend time with him and bend his ear now that I write almost all the songs I do. Mickey would blow you away with his ideas, but his melodies were just monsters. My melodies are probably the strongest part of my songwriting, and Mickey was a big influence on that. Newbury was a different thing. The songs would take you on a whole new trip. They helped me get into my peaceful side.

We went to see Mickey play one time. A top local disc jockey was really drunk at the show. He was doing all kinds of stuff, but we tried to ignore him. Mickey was going to this private bar party later on Music Row. He told us where it was, and we said we'd meet him over there. David drank a little too much, so his wife took him home. I had a brand-new white jacket that I had bought to go see Mickey. Anyway, we got to the place before Mickey did. We were standing on the sidewalk right out front. My sister, wife, and other family members were with me. That drunk guy showed up and ran right into me. I said, "Hey, man. Stay in your own little circle there." He came up and got right in my face. I said, "You need to get out of my face." He wouldn't quit, so I hit him up and down. He got up and was whining like a baby.

"Man," he said. "I make a living with my mouth." "I'm sorry," I said. "Gosh, you got right in my face. You've been trouble all night.

What do you want me to do?" "Who are you?" he said. "Who are you? Give me five hundred dollars, and I'll forget about it." I hit him again. He went down. My jacket was polka-dotted with blood. We went across the street and got into my car. He yelled, "I'll never play your records again." I said, "I thought you didn't know who I was." My wife was up early the next morning and turned on the radio show. "I'll say one thing," the disc jockey said. "What's-his-name sure has one heck of a punch." I told Mickey later what happened and he laughed. He'd bring up that story every time I saw him after that.[2]

Allen Frizzell has written songs recorded by Merle Haggard, George Jones, Willie Nelson, and Keith Whitley. His brother was country music pioneer Lefty Frizzell.

ED BRUCE

Mickey and I were friends for years until he burned out. We met through Hank Cochran and spent most times hanging out on Mickey's houseboat with our guitars. Sometimes we'd have both our boats out and meet somewhere in a little cove and get the guitars out and swap songs back and forth. We didn't do anything particularly outrageous, but I can tell you Mickey didn't go along with the accepted way to dock a boat. He'd come roaring in and flip the wheel, turn the boat sideways, and slide it into the dock. It was exciting to say the least, especially if you were standing on the dock, but ours was a real calm, laid-back, easy friendship. Mickey didn't seem to like Nashville. His wife, Susan, seemed unhappy with the people he hung out with.

We enjoyed each other's music. Mickey never seemed to have any agenda. I liked his approach to writing. Melody was important. He wrote some beautiful melodies and conversely some beautiful songs. I always admired his voice. Mickey, [University of Texas football] Coach Darrell Royal, and I spent some time together on the golf course. Mickey would always have a new song and talk about it. He had a way with phrases. He wrote songs that were wonderful lyrically and melodically. "San Francisco Mabel Joy" was the first one I heard. What a wonderful song. I heard that years before even Mickey cut it. Mickey wrote songs so well that other people were afraid to cut them because they were so incisive and said so much. Sometimes you wouldn't even understand them.

No one else combined voice and feeling like Mickey when he was singing his own songs. I think that's true with most writers and their songs. Nobody can do them the way the writers can. There's nothing new to say or add. Why extend the effort to do a Mickey Newbury song when you couldn't do it as well as him? Can you think of the hits done better by the other singer? Jerry Lee Lewis did a good job on "She Even Woke Me Up to Say Goodbye," but not as well as Mickey. It's filler if you can't feel and sing a song like the songwriter. You're putting it on an album to have another song on there. Mickey wasn't just hard to beat. He was hard to even match.

You had people who would get together and swap songs and ideas in Nashville back then. Publishers would go to different songwriters, and you had songwriters who would go for a partic-ular artist. I heard a story one time about this one particular art-ist. An artist would come to town and immediately be captured by someone at the airport and put up in the motel. You wouldn't see him for three or four days. The writer was writing and pitch-ing songs to him. You didn't have a chance to get a song cut if you didn't have access to them.

Anytime you got a song cut was exciting. Kenny Price cut my song "Northeast Arkansas Mississippi County Bootlegger." I had gone up to Cincinnati to do the television show that Henson Car-gill was hosting at the time. I had just written the song, and Kenny liked it. I said, "Well, cut it." I made a copy and got it down on tape with the lyrics. He cut the song the next week, which was pretty cool. My first Tanya Tucker cut was a major surprise. I had two that were Top 10, "That Man That Turned My Mama On" in 1973 and "Texas (When I Die)" in 1977.

I went into the Columbia office in Nashville at three o'clock on a Monday afternoon. Billy Sherill was sitting there in the foyer. "Ed," he said, "how are you doing?" "Fine." "You have anything for Tanya?" I thought about it for a minute but couldn't come up with anything. "Well, no. When are you recording her?" "Tomorrow at three." "Golly dern," I said. "That's not much time." Didn't have a thing. I said, "What if I come up with something?" He said, "Bring it in to me in the morning. Leave a copy." It wasn't so much a deadline as the opportunity was here now. Do it. Write something. They'll cut it if it's any good.

I didn't have the first idea, but I went home and got my guitar. I went out and sat out on the bus until I came up with the lick. I said, "That's pretty good." I put some words to it and took it in at ten o'clock the next morning. She cut it, and it was a Top 5 record. That's how songs get cut a lot of times. I knew from the first time through on the chorus that I had Billy. I looked up and he had leaned back and closed his eyes and was producing. I'm sure that's how it happened with Mickey lots of times. The opportunity was there. You take advantage of it.[3]

Ed Bruce wrote the popular song "Mammas Don't Let Your Babies Grow Up to Be Cowboys," released by Chris LeDoux in 1976. Waylon Jennings and Willie Nelson reached number one for four weeks on the country charts with the song in 1978.

DALLAS FRAZIER

I had a boat at Anchor High Marina when Mickey and Susan were living on their houseboat there. We had some interesting conversations about songwriting out on the boats and would compliment each other's songs. Of course, I knew him because he was one of the more successful songwriters in town and one of my all-time favorites. I lived on the Cumberland River in Madison, Tennessee, and remember playing "Poison Red Berries" in my den. The song carried me away, so moody and with such a feel. I had never heard anything like that. Mickey was a prolific songwriter. I remember "San Francisco Mabel Joy" and the Jerry Lee Lewis hit, "She Even Woke Me Up to Say Goodbye."

Mickey was a really deep songwriter and definitely a loner. He wasn't unsocial, but he had his own bag going. He wasn't a troublemaker, but he could take care of himself if he got in a scrap. I like that his songs were sad. He could identify with people who had a burden. I could feel the weight on my soul when I listened to "Poison Red Berries." He was identifying with people who had hardships. Not every song was like that, but that's what I remember. I wasn't the happiest guy in the world back then, so maybe that's why I connected to them.

I got the idea to write [the Oak Ridge Boys' 1981 crossover hit] "Elvira" from a street sign in East Nashville. I was coming home late one night with my publisher Ray Baker in late 1965. We were on Gallatin Road and I saw a street sign that said, "Elvira." I've always been a connoisseur of earthy, funky names. I knew I was gonna turn that sign into something. I started writing "name" songs when I was a kid. I was nineteen years old when I wrote "Alley Oop" [a number one hit for the Hollywood Argyles in 1960 and recorded by the Beach Boys in 1965]. I wrote "Mohair Sam" by Charlie Rich in 1965. My big songs are over fifty years old.

I was quite honored to be inducted into the Nashville Songwriters Hall of Fame in 1976. Guys who are inducted into the Hall have paid their dues. I started in this business when I was twelve years old, and I'll be seventy-nine this October. Getting inducted is a boost to your career and being a part of that is really nice. I really appreciated it, but I heard a calling from God to be a minister. I was out of the business for thirty years until 2006. I stayed in touch with the business some, but I went to Bible school and became a pastor. I did that for a while and I still speak at churches. That's what I wanted to do.

I still had some unfinished writing to do so I got back into it in 2006. It doesn't matter that much whatever happens to the new songs. The main thing is that I have to do them. I've been writing a few things. I'm enjoying it. I threw the baby out with the bathwater. I just quit completely when I got out of the music business. I didn't take *Billboard* magazine anymore. I didn't have any contacts, but I felt like I had things to say after thirty years away. So, I'll do those and then I'll hang it up in maybe another four or five years. I stored up a lot of ideas over the years. I'd write down a title or idea and start to thinking, Well, maybe I'll get to working again and I might need this. I haven't been working hard, but I have been thinking. I'm writing songs right now that I'm really looking forward to.

Mickey was one of the favorite guys back when we met. His wife, Susan, was a real sweetheart. She was a lady, and we all talked often. I was so surprised and disappointed when he died at just sixty-two years old. I felt very bad for Susan. He was a fortunate man to have her and vice versa. She had a good man who was a great songwriter. You know, we were in the business to get cuts. I had five songs cut by Elvis Presley, and they don't come any bigger than him. Those cuts have always been good plugs for me. I've had about seventy songs cut by Connie Smith, a few by Jerry Lee Lewis and Charley Pride. You always get a tremendous boost as a songwriter when a star cuts your song. Mickey was one of the best.

Some songwriters make a big splash. Others are really respected in the music community. Mickey was both. He was known as a songwriter's songwriter. We all appreciated his music and envied him. I know I did. There wasn't anybody else like him. He appeared on the scene and was nobody but himself. He was a cut above the three-chord country songs. I'm not knocking those. I've written a bunch myself, but he was above that. He was definitely a polished songwriter, but his songwriting wasn't the most commercial. I'm sure that cost him. You have to jump in the mainstream, get with the program, and do what the producers are hollering for in Nashville. He didn't fit that pattern. His stuff was different. "Poison Red Berries" should have been a Top 10 hit.[4]

Nashville Songwriters Hall of Fame member **Dallas Frazier** might be best known for writing the Oak Ridge Boys' smash hit "Elvira," but several others including George Jones, Engelbert Humperdinck, Jerry Lee Lewis, Connie Smith, Charlie Pride, and Elvis Presley also recorded his songs.

PAT ALGER

Mickey was special. Everybody who listened to anything beyond the obvious radio country music in the seventies thought so from the very beginning. His songs became legends in their own right. In retrospect, I don't know if they were that earth shaking, but at the time seven-minute songs like "Frisco Depot" and Shel Silverstein's "Rosalie's Good Eats Cafe" that Bobby Bare recorded had this narrative where you went, "Whoa. You can do that in a song?"

They were eye openers. Mickey was the one who was writing these right at the beginning of my writing career when I was deciding where to go with it. He really made me realize that you could make your own rules.

Mickey was an outlaw, but he was an outlaw about not being like the outlaws. He didn't want to be them. That wasn't his lifestyle. Mickey was a handsome, clean-cut guy. He looked more like a high school quarterback than a dangerous country songwriter. His being different appealed to me. Of course, I wasn't living in Nashville then. Curiously, right when I was getting here he was gone. I did finally meet him in the nineties when he tried to make a little comeback. I was president of the Nashville Songwriters Association at the time, and we were courting a Texas person to donate money to the organization. This person's request was a command performance with Mickey Newbury and other popular songwriters of the day.

The nineties were my peak era as a songwriter. I remember we did this performance in a room at the Loews Vanderbilt Plaza, which was probably the nicest hotel in town. It was just Mickey, Roger Murrah, me, and this Texas guy and his wife. It was a big thrill for me to sit next to Mickey. He was pretty well suffering with his lung issues by then, but he still had that hypnotic voice. It was interesting. He didn't want to play his hits. He wanted to play the songs he was working on right then. He played one that had to be seven minutes long and we all went, "What was that?" We were scratching our heads. "How do you do that?" Mickey was one of those legends who actually earned the legend name. He had an aura.

Mickey was a prickly guy. He really thought he was an artist more than a songwriter. He's like anyone else. You write a song that becomes a hit and money starts coming in, so you think of yourself as a songwriter. You go, "I wasn't making any money before that." Mickey really was an artist at heart. Listen to his records. They're very eccentric with their instrumentation. I think Mickey was looking for something that wasn't gonna pigeonhole him as a classic country act. I think he went beyond the modern country musician. He wasn't sitting there with any attitude that night in the hotel. He was happy to be sitting with us, listening to our songs, and commenting.

Mickey was only in his fifties when we played together. The guys I had hung out with were like Harlan Howard and Hank Cochran. They always seemed like old guys. Mickey seemed like he was still pretty vital even though he obviously was not well. You could tell he was struggling with his breath. I met many guys over the years in this business who had those lung problems. I'm just an admirer and fellow member of the Nashville Songwriters Hall of Fame, which blows my mind sometimes. I always rank myself pretty low in that group, but I'm in the group. Mickey would certainly be one at the top.

Our self-confidence level is always just slightly below the equator trying to get up to the North Pole as songwriters. I was shocked and gratified to be inducted. I was an outsider who didn't play the Nashville game in much the same way as Newbury. My success came with a very small company of very opinionated people who only liked really great songs. Their endorsement was the first key to my success. I knew if I could please them then the songs I was writing probably were good. I was proud that I came at it as a slightly less mainstream part of the business here. Interestingly, the first time I came to Nashville was in 1970, and I went to meet a producer named Elliot Mazer at Cinderella Sound.

Cinderella was cool and totally going against the Nashville session model. It was interesting that Mickey had had the same experience. I was living in Atlanta and a friend told us to contact Elliot, who had produced Linda Ronstadt's first album. He was outside the mainstream, too. I called him and he said, "I'm producing a session. Why don't you come see me at Cinderella Sound?" I went out there and it was funky as hell. Elliot would just nod occasionally. When the session was over, he listened to our tape and gave us advice. He didn't think my stuff was gonna make it in Nashville. He was probably right with what I was pitching at the time. Anyway, everybody's in little rooms with baffles at Cinderella. A sign came on that said "pick" when it was time to play. I thought that was neat. Everybody was trying to record at Quadrophonic and all these fancy studios, and here's a hot producer cutting out in the country.

Mickey was a prominent influence on many songwriters. His lyrics weren't the cornball lyrics that we would deride as classic country in those days. We've come to appreciate those on their own level since I've been here, but I was coming from Woodstock, New York. My first hit was on the pop charts like Mickey. I was coming to Nashville looking for someone to admire with some meat on his lyrics. That was Mickey. I think if you look at his lyrics today separately from the music they don't necessarily knock the top of your head off until you see a couple of lines or a metaphor. You go, "Oh my God, nobody else would've said it that way."

So much was the careful way he did things. "An American Trilogy" is so subtle and so quietly done. Mickey's "An American Trilogy" is so much more powerful than Elvis's version. You could really imagine those three songs sung together during the Civil War the way Mickey did them. He was unique. It's such a shame he died so young. I'm about to be seventy-one, and it would have been interesting to see what he would have done at my age. I would have liked to see what would have developed down the line.

I had the idea for [the Nanci Griffith hit] "Lone Star State of Mind" when I was living in New York. Billy Joel had this big hit with "New York State of Mind," but I was like, "Nobody calls it the New York state. They say the Empire State." I casually mentioned one day that if I was gonna write a song about Texas, I wouldn't call it "Texas State of Mind." I'd call the song "Lone Star State of Mind." I thought that sounded pretty good. I had never been to Texas when I wrote that song. I called my friend Richard Dobson, who was in Houston, and said, "You've been to Corpus Christi, right?" He said, "Yeah." I said, "That's really on the coast, isn't it?" I wasn't sure. I somehow captured the flavor of that area writing the song with Fred Koller. We got lucky.

I saw Johnny Cash for the first time in 1969. He was introducing Kris Kristofferson at the Newport Folk Festival. God, the guy knew how to carry himself onstage and also was generous to bring out a guy like Kris Kristofferson, who wasn't a singer in any sense of the word. Johnny didn't have a problem putting him onstage. Kris told me that was a big deal. The crowd reaction was interesting. Kris was rough as a singer. He made Woody Guthrie look like a singer. Kris was very much influenced by Mickey Newbury lyrically. The thing that separates them, though, was melodies. Kris's were old country melodies. Newbury's were so totally modern.

Mickey got drunk sometimes. I'm sure he got high. I don't think that was his goal in life, though. I think his goal was to be a good family man and pay attention to his kids. I never heard anybody talk about him as a ne'er-do-well. My impression was that Mickey didn't think much of the outlaw country movement. You had to be a real singer to sing a Mickey Newbury song. I think that's why he had early success with people like Tom Jones. "Sweet Memories" is like twelve lines and isn't even really a lyric. Mickey was the consummate musician. He was playing the correct bass notes and descending the lines with the right chords and singing a melody on top. There aren't many guys who are very sophisticated musicians in terms of harmony and understanding the arrangement in a great song. Kris's melodies were simple, but they lent themselves to enormous amounts of interpretation.

Don Williams did the same thing as Mickey. He found a tuning that worked and if you wanted to write a song for Don you had to do it in that tuning. One of the things that's hard to believe is the number of interesting melodies Newbury wrote in one key. One thing I teach kids in my class at Belmont University in Nashville is to change keys if your melodies are starting to sound alike. Your melodies will change. Mickey didn't even really try that evidently, but he was really eclectic. I don't think he cared what genre he was writing in. He had a hit with Solomon Burke, for Christ's sake. Harlan Howard was like that. He was known as the quintessential country songwriter, but he made most of his money on the pop chart with people like Burl Ives and Ray Charles. John D. Loudermilk and the Everly Brothers are others who were country songwriters but got huge hits on the pop charts. Clearly, the Everly Brothers were huge on the pop charts. Nobody was more surprised when I became a country songwriter than me. It was amazing that somebody could be as good as Mickey and then just disappear. It's hard to disappear in this world, but Mickey managed to do it.[5]

Pat Alger has written or cowritten hit songs for Kathy Mattea ("Goin' Gone"), Garth Brooks ("Unanswered Prayers," "Thunder Rolls"), Hal Ketchum ("Small Town Saturday Night"), and Don Williams ("True Love"). He was inducted into the Nashville Songwriters Hall of Fame in 2010.

JOHNNY LEE

I was blown away to meet the one and only Mickey Newbury at a golf tournament. I had heard Mickey on the radio when I was working at Gilley's. He was nice, down to earth, and smoked Camel cigarettes one right after another. The stories he could come up with and put down on paper for music amazed me. Then to get to back up an artist and writer like him onstage in the midseventies [as a guitarist]: wow. He was a heck of a guitarist himself, so I just played rhythm behind him. What an honor. He was mesmerizing. I just soaked it up.

[*Esquire* magazine writer] Aaron Latham came to Dallas because he heard stories about Gilley's nightclub being unique. He met Bud and Sissy and was mesmerized like all of America with the lifestyle, and he wrote ["The Ballad of the Urban Cowboy: America's Search for True Grit"]. Paramount Pictures saw the article and next thing you know they were down there scouting it out. Texas is where all the beautiful women are, and Gilley's was mostly blue-collar people, good old boys and good old girls. There wasn't any other place like it. Next thing you know, there's gonna be a movie. I said, "Yeah, right."

[Legendary music business executive] Irving Azoff came up to me on one of my breaks and wanted to talk. I said, "Yeah, buddy. Sure, sure, as soon as I finish my watermelon here." It's like, "Get the fuck out of here, and leave me alone." Talent scouts coming out had happened before. They're bullshitters. You'd find their business cards all over Gilley's at the end of the night. Anyway, they said John Travolta was gonna show up. Jesus Christ. Next thing you know, Travolta shows up incognito. Sissy Spacek was supposed to be Sissy in the movie, but she turned it down. Deborah Winger took it, and the rest is history, man.

I knew "Looking for Love" was a big song, but I didn't know whether it was gonna be a hit. That's the way the music business is. There are great songs that have been cut that people haven't heard before. I knew it was a hit and I couldn't believe I didn't write it myself. I just changed up some music and made the song what it is. Meanwhile, Newbury and I stayed in touch through golf. He was at the Houston Open with Larry Gatlin, Alex Harvey, Red Lane, and myself. Every once in a while I'd call to check and see how he was doing. He was a great guy. I loved him to death. He was one of us but had extraordinary talent.[6]

Johnny Lee gained fame from his huge crossover hit "Lookin' for Love" from the soundtrack to the film *Urban Cowboy*, which was shot in large part at Gilley's, Mickey Gilley's club in Pasadena, Texas. His other hits include "The Yellow Rose" and "Pickin' Up Strangers."

MICKEY GILLEY

Mickey Newbury and I were recording at the same little studio called Jones Sound Recording in Houston, Texas, a normal recording studio from the sixties and seventies that had a twenty-four-track machine in the console if you wanted to do overdubs. You could layer the sound by adding guitars, bass, drums, and then you could mix it. Mickey and I became friends, and he was writing songs at that time. I remember when he came in one day with his twelve-string guitar and a song called "Just Dropped In (To See What Condition My Condition Was In)." I said, "What were you drinking or smoking when you wrote this one?" He laughed. Such an oddball tune. I didn't think too much of the song until Kenny Rogers had a hit with it. Gee, that was a hit song? I could've recorded it.

I don't know what brought out all the music in him, but I always thought Mickey was a tremendous writer. "She Even Woke Me Up to Say Goodbye" was one heck of a tune. I wish it was given to me, but at the time Jerry Lee Lewis had the hits. I didn't. I wouldn't have had the same hit with it. I remember one of Mickey's ultimate goals was to have Ray Charles cover his tunes, and he lived to see that happen. "An American Trilogy" was really an awesome tune, but I wasn't around then. He had written that after I had left the recording studio and opened up Gilley's. It was amazing to have Elvis do that song. Mickey was having good things happening for him.

We lost touch when I opened Gilley's. He left the area, but we never hung out much even in Houston. We'd go have coffee at a little place called the Pig Stand, which was about six blocks from the recording studio, but other than that we didn't socialize that much outside of chatting about music in the studio. We mostly talked about his songwriting and getting the major stars to record his music. He accomplished that. I thought "How I Love Them Old Songs" was a pretty good tune, and we recorded it [on Gilley's 1975 album *Movin' On*].

Look at Larry Gatlin. I always said you hear a lot of Mickey Newbury in his vocals. I heard Mickey do the demos, and then Larry comes along and starts having hits with his brothers. It was awesome the way his voice reminded me of Mickey's. Larry's a great guy, an awesome entertainer and singer, good songwriter. Mickey was just interested in doing his music. When he got the deal with Acuff-Rose, he had a lot of success and we were all very proud of him. I didn't have a hit until 1974 with "Room Full of Roses." I recorded that at the little studio where Mickey was writing all his songs.

I had a number one song after struggling in the music business for seventeen years. I went on the road with Conway Twitty and Loretta Lynn after that and wasn't paying much attention to what Mickey was doing, except I ran into him at one of the big deal Fan Fares they had in Nashville. That was the last time I saw him. Your life changes quite a bit with a number one hit. I was just a struggling musician up until that time. I went in to record the Harlan Howard tune "She Called Me Baby All Night Long" with the flip side "Room Full of Roses." I didn't think anything about it. I grew up singing that song with my cousins Reverend Jimmy Swaggart and Jerry Lee Lewis.

I never dreamed that song would be a national hit. I went in, did it, and didn't think anything about it. That song became one of my biggest recordings. Conway Twitty came down to the club to hear me do the song. He hadn't put together that Mickey and Gilley's were one and the same. I had a guy come down from Nashville two days later to sign me up with his agency United Talent. He and Loretta Lynn owned it. My dream finally came true. I was out on the road two weeks later opening shows for Conway and Miss Loretta. Of course, I got another boost when John Travolta came down in 1979 and 1980 and did *Urban Cowboy*. It's too bad that Mickey and I weren't closer at the time. I'm sure he would have gotten some music in the film.[7]

Country star **Mickey Gilley** has landed more than forty songs on the country chart including "Room Full of Roses," "Don't the Girls All Get Prettier at Closing Time," and "Stand by Me." His cousins are the singer Jerry Lee Lewis and evangelist Jimmy Swaggart.

JOE HENRY

Meeting Mickey Newbury was the most amazing happenstance in my musical life. My foundation was being John Denver's main cowriter for his whole career, so all my business had been done between New York and Los Angeles. I was an ASCAP writer and they were always putting me together with collaborators because I'm strictly a lyricist. I had had a real bad accident and couldn't do anything for about six months. I went to New York and had a big meeting with ASCAP when I got back on my feet after the accident. They said, "Man, you've got to go to Nashville." "I don't know anybody in Nashville," I said. "The only music people I know are in Los Angeles and New York."

I had a ticket the next day to fly to Los Angeles. They said, "We'll pay to change your ticket if you'll fly from here to Nashville. We'll set up as many meetings as you want for twenty-four hours." Bob Doyle, who would become Garth Brooks's manager, was working for ASCAP and met me. He picked me up and brought me back to his office. He had a whole schedule of appointments for me for the next two days. Then I was going on to LA. My last meeting at the end of that day was at Acuff-Rose with Ronnie Gant. I was sitting in his office, and there were all these Newbury album covers on his wall. I said, "Why do you have all these album covers on your wall?" He said, "We publish Mickey."

I have my folder with a couple of hundred lyric sheets in it when I'm at meetings. "I gotta tell you," I said, "Newbury's music has been my touchstone for the last five years." Ronnie said, "Well, if you could show anything to Mickey, pull three lyrics out and show me." I went through and pulled three out, and he made copies. We shook hands and moved on. I had another meeting. There was a message from Ronnie when I got back to Doyle's office. I called back. "Look," he said. "I called Newbury. He's got a cabin out in Hendersonville. I read him those three lyrics. Newbury said, 'If he can write words like that, I want to meet him.' Do you want to meet Newbury?" "Absolutely."

"He's not doing anything the next couple of days," he said. "Go up there after lunch tomorrow. I'll give you directions." "Okay." I called Mickey. We'd never met. "Be here at three," he said, "and we'll talk." I had my satchel of lyrics with me, and he met me at the door. It was like we already knew each other. I was supposed to have a dinner date that night with a lady friend at eight o'clock. We sat down and talked for a few minutes in his living room, which had this big fireplace. Opposite the fireplace was a couch. We sat on that couch, and he said, "Show me a couple of those lyrics." I pulled my folder out and started flipping through pages. "No, no," he said. "Let me see that folder."

He took out his guitar. He put like three hundred lyrics next to him on the couch and looked at the first lyric and played the song. He did that with a hundred fifty songs. I was stunned. There was no recording device. We finally finished about three-thirty in the morning. I was so blown away. I thought to myself, This is one of those things where I'm the guy out on the ocean by himself, and he catches the most monstrous fish that's ever been caught. That's all he can tell anybody. "I caught this fish. Now it's gone." I have no proof of what I'm talking about. I was supposed to go to LA the next day and I ended up staying in Nashville for two months. We got together every day.

Mickey was starting to put together songs for [*After All These Years*, 1982], which I believe was produced by Norbert Putnam. I was with him every afternoon and evening. He was gonna cut three of my songs that he put music to on the album, but then he backed away. He said, "You know, I've never really written songs with people before. I write my own songs. I'm afraid it won't be a Mickey Newbury album having three songs with another writer." He ended up putting our cowrite "Over the Mountain" on the album. He was staying every night at this famous old place called the Spence Manor while he was recording *After All These Years* in 1981. The swimming pool was shaped like a guitar. Mickey didn't drive, so I'd pick him up at the studio in Franklin every night, get something to eat, and take him back to the Spence Manor.

I later spent eight days living with them in Vida, Oregon, and we had conversations. He was so revered by songwriters and had so many cuts by different people, but I don't think he could believe that he wasn't as famous as Jerry Lee Lewis and Elvis. I think the business machine really killed him. There was another thing that was colossally hurtful to him. Wesley Rose always presented things as Mickey was his son. There probably weren't legal documents. Everything Mickey did he gave to Wesley. Hearsay said that Wesley said in later years, "You're like my son. If I ever get to the place where I'm gonna retire and sell this company, you'll be well taken care of." Wesley sold Acuff-Rose and Mickey got nothing. Zero. Wesley disappeared. That was a killer.

Mickey was completely defeated when he left Nashville. He sold his big log house on the lake in Hendersonville. He told me that he sold everything he had and was going back to Oregon. I got a phone call from Susan one night. She said, "Do you remember the coal bin that's down in the basement?" "Yeah, I do." She said, "Well, Mickey put his five guitars in the bin and locked it. He gave me the key. He said, 'No matter what I do, what I say, don't give me that key. I never wanna see those things again.'" That's what made me want to write this big, long letter to Mickey in February 1984, the longest letter I've ever written. I wanted him to know that I've worked with John Denver, Frank Sinatra, Garth Brooks, and no human being I've ever met is as close to being a bird as Mickey Newbury.

Music came out of him without even thinking about it. "Over the Mountain" happened the same as the others that night. He took the lyric sheet and put music to it. The two other songs Norbert wanted to put on that album are "The Boatman" and "Seven Candles." I could regret not being able to record that the rest of my life or I could give thanks. A mandala is a sand painting that was a sacred healing circle to ancient Indian tribes. Buddhists still do them. There are pictures of incredibly intricate, beautiful mandalas. They sweep it away when it's finished. That night with Mickey was like a mandala in my life that happened between Mickey New-bury's soul and mine.[8]

Longtime John Denver collaborator **Joe Henry** has had his lyrics performed by several dozen artists including Garth Brooks, Rascal Flatts, and Frank Sinatra.

MARK GERMINO

I was working construction in North Carolina during the fall of 1971. I was listening to the area's country station WGBG one Wednesday night, and the disc jockey said, "Gonna let you hear a new guy. Here's something a little different." Damn sure was. Mickey cut into "Frisco Depot," and it absolutely knocked me to the floor. I think I actually lay on the floor because I was so damn happy at what my ears were hearing. I went straight to the record store the next day and saw an album by Mickey Newbury in the rack and wondered who he was. I bought *Frisco Mabel Joy* for $3.99. Then I went home and had a beer and a bowl of cornflakes. That was all I had left in my refrigerator before being paid on Friday.

My girlfriend and I got drunk on Fleischmann's blended whiskey that Friday night and played the album until three in the morning. I haven't been the same since. I never heard Mickey Newbury on that station again either. Mickey had a lot of musical strengths—his timing as a singer, willingness to establish a great first line that neither dazzled nor sold the song out. There was nothing easily predictable in his words or rhyme schemes and his willingness to wait for a form-fitting melody to surround those dagger words. His melodies were both lazy and energetic. His greatest strength was his ability to write a truly indescribably painful broken love song.

Mickey has no harbinger in his music ever. Whatever journey he decided to take you on, there was never any need to warn you or prepare the listener for the next line, the next phrase, the next mix level, or the next song. Nothing was predictable. I loved that he never gave any indication of what might follow within a song. I'll never know if that was intentional or not, and I really don't care. He had omitted that convenient creative characteristic in his writing. He never made it easy for the listener. He engaged and involved you. There was another level of acceptance and understanding that you had to be ready as a listener within Newbury's songs. They were spooky at times.

Mickey had no gimmicks as a performer, no secrets or traps to hold an audience's attention. He just sang, and that's not an easy thing to pull off. He was never a comedian or a man occupied with lamentation, but he could make you laugh or cry. He made you feel good about being there, and for my money it was his ability to render a song that had sweet components running through it without ever sounding fluffy, syrupy, or perfumed in any way. His music was beautiful in a tough way with a slightly jagged edge, but it was never harsh. I love ninety-five percent of his songs, and I don't like that many of the Beatles, Elton John, Hank Williams, or even Bob Dylan.

As I wrote in the liner notes for his album *Nights When I Am Sane*, experiencing Newbury live can go something like this: You sit there and realize you are hearing a piece of work so meaningful in its intent that you fail to notice you are being subjected to a dose of exhaustion so punishing yet so generous with its oxygen. You are not even aware that the ice has completely melted in your drink. You hang there suspended in gratitude, not wanting to be the first to break the spell Newbury put you under. Yet you desperately wish for someone to jab you in the ribs to bring you back to earth long enough to reclaim your bearings so you can have a fighting chance to account for how you have been touched.

Mickey's music helped shape me as a songwriter. Ingesting his music over twenty years and regarding it as soulful and entertaining meant that his artistry has intrigued me for that long. That's a hard thing to do. He's had two decades to seep into my mind. I love "33rd of August," "Apples Dipped in Candy," "T. Total Tommy," "She Even Woke Me Up to Say Goodbye," "The Future Is Not What It Used to Be," "Love Look at Us Now." However, as much as I am a fan of his, I didn't come to Nashville to write Mickey Newbury–type songs. I witnessed many songwriters try that from the early seventies through the early eighties and generally everyone who tried to emulate him failed. Newbury was not meant to be impersonated.

Mickey was meant to be appreciated. He was too original to be successfully copied by anyone. It has been my observation since arriving in Nashville in 1974 that Mickey Newbury is thunderously admired and respected by a vast majority of both run-of-the-mill Nashville songwriters and some extremely jaded listeners. It was heightened when I arrived in Nashville and Newbury was gathering fame. I'm pretty comfortable thinking how I may have actually ripped him off a couple of times, but I can't evoke any certain instances.

I had breakfast with Mickey one morning while I was in Portland, Oregon, and he brought up not being better known. He mentioned that he never liked the road on anyone else's terms but his own. He had no desire to paint by numbers or go through motions when it came to giving live performances. Giving it all was paramount to him, and he didn't think he could do that night after night and maintain his sanity as a responsible performer. Quality was more important than quantity. Taking such an unselfish professional posture may have had an effect on saturating his name on the level of Gordon Lightfoot, Joni Mitchell, Dan Fogelberg, even Kris Kristofferson.

Owsley Manier and Steve Roberts wanted to start the Winter Harvest label for Mickey [in the 1990s]. Both were huge Newbury fans, and Owsley was Mickey's old friend. Their concept was founded on the idea that Mickey's creativity was being wasted and generally ignored. They believed that he had a lot left in the tank. They also believed there were other artists who deserved a place on their label. Naturally, all those noble dreams required dollars, which they were still attempting to accumulate from well-off and like-minded independent investors. That aside, there was never any question about their love for Mickey and his music. They were dedicated to his resurgence.

Those guys caught me performing one night and were captivated. Both knew I had made some albums for RCA/BMG and saw me on the David Letterman show and knew that I lived in Nashville, but they knew very little about me personally. Eventually, they asked me if I would record an album of my songs for Winter Harvest Entertainment. Steve Earle had signed a one-off for *Train a Comin'* about the same time. Steve was really their inaugural move into the music business. His album *Train a Comin'* was probably instrumental in allowing me to get on the Americana radio chart. Mickey was hanging around the studio while I was recording *Rank & File* [1995]. Steve Roberts realized that I had yet to sign my contract with Winter Harvest and Mickey was there. So, as I signed, Mickey's signature is on my contract as a witness to my signing, which is kind of cool. Mickey and I later did a show at the Ace of Clubs in Nashville with me opening, a fascinating evening.

My personal relationship with Mickey was both highly enjoyable and relatively short lived. He journeyed on back to Springfield, Oregon, after we spent some time together on Winter Harvest to be with his family. He seemed to settle in there for a while. I wasn't one to keep close tabs on him so most of my updates on anything he did came from Owsley. Mickey did, however, call me from time to time as he did with a lot of people. That really lit me up. The conversations lasted more than two hours more than once. Our discussions were typically wide ranging as he would often hold forth on various subjects from his early days riding in a beat-up car through the South and writing songs to UFOs. We mostly talked about writing.

We discovered that we shared the opinion that a song is never really finished. A song can grow and evolve just like a plant or change, expand, or develop as the years roll by. That explained why Mickey was always carefully tweaking his own work and expertly recording the same song several times if he felt like it. I think he enjoyed exploring his own music that way. He'd bring his own song lines as conversation and sometimes astonish me by bringing up mine. He sat his phone down one time in a position he had perfected and started singing "In '59." He blew me away with not only the song, which I had never heard, but with his amazing sound quality presentation over a phone. I remain amazed to this day by what I heard that afternoon.

I learned about his life-threatening chronic obstructive pulmonary disease over one of those phone calls. I felt comfortable asking him about his life expectancy. He readily answered, "About five years, Mark." He was pretty accurate. I always saw joy in the man whether I was around him in Nashville or Portland or at the Flora-Bama. I always found him personable to everyone he was in contact with. I'm still amazed at the love he showed to my nine-year-old daughter when he met her one evening before he went onstage. It was simply a lesson in how you should care about people. The man shined like he had been tapped from on high. He also had a deeply rooted attachment to his family back in Oregon.

His attachment never wavered. There was never any, "I'm out of town, so I'm not thinking about you." He would speak about his wife and family as if they were in the next room. They were totally connected. I'm guessing that his Texas roots were similar in strength. I got a firsthand glimpse into that after Mickey had passed. His mother, Mamie, came to my show at the Crighton Theatre in Conroe, Texas. I didn't even know her, but she danced up to me in a red cowgirl dress at eighty-plus years old. Emerging from a family like that sure enough explains where the love he showed others came from. Mamie danced up. "You were a friend of Mickey's, so I came to see you," she said. "Now I'm going dancing. You want to come?"[9]

Mark Germino's high-water mark *Rank and File* was released on the Winter Harvest record label around the same time as Mickey Newbury's *Nights When I Am Sane* in the midnineties. Germino has written songs for Kenny Chesney, Paul Craft, and Emmylou Harris.

RICHARD LEIGH

I was twenty-two years old and in college at Virginia Commonwealth University in Richmond, Virginia. A local songwriter went onstage at a coffeehouse and started singing the most beautiful song I'd ever heard: "San Francisco Mabel Joy." I almost knocked over my Diet Coke. I said, "Who wrote that?" He said, "Mickey Newbury." That's how I first heard his name. I was amazed that [the singer] didn't write it. For the song to translate so powerfully through a local songwriter really showed its strength. "San Francisco Mabel Joy" was the bar for all songs after that. I would be surprised if I'm ever moved by a song that much again.

I moved to Nashville in 1975. The city was fabulous then. I was living in a little duplex, and my neighbor kept playing "She Even

Woke Me Up to Say Goodbye." "Who wrote that?" I kept running into this same genius writer. I'd heard the Kenny Rogers hit "Just Dropped In (To See What Condition My Condition Was In)" in high school. I discovered Mickey wrote that, too. I thought he was the most brilliant, original lyricist I'd heard in a long time. I kept bumping into his music around town. People all talked about Mickey, Townes Van Zandt, Guy Clark. Mickey had a plaintive approach to singing and songwriting that was even greater than Hank Williams Sr. Hank could kill you with his sadness and dark-side-of-the-street songs, but Mickey took it to a new level.

Guy and I were having drinks one day in Nashville over by the old Catholic cathedral and St. Mary's bookstore. Harlan Howard used to camp out there every afternoon. Guy got up to get more drinks and this other guy sat down in his seat. "Hi," he said. "I'm Mickey Newbury." "Nice to meet you. I've heard lots about you." He looked around the room a while. I was fascinated by him. He was so polite and included me in the conversation as if we were old friends. I ran into him once or twice more around town. I thought Mickey was exactly who he appeared to be. He was sincere with his feet on the ground in spite of all the wonderful things people were saying about him. I guess that's why he appeared so honest in his songs. My impression was that he was honest in everyday life. He was a good one.

Those guys were kings during the wonderful seventies singer-songwriter moment. Then they went on to a slicker sound, but music and writing songs really saved my life. I was a sad son of a gun, an orphan boy and twice a foster kid. I heard Hank Williams Sr. and thought it was the saddest music I'd ever heard. "Where is this music being made?" I can identify with that music. I loved the way they had Mickey's gorgeous, incredible, plaintive vocals way out front on the records. I didn't identify with Elvis singing about girls or the Beatles singing about dancing. I wasn't there yet. I wanted to talk about how life had ripped my heart out as a young boy. I heard Hank and went, "I'm going where he was."

I found a couple more songwriters like Townes and Harlan. I loved those songs. It made me happy to be sad. Mickey was a kindred spirit. I doubt the current "bro country" songwriters have even heard of him, but everyone talked about him in the seventies and eighties and early nineties. Everyone loved him, but the media is the media. They let him go. People all the time ask about an artist, "What happened to so and so?" Well, they're out there playing. They're just not on the radio. They were gigging and doing corporate jobs. Man, he could sing and when he was on TV everyone would talk about him.

I thought I'd heard a short story when I heard "San Francisco Mabel Joy." It was so beautifully written and created a mental video. The song ended like a book. "Oh, man. It's over? I wish I could start it again." You felt like there was a whole lot of stuff in there. He had a powerful lyrical style that was deceptively simple, but every word counts. His economy was such that he could fit a huge story into a few minutes, which was great and so artistic, yet commercial at the same time. I was drawn to that as a guy trying to make a living in commercial music. I found the key to connecting with an audience is brutal honesty. If you can say something honestly it touches people, and they immediately know what you're talking about. It's so popular and yet everyone thinks it's so original. What's original about it is not that you've touched a human being but that you had the guts to say it. Mickey did. He was a master.[10]

Richard Leigh might be best known for writing Crystal Gayle's Grammy Award–winning song "Don't It Make My Brown Eyes Blue," a song that friend and fellow songwriter Guy Clark frequently noted was written about Leigh's pet. "Dog had cataracts," Clark would quip.

JAY BOLOTIN

Mickey indefatigably supported my writing. I'd often stay at Mickey and Susan's house near the lake in Hendersonville, ride around in his Mercedes, and have a good time. Mickey would tell me to drink coffee right before bed when I would stay overnight. I didn't stick with that regimen, but I tried it out. He had advice, was quite the loquacious host, and was a great talker. He'd want to talk about politics and had advice on what shampoo to use on my beard. He'd

sometimes very convincingly say, "You know, there are voices in this
room that we can't hear." I'd look around. He'd turn the volume up
on the radio and laugh. "See?" That seemed to make some important point to him. Staying with Mickey was always an adventure.

Mickey got a call one time when I was staying over. He hung up
and said, "Come on, Jay, we've got something to do." "Where are we
going?" "We're going to meet a chiropractor at a 7-Eleven." I distinctly remember that Mickey couldn't start his brand-new Mercedes but finally figured out how to turn it on. Off we went to meet
the guy. Sure enough, it said "chiropractor" on the panel van. He
said, "Merle Haggard's in town to play a concert tomorrow, and he's
got a crick in his neck. We're gonna go over to his girlfriend's house."
Merle and his girlfriend were there as well as a little boy and a Chihuahua. Everyone but the little boy, the Chihuahua, and me went
in the other room. They came out and Mickey said, "Play Merle a
song." I did. Merle didn't say much. Then Mickey and Merle went
back into the bedroom and when they came out Mickey said, "Play
another one." Merle said, "Okay. We're gonna record you." Mickey
would go a long way to introduce people to my songs. Mickey and
Merle were both very much gentlemen and American music afi-
cionados.

I'd sometimes sit in when he was doing sessions over at Acuff-
Rose. He was an adventurous fellow in terms of recording. I remember one session at Acuff-Rose when he couldn't find the rain
tape he recorded so he said, "Well, here's another album where I
recorded rain. Just record that." The engineer balked at that, but
Mickey said it'd be fine so that's what they did. Mickey seemed to
be in charge. I opened the show one of the few times he played
Nashville. Boy, the place was packed. The show was at the Exit/In.
Kristofferson came back into the dressing room quoting lyrics of
mine that he had just heard for the first time. I thought, Wow, these
guys are serious about songwriting. That was Mickey's doing. He
made Kris come and listen to me.

I didn't quite get Nashville. I lived there about two years, and
the longer I was there the more I seemed to notice that songwriters would start to write songs about writing songs. I didn't wanna
write songs about writing songs or life on the road. I wanted to

live life and come from that point of view. That's the good version of the story. If someone were prescient, they could also say, "Yeah, you also got fired from two publishing companies." Well, that's true too. I remember sitting with a lovely guy at BMI once who asked me to come in to play a few songs. He'd heard me playing in clubs. I played him two or three songs and he looked at me intensely. He said, "You really do write songs for some other reason than to make money, don't you?" "Yeah, probably." That didn't faze Mickey.

Mickey believed in my songs even though they weren't commercially viable. He called everyone idiots on Music Row in an article in the *Tennessean*. People would introduce themselves for years after that by saying, "I'm one of those idiots on Music Row. Nice to meet you." Mickey enjoyed his success. He said, "My wealth comes in eighty-dollar checks." He had so many cuts by so many people. I don't know why that is. Obviously, he wrote lovely songs, but he was also a lovely person. People loved Mickey. If I played a new song to him, he'd sing along the way he would do it. I played him a song called "Ripples in a Pond," which is about a guy who throws a rock in a pond and comments on the ripples, but then they're gone and the rock is, too. The next time I stayed with them, he gave me a polished rock. He said, "Here's your rock back." How thoughtful is that?[11]

Jay Bolotin earned fans such as Merle Haggard, Mickey Newbury, Norbert Putnam, and Porter Wagoner during the seventies and eighties, but he has remained largely on the fringe. Dan Fogelberg recorded his song "It's Hard to Go Down Easy."

DAVID SHEPHERD GROSSMAN

I opened for Mickey Newbury at the Sweetwater [Music Hall] in Mill Valley, but I didn't know who he was. My roommate told me it would change my life. I was like, "Whatever." I was backstage before the gig tuning to my harmonica. Mickey says, "What are you tuning to, son?" "My harmonica." He goes, "You don't have an electric tuner?" This was in 1987. Nobody had those. "No." He goes, "You can have my electric tuner." He just gave me his electric tuner before he even saw me play. It was amazing. I was so blown away. He played after my set and was the best solo act I'd ever seen before or since. I've been doing music for forty years. He was the best songwriter and balladeer ever. We stayed in touch the rest of his life.

Mickey called me every four to six months and played songs over the phone while we talked. Amazing. I've opened for a lot of people, but he's the only one who kept in touch. I wouldn't have called him. It would have been like me calling Bruce Springsteen. He called me out of the blue. I talked to some people who knew him in the meantime like Scott Turner in Nashville, who wrote songs with Audie Murphy. He told me, "You don't let that man out of your sight. He's a teacher." He was. He taught me how to write ballads. There's a guy named Ernie Bunch, who's the mayor of Cave Creek, Arizona. He was really good friends with Mickey. I could play him twenty of my songs and he'd go, "Play another Mickey song." People who knew him loved him. That was the great thing about Mickey Newbury. He was so down to earth. I used to tape the songs he used to play for me over the phone. He'd call and sing four songs. "These are new, Dave," he'd say. "Let me know what you think."

He used to say he was gonna hand out razor blades at the beginning of his shows. He really thought he was a downer, but he enriched me with the songs. I play "Frisco Depot," "Apples Dipped in Candy," "Willow Tree," "She Even Woke Me Up to Say Goodbye" when I play here in Studio City, California. Musicians who hear me do those songs want to know where they came from. They ask me all the time if I wrote them. I'm like, "No, no, no. That's a Mickey Newbury song." They go online and find out about him. I think he'll be more popular as more people find out about him. He gave up toward the end. He felt like time had passed and people didn't know about him anymore. It was sad. He really deserved a bigger audience.[12]

David Shepherd Grossman is a singer-songwriter based in Studio City, California. He performed with Mickey Newbury in the late eighties, and they maintained a friendship for years.

FRED KOLLER

I was making a record with Bobby Bare when he was producing Mickey's album *Rusty Tracks* in 1975. We spent a lot of time
together. The songwriting community was much smaller then and
most people knew what others were working on. Mickey cut my
song "Show Business Has Sure Been Good to Me" at the old Acuff-
Rose building over on Franklin Road. Then we got to spend the day
listening to him and a small band go through a bunch of songs he
liked for a new project. Always great to sit across from Mickey and
hear him play and tell his endless stories. A typical conversation
with him would go from a sandwich he had in New York to UFOs
in Bend, Oregon. He was all over the map, but he really listened
to other people's songs and encouraged everyone he was around.
I heard his records for years and loved *Rusty Tracks*. I was thrilled
to get to spend time with him.

There was mutual support when Newbury lived in Nashville.
Everything changed when Belmont came into Music Row and
pushed that to the side. Belmont is a very Christian school. Mike
Curb started supplying his interns who had grown up listening to
more contemporary Christian music rather than Lefty Frizzell and
George Jones. You weren't able to be unattractive and be a country singer over a period of time. All the songs took on a generic
rock-and-roll feel. It was sad to watch so many great singers get
pushed to the side starting in the early eighties. They still have a
music program there, but I can't say that the music has improved
with these people. I understand that they're trying to sell records,
but they have the same six people on the awards shows year after
year after year now.

Somebody new looks exactly like someone who's already been
there. The business is no longer song driven. The producer and publisher have four writers and they're gonna sit down and write a song
for Jake Owen that'll never get covered again. Mickey should've
been a bigger artist. He started out with songs like "Just Dropped
In (To See What Condition My Condition Was In)" that really made
careers. I liked "Cortelia Clark" and "Leaving Kentucky," which they
did on the *Rusty Tracks* record when I was in the studio recording.
I remember Larry Gatlin coming in. Everyone was so excited just
to have Mickey in town making new music.

Mickey was a giant, a songwriter-performer who could go out with the best people like Red Lane. Red was playing classical guitar and had a great voice like Mickey. Everything fit together. Mickey was the consummate showman every time I saw him at a time when there were people in town who couldn't play their instrument. I'm sure he influenced all my songs because he was a great storyteller. I've always tried to tell a story in my songs like "Jennifer Johnson and Me," which Robert Earl Keen covered on [his 1989 breakthrough, *West Textures*]. I'd play that song if Mickey walked in right now and asked me what I have that's new. I had the idea for "Jennifer Johnson and Me," and Shel Silverstein and I just rode around and wrote the song. He and Bare had just done *Lullabys, Legends, and Lies*. Mac Davis did a version of "Jennifer Johnson and Me." So did Conway Twitty.

Shel was a very fast writer. It was hard to get him to stop when he got on a roll. We'd get together and write ten songs in a week. We were just eating and writing all over Northern California and in Martha's Vineyard. He was always polishing and improving his songs. He called me two nights before he died and was still polishing a song that we had started doing fifteen years earlier. "We should do this. We should try that." He really believed in his songs. Shel didn't quite fit into the bounds of country music for some people, but when you look at his catalog you see that he was writing songs for Ernest Tubb and Loretta Lynn along with Dr. Hook. He was writing good songs. Mickey and Shel were always just coming through town even when Mickey lived on the lake.

Mickey probably wasn't better known because everyone thinks that Elvis wrote "An American Trilogy." They think Kenny Rogers wrote "Just Dropped In." Mickey's songs fit the artist who cut them so well. You never dreamed that those people didn't write them. Country music radio didn't really seem to be jumping on records with rain sound effects and the production he was doing even though they were beautiful records that I still play all the time today. I've encountered it so many times: "Here's Robert Earl Keen singing a Shel Silverstein song." "No, we wrote that one together." Same thing over and over.

I could easily see more pop singers doing Mickey Newbury songs. Miley Cyrus could do a great album with his songs. I would much rather listen to that than somebody all rhinestoned up singing songs that are nowhere near that quality. I think that his music will survive even though I don't think he has anyone actively working his catalog. Unfortunately, the new writers would stare back at you if you asked any of them about Mickey Newbury. Gretchen Peters recently recorded an album of his songs. Fabulous. She's very well respected. Sometimes that's what it takes, like when Jennifer Warnes did that Leonard Cohen record. That really showed a whole different side of his songs. I think that Mickey's songs are so good. I don't see them going away quickly.[13]

Fred Koller has written songs recorded by Bobby Bare ("This Guitar Is for Sale"), Robert Earl Keen ("Jennifer Johnson and Me")," Jerry Lee Lewis ("Circumstantial Evidence"), and more. He's best known for his collaborations with cartoonist, children's author, and songwriter Shel Silverstein.

INTERLUDE: A SONG FOR SUSAN

Kenny Rogers and Mickey went to different high schools in Houston but knew each other well. I was in the New Christy Minstrels, and we were sent to Nashville to spend time in the studio. Kenny went on and on about his friend in Nashville. He said he was trying to break into the music business, and we really needed to help. Kenny's always been a promoter and spins things. We were supposed to record one of Mick's songs but found out he had four different songs in the number one position on different charts when we got to Nashville: country, soul, R & B, and easy listening. Mickey needed no help from Kenny. We never did do his song. The songs he wrote weren't like what the Christies did anyway. Anyway, Mickey and I were introduced in the locker room at Vanderbilt before the concert that night. I thought he was cute but didn't really think about him again, and then I left the Christies a few months later. I was tired of the road and wanted to go back to school.

Kenny pointed out Mickey on the television on *The Joey Bishop Show* one night when I was nannying for [Rogers's third wife] Margo [Anderson] and him. "You met Mickey at Vanderbilt," he said. "We're going out to dinner with him tonight." I said, "No." "You will," Kenny said, "or you're fired." "Okay." We went to dinner and saw *2001: A Space Odyssey*. Mickey and I had just ended relationships, and I don't think we said four words to each other. Kenny drove to Mick's hotel across the street from Grauman's Chinese Theatre to drop him off. I got out to let Mick out. Kenny just waved and took off in the car when Mick cleared the door. I was so mad, but that was typical. Kenny and Margo were matchmakers. Mickey was so embarrassed. My car was at Kenny's house, but Mickey was the perfect gentleman. "I can't believe Kenneth would do that," Mickey said. "I'll get you a cab."

Mickey promised the cab would be there soon. He asked if I would come upstairs and listen to a new song he had just written before it arrived. He was so genuine. He was writing what became *Looks Like Rain*. I listened to almost all those songs before I went home and was blown away. I hadn't heard lyrics and music like that. We were singing "Green, Green" and "This Land Is Your Land" in the Christies. I couldn't believe how good he was. I had never heard him sing that way even though I had seen him at Vanderbilt and on *The Joey Bishop Show*.

I would stop occasionally at Kenny and Margo's and would ask about their friend from Houston, but I didn't see Mickey for two years. I had decided I wanted a career, which meant no relationships. Then I was coming back from a stint in Tahoe and was headed for Casper, Wyoming. Mickey and Kris Kristofferson were there. It was like coming home. I didn't even see Kris in the room. Seeing Mickey rattled me so badly that I got in my car after dinner with them, drove all night to Oregon, and didn't even call to cancel the date we had set up for the next day. We had been in each other's company for eight hours total over a two-year span. My feelings scared me.

Margo called me two days later and read me the riot act. Mickey had been writing the *John Hartford Special*, but he walked off the job and drove to Houston after I went back to Oregon. His mom said he was silent for two weeks. I was sent to Nashville not long after, and Mick was at the gate when I got off the plane. Kenny had called and told him. Mickey said to me, "We're going to Gallatin and getting married. You know that we're going to mess this up if we don't." We were married by three o'clock that afternoon. I knew marrying Mickey was the right thing. I can't tell you how, but I knew. Most women fall head over heels for Kristofferson. I hardly remembered that he was there. Mickey was my focus. Singing fell by the wayside after we got married. I didn't go back to Los Angeles. I called my roommate and my sister and said, "Guess what? I'm not coming home." "What?" Mickey and I had four kids and were best friends for thirty-two years.

Mickey was always looking for a common thread running through experiences no matter what culture you were brought up in. He had had a crazy upbringing. Mickey's family was very close and loving, but they had some crazy stories. His parents listened to all music. His dad would take him to visit his aunt Mattie in Kountz. Mickey would sneak off and listen to the music in black churches. Mattie lived next door to Jerry Lee Lewis, Jimmy Swaggart, and Mickey Gilley's grandmother, and Mickey would listen to those three playing music on the front porch on hot summer nights.

He would hang out in Bossier City, Louisiana, with Percy Mayfield and other black writers before we were married. The Ku Klux Klan ran him out of town and threatened to kill him. He didn't hang out with the traditional writers. He wasn't looking for fame or fortune. He was looking for people he could communicate with. He would get an idea and start humming something. He never really wrote with anybody. His process was too internal. Songs took a long, long time.

His favorite album was *Looks Like Rain*. He really liked *Lulled by the Moonlight*, too. He was such a Stephen Foster fan. That whole album was his concept of Stephen Foster, Americana music, and its simplicity. He didn't care that the album wasn't a hit with other people. He did it for himself. I like *Stories from the Silver Moon Cafe* probably because the songs are very personal to me. "A Storm Is Comin'" was most personal to us. People don't realize that there are multiple levels in that song. Mickey was a political animal. He was in special forces in the army and ended up in some crazy parts of the world like Thailand, Cambodia, the Congo. He was a radio operator, but he was a risk taker and would volunteer to go on those things. He didn't have a family and made great extra-duty pay. I also really liked *Blue to This Day*. Those were my last years with him.

He wrapped many experiences into one nice package in writing "So Sad." Women loved Mickey because there wasn't anything predatory about him. He was a safe place. I can't tell you how many country females gravitated toward him. He was their best friend and would always listen. Mickey spent hours on the phone talking them through divorces and other problems. He was just saying how sad it is when relationships fall apart in "So Sad." He wrote another song about Hank Cochran and his wife, Jeannie [Seely]. They lived together for years in apartments next door to each other. Hank took a chain saw and carved a doorway between the apartments. I guess he paid for all the damages. They lived together like that all these years and all of a sudden they decided they wanted to get married and their marriage fell apart within six months. That piece of paper made all the difference in the world. It was ridiculous. Mickey's song has the line, "Once they were lovers, but now they're not friends / She's found another, he says it's the end / To think they once tore down a wall for a door / Now they don't speak anymore."

Mickey was constantly rewriting. Songs were never finished, which drove me crazy. He'd do my favorite version and then combine it with something else. Some songs would come overnight. We were on the beach with our six-month-old son, Chris, in Surfside, California, visiting friends one time. They'd gone to work. I remember sitting Chris down on the sand. He would take handfuls of sand, let them go, and watch the wind scatter the sand. He did that for ten minutes. Mickey looked at me and said, "I'll be back in about thirty minutes." He took off and went back to the apartment. He had written "Willow Tree" by the time I got back. Another time he woke me up in the middle of the night and he said, "You have to listen to this." He was working on a melody and sang it. "You have a problem," I said. "That's the Pepsi commercial on the air right now." He was so mad.

Also, Mickey was really good with the music business. He could read a contract like you could not believe. People would come to him with theirs. Mickey would go, "Okay, be careful of this and that." He had an incredibly good business sense, but that also put him in the crosshairs because the companies thought he was hard to get along with. He would not jump through their hoops and play their games. They'd say, "We'll advance you two hundred thousand dollars." "I don't want you to advance me two hundred thousand dollars," he'd say. "If you do that, I'm your monkey. I don't want to be your monkey. I want a decent wage for what I do."

Mickey would give you the shirt off his back. We were on a road trip in Kentucky one time, and this kid filled our car with gas. He was trying to be a songwriter. Mickey turned around and picked up his twelve string from the back seat and gave it to him. He wrote so many good things on that. I wanted to throttle him. "Nope," he said. "It'll do him more good than me now." There was some young kid on our couch at least once a month in Nashville. They'd come to town and we were in the phone book. They'd call, and Mickey would go get them. They'd stay for a couple of days and then Mickey would take them downtown and introduce them around. He'd grown up in a big family who always helped each other out. He believed that's what you did. I used to joke that our phone number was on the wall at the Greyhound station.

We didn't listen to music in the house. The kids had to listen to their music with headphones in their rooms. Mickey didn't want that pollution. He didn't want to get hooked on something that had already been done. He thought of his songs as his children. He told me before he died, "Please don't sell the children." His one frustration was he knew he'd be known for "An American Trilogy" and not something he wrote. He'd written so many other songs, but that's what he'd be remembered by.

Writing was his communication. He'd write whatever communicated with the people we were hanging out with at the time. He understood people. He could play blues, bluegrass, country, rock and roll, anything he wanted to. We went to some big shindig in Steamboat Springs, Colorado, one time. He had a friend in the oil business named Jakey Sandifer. Jakey had put this group together of people who had grown up as teenagers in the fifties. Jakey flew all these songwriters out to perform. These writers got out in front of this crowd who couldn't care less about country music, and they all bombed one after another. Mickey was watching backstage.

I thought, What's he gonna do? These people are getting drunk. Nobody's listening. Mickey goes out and starts with a story about how he was in a doo-wop band called the Embers in the fifties and talked about how songs used the same three or four chords. He did all these old fifties songs. I swear he had them all eating out of his hand within ten minutes. The place was totally locked in on what he was doing, and he never sang one of his own songs. He walked offstage with the biggest grin. I said, "I can't believe you pulled that off." "Ah, you just give them what they want. They don't wanna listen to lyrics. They want to relive their teenage years."

He'd perform with Willie or Kris, and they'd have all these guys onstage. The mikes would be wide open in an auditorium. You couldn't understand anything. Mickey would walk out with just his guitar and one mike and people would be spellbound and listen. He was that good. He knew what he had to do to get the audience, which came from all those years performing in high school. He loved the Embers because he got the girls. There were fan clubs. He was a skinny white boy in a school that was eighty percent black and seventeen percent Mexican. White kids were the minority. So, he thought having a group like the Embers and girls wearing the same color sweater behind them because they were the fan club was great.

Waylon found [his wife] Jessi [Colter] about six months after we got married. Kris was singing duets with [his wife] Rita [Coolidge]. Joan Baez and Dylan weren't really hanging out anymore, but she was singing with other guys. There were all these duos happening. Mickey turned to me and said, "Well, I guess we should work on some things together." I looked at him and said, "Are you nuts? I would never go onstage with you." "Why?" "Because you're too good. There's no way. You can forget that right now." The relief on his face was magic. He was so grateful he wasn't gonna have to go through that. I said, "You go be onstage. You go do your thing. I'm fine. I'll stand backstage and whisper lyrics to you or whatever." I didn't want to go onstage. He was too good by himself. People wouldn't sing after him.

We talked about *Live at Montezuma Hall*, but that record wasn't his favorite by a long shot. He would have recorded more by himself and the guitar in the studio if the labels were okay with it. Elektra wasn't. RCA certainly wasn't. They jazzed everything up, which is why he didn't want to go back to them. He was really into the sound effects. He liked flow and the concept album. His favorite Willie Nelson release was *Red Headed Stranger*. He loved the Beach Boys' *Pet Sounds*. We probably listened to the Beatles' *Yellow Submarine* more than I can remember. He was more into concept album theatrics. One thing about *Montezuma Hall* is the talking. He wouldn't talk onstage up until that time. He wouldn't tell stories. He went from song to song to song. "They put out a tape recorder that night," he said. "I can't wait to hear what that shit sounds like." I remember him telling me that he talked more onstage that night and he was okay with that. He felt good opening up.

I loved the houseboat. We lived on the boat for five years. Guitar pulls were regular: Hank Cochran, Ferlin Husky, Merle Travis, Red Lane, Dallas Frazier, Dottie West. Tanya Tucker slept on our couch for a little while, as did any new songwriter trying to find a place to hang. Townes, Guy, Sonny Throckmorton, and David Allan Coe hadn't come to town yet. It kills me to hear Kris talk about how he took care of Mickey. That is the biggest laugh of the century. Kris was a mess. I still tease him about it. Mickey was a neat freak because of his years in the military. Kris couldn't live with Mickey because he polished the brass screws in the headliner of the boat. Mickey had four pictures symmetrically on the wall. Everything was tidy and put away. Kristofferson is the exact opposite. They tried to stay together on the boat and they went to Los Angeles a couple of times. They wanted to kill each other.

Kris says, "I was always there to take care of Mick." "Kris, you don't know what you're talking about." Kris couldn't even take care of himself, but I love him. Mickey was always there for people to bounce ideas off. Kris and Mickey had a love-love relationship. Kris loved Mickey's writing and Mickey felt the same way about his. Mickey talked Kris into staying in Nashville when he was on his way to West Point to teach and stopped in Nashville to show some songs. He ended up at Bob Beckham's at Tree Music. Mickey heard him there. He was like, "Dude, you can't leave this town. You're too good." "Well, I'm married and have kids," Kris said. "I have to make a living." Mickey said, "Go get yourself a job as a janitor." So, Kris did. He went to Columbia Records. Unfortunately, that ended his first marriage.

People were really drawn to the boat. That was the thing: come to Nashville, go see Newbury's boat, and hang. Liza Minnelli spent the night with us. Ricky Nelson came out. Mickey liked that. He didn't like to go anywhere. We didn't even have a car the first two years we were married. I went to the grocery story with the gal whose husband ran the marina. There were a couple of restaurants on the lake, and we'd eat there occasionally. We were usually on the boat. He loved it. We'd go find islands and pull up for a day or two. Mickey loved to fish. He liked the peace and quiet. He didn't feel badly because people would say they were coming over and he'd say, "Sorry, we're up the lake." He liked the solitude, but we also had a really tight group of friends from all professions on the lake. John Cash and June Carter Cash would go fishing with us on the boat some Saturday mornings, or we'd go get them when they had people lined up around their house looking in their sliding glass door.

People crashed all the time. I can't tell you how many times we'd wake up and find Dallas Frazier asleep on the couch because he'd gone out and bought a dump truck or big excavator and didn't want to go home and tell his wife. I'd wake up and look in the parking lot and say, "Uh-oh. Dallas is in trouble again." He'd have to return it because his wife would be mad. The boat was a small space, but it was perfect for us before we had kids. Also, guitar pulling started between Hank Cochran's house and our boat. I'd sit in the galley and watch. They loved to drop lines in front of each other. Mickey would save lines to drop in front of Cochran. Cochran would look all squirrelly and say, "I'll be back in an hour." Mickey would laugh and say, "I knew Hank would want that one."

They loved playing songs for each other. They'd help each other out with their ideas. Many times they'd all be working on the same kind of song at the same time. Who knew what planted that seed. There was one night not too long after we got married where we had this ridiculous, scary, and violent thunderstorm. There was lightning and it was raining like crazy. Mickey was in the shower around ten o'clock at night. Somebody banged at the door. "Oh my gosh, what is that?" I cracked the door, and on the other side is this full, black beard with a shaved head: Shel Silverstein. "Is Mickey home?" I thought I was gonna die. I didn't know who he was. I'd read his stuff, but I'd never seen him. You never knew who was gonna drop by at any time.

Townes frustrated Mickey so badly. We'd get calls from him in later years here in Oregon. Townes would be melodramatic and telling Mickey good-bye. He'd tell Mickey he'd overdosed. Mickey would be so furious. Townes wouldn't tell him where he was, so Mickey would have to get on the phone with the police and they would have to start narrowing things down. Where was his credit card used last? What hotel was he in? I remember one time Mickey was so upset with him because they barely got to him in time. They ended up breaking down the hotel door. Townes would do this melodramatic farewell stuff and get everybody all upset. What's Mickey gonna do from two thousand miles away?

Mickey didn't want to raise a child on the boat when I got pregnant with [our first child] Chris. He bought a cabin on Old Hickory. When I was eight months pregnant, he said, "We're not raising kids here. We're moving to Oregon." "I'm not going anywhere," I said. "I'm eight months pregnant." Mickey asked me how soon could I travel. I told him probably about six weeks after the baby was born. He sent me to Houston to see his folks for about two weeks and then asked me to fly out to show the baby to my family in Oregon. "Your mom and dad really want to see the baby," he said. "I know your mom saw him when he was born, but your dad really wants to see him." He picked me up from the airport and then drove past my parents' house to this gorgeous mountain chalet about half a mile down the street. I was confused. "Who lives here?" I asked. "We do," he said. I walked in, and everything out of our cabin—including the sixteen-foot credenza that he had bought in Portland and shipped to Nashville and shipped back—was there.

He had packed everything and moved clear across the country while I was in Houston. My mom said they unloaded the moving vans and they had trash cans that still had garbage in them. He paid them to pick up and move everything. We loved living there. My brother lived behind us. My sister bought a house on the road. Our kids grew up in this fantasy land in the woods with family all around. You learned not to be surprised about anything Mickey did because he was pretty spontaneous. The only thing I had said before was, "Don't bring me back to Oregon and then tell me you can't stand the rain." I love it here. He said the rain wouldn't get to him, but it did. There are a lot of songs about rain, but he was willing to make that sacrifice because he saw how good it was for the kids.

We were on the road quite a bit during Chris's first three years. We tried traveling on a motor home after Leah was born in 1977. Nashville had changed, and Mickey didn't want anything to do with big labels anymore. Rumors flew that he died. Rumors flew that he was a drug addict, hence "People Are Talking" [from *Rusty Tracks*]. Mickey was an amazing father. He always took the whole first year and changed all the diapers, got up in the middle of the night, sang to them, put them down for naps on his chest singing to them, and just stayed around, except to play fifty-four holes of golf at five o'clock every morning. Mickey laughed at those guys who chased the little white ball for years when we first were married. You wouldn't have ever caught him playing golf.

Then he started having severe back problems. He found a

great doctor in Nashville when Chris was six months old, and he fixed everything. He told Mickey he had to get exercise and not sit hunched over the guitar all day. "Where in the world," he said, "am I gonna walk?" Not long after that we were in Louisiana with Mickey's best friend from high school. He said, "Hey, come walk with me on the golf course. You don't have to play. Just walk with me." He put a golf club in Mickey's hands that night. He was an addict from that day on. Mick played fifty-four holes every day and walked every chance he could get. He would go out in the rain, sleet, snow. He loved charity tournaments. They were a great way for writers to connect. We didn't see friends from Nashville anymore. They were on the road, but people would play golf tournaments and then spend all night singing to each other.

Darrell Royal loved Mickey. Mickey didn't care a whit about football. He never asked Darrell about football, but he'd sit and sing to him for hours. They met because Mickey was playing a charity golf tournament in Texas. He didn't have that connection with men in particular, but he got that playing golf all the time. He told me one time, "You buy too much fabric." "I'll put one yard of fabric to every golf club you have," I said. "I'll bet you come out the winner." "I don't want to talk about it." He loved refinishing golf clubs. He would take old golf clubs people didn't want or were throwing away, and he'd dismantle the club, refinish, glue, and reset it. Then he'd give it away. He refinished hundreds and hundreds of clubs.

Mickey didn't like to travel and be away from home. He didn't care about being famous. Kenny Rogers could never understand that about Mickey. He'd take him on the plane and say, "Don't you want one of these?" "No," Mickey would say. "Way too much responsibility. No, thanks. Don't want one of these. Don't want forty people depending on me for their next paycheck. Kenny, you're an idiot. You're gonna have to lay all this down one of these days." That's one reason he liked playing by himself. He didn't have to worry about paying someone else. So, sometimes he liked to perform. Sometimes he didn't. Many times that depended on the audience. He would sit in our living room and sing for friends for three and four hours at a time.

Mickey felt deserted by the industry after we moved to Oregon. He wouldn't do their song and dance. Kris used to get so frustrated.

Mickey would say, "Kris, you're not writing anymore. You only have so much energy and if you go out on that stage every night and re-create those songs, you're using that energy. You're not gonna have any kind of energy to write new stuff. You gotta get off the road." "Oh," Kris would say, "the money's good." "Okay. Decide which piper you want to pay. You're not gonna be a great writer if you're out there carousing every single night." Mickey felt people had moved on to other things after we moved.

Texas took years to finally acknowledge Mick as a native son. Ralph Emery wrote a book about country music and never mentioned him. The new Ken Burns documentary about country music does the same. Mickey fell between the old and the new, and he was always more Stephen Foster and Americana than traditional country. Labels were always a problem for Mick, but he truly didn't care. His writing was about communicating with whomever he was hanging with. He could hold his own with Carol Channing, Shel Silverstein, Liza Minnelli, Dinah Washington, Roger Miller, Ricky Nelson, Percy Mayfield, Ray Charles, Johnny Cash, Andy Williams, Stevie Wonder, Joan Baez, Joni Mitchell, and Bob Dylan. Those people were all on our boat at one time or another, as friends who came to listen to music. These friends would always sing first. Nobody liked to follow Mickey.[1]

Former New Christy Minstrels singer **Susan Newbury-Oakley** was married to Mickey Newbury, and the couple had four children.

CHRIS NEWBURY

We had a pretty ideal childhood. We grew up in the Oregon woods on a beautiful river. We did all the stuff kids do—threw shit, blew up and shot stuff. People didn't know who Dad was in Oregon. We weren't celebrity kids. We had everything a kid could possibly ask for and lived in an open, two-story, large, all-cedar wood cabin, which was real dark and rough. Some people didn't like that because you couldn't rub yourself along the wall without getting a thousand splinters, but we thought that was cool as kids. We could throw Chinese stars, shoot BB guns, and do stuff to the walls without hurting them. Plus, we had a twenty-foot Christmas tree every year.

My parents took turns being the disciplinarian. Dad never had to whip me. He'd just give us the look. Mom did with whatever she could grab like her hairbrush from her purse or wooden spoons for a while. Then she caught me burning wooden spoons in the fireplace. I think she thought that was funny and figured out that I'm more of a carrot instead of a stick kid. It worked. I wanted to work, get a car, and have a license. I did what I was told for the most part. "Do you want to talk to your dad? Should I call your dad?" "No, no, no. We're good." He had a piercing look, man. He could scare you into submission, so he never had to touch us.

He would have been on the road all the time if he did what the record labels wanted him to do, but he was home most of the time instead. They moved to Oregon right when I was born, but he'd still come out with a new record every year or two. He'd go to Nashville to hammer it out, and then he'd come home for long periods of time. He just hung out and played golf when he was home. He was a regular dad, then he'd go for months to Nashville to get things done and then come back. He was recording in Nashville until about 1978. Then he experimented with recording outside Nashville. He did one record in Oregon, then another somewhere else.

His life changed when he met Joe Gilchrist down here at the Flora-Bama. He was sick of Nashville and the music business and was thinking about permanently retiring, but he found a niche down here with Joe and the community. They loved him. Joe knew how to set up the atmosphere for songwriters like him and Hank Cochran. They felt comfortable and welcome down here and loved it. He was planning to come right back the first time he came here, but he ended up staying a couple of weeks longer. He went home for a few months and then came straight back here to the Flora-Bama. He liked it there.

Dad was finally having a good time. The eighties were rough for him with Acuff-Rose going out of business and his dad dying. He had a rebirth when he came to the Flora-Bama, which kept his career alive much longer. He realized that there were still people around here who wanted to hear him. It was also when the internet started coming around. He was always ahead of his time with everything and especially technology. He was one of the first people to have an active website up and running. He had a message board that was very active with dozens and dozens of people posting before most people even had a website. They didn't really know what the internet was. People from that web board started the first gathering down here in 1999 and have been ever since.

Dad always wanted the newest toys. He was cutting edge. He and some investors bought this fancy new box called an analog-to-digital converter, a modem, but it was a huge, heavy box that cost something like twenty grand. He had one of the first Kurzweil [electric keyboards] when they came out. He was doing midi stuff on his guitar before anybody had been doing that. Chet Atkins got the first solid-body gut-string Gibson guitar, and Dad loved it. He could hook it up to a midi and do all this stuff. He was always cutting edge in the studio, too.

I was too young to be there, but I hear stories that he was always experimenting with new toys. He was using them as a tool to complement the songs. Dad just missed his ideal scenario by a few years. He was always envisioning a day when you could email tracks to each other and all the amazing stuff we can do now and take for granted. I remember the days when he had to mix the albums by calling the engineer and saying, "Okay, this is too loud, this isn't loud enough. Do this. Do that. Send us another CD in the mail and we'll talk about that mix." He was very specific later in life by calling them the engineer. He knew he was the producer.

Looks Like Rain was the first album he actually claimed as his. They were like, "This kid is gonna be the next Elvis. He can sing and write his own songs." They were grooming him, and he was feeling all this pressure. He hated and disowned *Harlequin Melodies*. I think it has some great songs on it, but I can tell where things weren't his flavor and that he did things that he didn't like. He was already a successful songwriter so one luxury when he started working with Wayne Moss is that he didn't have the pressure that these kids have on record labels. They have to do whatever the label says.

My parents moved from Nashville to Oregon because he was fed up with the music business, but as I get older I realize he moved here for me and my mom as much. I've never heard her say it explicitly, but I'm pretty sure my mom said, "We're not gonna live in Nashville." They probably both decided that it would be better for me to grow up in Oregon. It was. I'm glad I didn't grow up in Nashville. Dad wasn't a friend of the establishment. He was blackballed at some point way later when he started making his own records. He did an interview in one of the Nashville papers and said, "This city's a scam. All these producers are ripping these kids off. They're spending money on these records and stealing all the money. I make my records for twelve thousand dollars, and it's as good as any of theirs." He was blackballed because he was always speaking out against the establishment.

Dad told me this story. He was trying to get Townes to go to Nashville, but Townes was from a wealthy family and really wasn't motivated financially to write. Dad thought, Okay, I'll get him to Memphis and we'll party. Then I can get him to go to Nashville from there. He says, "Townes, let's go to Memphis and listen to some blues." Townes said, "All right, Mickey, let's do it. My psychiatrist just gave me this experimental drug, though, so let's split it." Who knows how much it was, but it sounded like they were tripping out pretty hard in the story Dad told me. They were drinking at the same time. Townes got drunk and passed out. Dad thought, Okay, this is my chance to take him from Memphis to Nashville. Dad knew if he kept him in the car he'd probably try to jump out or do something crazy and make him wreck the car. Keep in mind, he was tripping on LSD, so he might have been paranoid. Dad put him in the trunk and had to take the spare out to put him in.

The line in "Just Dropped In (To See What Condition My Condition Was In)" says, "Eight miles out of Memphis, and I ain't got no spare." That's real life. They apparently got a flat and didn't have a spare because Townes was in the trunk. I don't know if they ever made it to Nashville that night. I never heard the rest. That story's confirmed, but my theory is that Dad coined the term "tripping on acid." He wrote the song before there was acid and there was the line, "I tripped on a cloud and fell eight miles high." I don't know if people used the term before, but he may be the guy who coined the phrase. Also, the acid craze was started by a bunch of people who idolized him.

He was jokingly called the hippie country songwriter because he was always wearing an Italian suit. He was such a poor kid that when he got money he said, "By God, I'm gonna dress sharp all the time." He taught me a lot about men's etiquette and how to tie a tie. He knew a lot about it, and it was always important to him. He actually was conservative in a lot of ways. He was a Republican. He campaigned with Nixon, which I think he regretted later. He did a lot of horse trading on his Cadillacs, but he wasn't spending a lot of money on them. I wouldn't say he was conservative with money, though. He was always generous with us kids. He was generous in general. He would give cars to people but would also see a guitar and say, "Hey, I love that. If you don't love it, give it to me." I've heard all kinds of stories about him giving people his boots, watches, cars. "Your dad. I couldn't believe it. He tried to give me his car."

I think he would be content and happy knowing how much respect he has within the industry and his peers even if he didn't sell another damn record. I also think he'd be happy if people recognized the artistry side of him and listened to him doing his songs. Let's face it. If you're an artist or a writer, you know it can be a curse. If somebody hears your song and goes, "Holy shit, I can't treat it anywhere near as good as that, I can't sing like that," they're not gonna do it. I know. I've heard songs and have gone, "I can't play like that on the guitar. I'm not gonna even do it." I'm sure he missed a few cuts because of that. His songs are very difficult to just play on guitar.

Live at Montezuma Hall is one of the best acoustic solo live performances of all time. People in Nashville would say the same as far as a guy live with no accompaniment playing his own stuff. He's playing what seems like simple stuff but it isn't. He was on top of his game when he was playing a lot. He wasn't up there just noodling. Of course, if you ask Dad what the best solo acoustic live album was, he'd say Townes's *Live at the Old Quarter*. I tell you what, though. Dad was a much better guitar player than Townes. Period. Then he started writing more and more on the keyboard a lot when he started coming down to the Flora-Bama, which was really great. Sometimes good writers can get hindered by their instrument.[2]

Chris Newbury is Mickey Newbury's oldest child. He lives in Pensacola, Florida.

JACK WILLIAMS

We drove toward Orlando. We were supposed to play in a few days, but we always planned several days between gigs for Mickey to rest. A friend had invited us to stay with him, and his wife was a nurse. She took care of Mickey. She said, "Mickey's gotta go to Tampa General. He's in bad shape." Mickey grumbled and bitched all the way to Tampa and missed the rest of the Florida gigs. He did okay in the hospital. Coincidentally, the head surgeon was Bob Rosemurgy's brother. What a strange turn of events. Mickey got great care.

We had played for seven years by that time. We originally met down at the Flora-Bama songwriters' festival in 1990. I had heard his name but didn't know who Mickey was. I heard Mickey at the festival, and he heard me. I found out who he was, what he'd written, and why I probably should have known about him. I had played a song or two one night and was about to go offstage and he jumped up onstage and grabbed me by the wrist and said something like, "This is what people should be doing. This is good stuff." He honored and humiliated me at the same time. Mickey could be overbearing. We got to be friends, though, and next time he asked me if I'd accompany him. I did.

We had similar background taste in music, with doo-wop that we'd sung in our early years and the R & B and jazz I played. We hit it off pretty well. I found it really easy to accompany him. He found out that I was pretty good at staying out of the way of a good voice and good melody and only playing when necessary. I ended up playing with him every time he played at the Flora-Bama festival. Then the Flora-Bama owner Joe Gilchrist made arrangements to make a bigger concert for the festival. He brought in more people from the community. Mickey asked me to play with him at a gig at an arts center in Gulf Shores.

You know, when we first met, Mickey said, "Who the hell are you? Where do you come from? You're almost my age. How come I've never heard of you?" "Well," I said, "I've never sought out any notoriety, fame, or fortune. I enjoy being under the radar. I play house concerts, festivals, shows of that sort." "Tell me about that," he said. "I wanna do that." So, I called his bluff and next thing you know, he was lying on the bunk in my van. He was already ailing by then. I was never quite sure what his illness was because he was such a hypochondriac. He was always saying he was dying of something. I can't even begin to name all the diseases that he was not afflicted with but thought he was. Eventually, I realized that emphysema was at the head of the list.

Anyway, I booked him, and we were traveling around. "Mickey," I'd say, "I'm going to Michigan, Texas, and Florida. Do you want to come along and do two, three weeks of gigs?" "Yeah, man. Bring me along." Most venues had never heard of Mickey, but they knew songs he'd written. Then they'd hear from the people at their venues that Mickey was something to lift your head up about. I accompanied him at most gigs for the last seven years of his life. The most important one was in 1995 when Bob Rosemurgy and Owsley Manier teamed up. Rosemurgy was the die-hard fan who had the money to back the *Live at the Hermitage* DVD. I was to accompany Mickey and showed up at the Hermitage Hotel ballroom in Nashville. Of course, we hadn't rehearsed and winged it.

I was involved with several of his albums after that show [including *Lulled by the Moonlight* in 1996 and *Winter Winds* and *A Long Road Home* in 2002]. I was definitely actively cowriting, coproducing, and performing on *Lulled by the Moonlight*. Mickey was really doing the producing. I was token producing. My job and Owsley's was to keep Mickey from doing what he did in the early days by piling production on top of his beautiful voice and simple playing. "Let's keep it raw, Mickey. Keep it simple." I was trying to hold on to some tight reins that were barely there as a producer.

I like bare bones. I spent my early years in eight- and twelve-piece bands with horns and organ, but I got rid of that sound around the late eighties and early nineties. I realized that playing by myself is what's good about what I do in this world. Mickey enjoyed playing by himself live, but when it came to recording it was like that scene in *To Kill a Mockingbird* where a poor boy's brought home to Atticus Finch's to have dinner with his family. He has meat, vegetables, everything. He looks up there and sees the maple syrup.

The kid takes it and pours it over everything on his plate. That was Mickey in the studio.

He was basically lying on my bunk in the van when we traveled. We went thousands of miles talking, singing, telling lies together. He'd be on oxygen and smoking a cigarette at the same time in my van, which scared the shit out of me. Anyway, Mickey wanted to play, but he didn't want to succumb to the music industry. They were saying, "Hey, Mickey, write another of those 'Sweet Memories.'" He'd say, "Hell, I've already written that." He didn't want the corporate bullshit brought down on him, which is why he left the industry. He missed performing, though. He missed the adulation. He missed having people love him and come up to tell him how much they loved him even though there were times he'd say, "Man, those people bug the hell out of me." He referred to people who bugged him as squirrels. Owsley would say, "Yeah, but he sure does leave a long trail of nuts." He wanted the adulation.

I think the first house concert we played was in Columbia, South Carolina, in 1995. The man holding the concert held these concerts in his mother's living room completely unplugged. The booking was last-minute, but Mickey filled the house on a Tuesday and Wednesday evening. There were Mickey Newbury people in the South Carolina Midlands, which I would have never believed. Mickey loved being among those people and playing. I told him how much we'd earned after we played. "Huh," he said, "we're not making any money doing this." I said, "Mickey, you don't have to do it. This isn't the Great American Music Hall. This is Jerry's mother's living room." He said, "The show was good." He would gripe often about the money we were making, but he loved playing.

I always say there's a curtain in the music world that hangs between me and certain people. That curtain divides the people who do not drink or do drugs and those who do. Someone at the Flora-Bama who drinks and finds out that I'm a teetotaler who doesn't drink, smoke marijuana, take cocaine, they're very nice to me and polite, but they don't really want me there because they feel judged. Mickey had given up the hard drugs he had done when we were at the Flora-Bama, but there were people there who he wanted me to keep him away from. He wanted to be with them, but he didn't. Mickey had lived a self-inflicted harder lifestyle than I did. Alcohol and drugs weren't the driving force with Mickey, but they were for these people. I had to contend with them.

Mickey was a different person in their presence. He was macho, a true Texas cowboy, but a dandy at the same time. He would sit down sometimes in my basement in Columbia and play piano in his silk bathrobe, smoking like a chimney, dreaming up melodies. He dressed to the nines every day. The people at the Flora-Bama were the only ones I ever saw Mickey in contact with on the other side of the curtain. Mickey adored and idolized Townes. A beautiful Texas tale: Townes was the dark, hard-drinking poet on the other side of my curtain. The people who drink listen to Townes because he's one of us and has hard times. Mickey admired that, but he wasn't that. Mickey gave up heroin on his own. He didn't have to go to rehab. He told me he quit cold turkey.

Mickey was on my side of the curtain by the time he toured with me, but he wanted to be Townes Van Zandt. He wanted to out-Townes Townes, which accounts for the dark nature of his writing. He wrote beautiful, great cinematic tales like "San Francisco Mabel Joy," but he never did achieve what Townes did. Townes had a huge cult of tortured alcoholic artists who will always listen to his music, but they'll never hear Mickey's. Mickey was a family man. I believe Mickey enjoyed fueling his own myth and legend, though. He enjoyed being mythological but was quite human at the same time.

Mickey was a devoted family man despite the fact that he longed to be out there traveling. I could tell he was devoted the way he talked about his children. As gruff as he was—he scowled even when he smiled—he would do something silly. I would say, "I didn't like this" about a song, and he'd stick out his lower lip, make it tremble like, "Oh, you hurt my feelings." I really admired his ability to be silly. That relaxed me around him, but I also knew the gruff Texas kick-ass side. He'd threaten to fight sometimes, and I could tell he was a brawler. He was short in stature and that could have led to his defensiveness.

For example, Mickey went into the Nashville Songwriters Hall of Fame one time because they'd spelled his name "Newberry." Something happened when he went in there. I've seen it many times when he gets like Robert De Niro [in Martin Scorsese's iconic 1976 film *Taxi Driver*]: "You lookin' at me?" His look said, "I'm gonna kick your ass." Apparently, some guy was looking at him as he went into the Hall of Fame and came over toward him. He would often say, "That guy over there's looking for trouble." Mickey pulled out his derringer and fired it through the ceiling. Of course, he was banned from there forever. I always thought, Good God, I'm gonna end up in a fight with this guy around. Fortunately, it never happened.

I think Mickey was looking for trouble as much as the people he said were. "Jack," he said one time, "I hear you're playing in Nashville." "Yeah, I'm playing at Radio Cafe over in East Nashville." "Oh, East Nashville? You wanna take my gun?" "No, Mickey, I don't carry a gun." He had that attitude. "Jack, that's bad, bad territory over there." Well, I've played over there several times. People would go by and wave from their cars if we were playing on the street corner. I never saw any trouble there, but that was Mickey's perception of the world. Somebody's out there to get you, and they're ready as soon as you put your guard down. Mickey's was always up.

I had three wishes for Mickey: I wanted him to play Kerrville, then see his mama, and then play the Bluebird in Nashville. I wanted Mickey to have what he told me he wanted to have from his fans, family, and friends while we drove around on tour. Mickey said, "You're going down to Texas? You taking me?" "Sure." I booked the gigs. I think this was 1997. I told him that I'd had him booked at the Kerrville Folk Festival because I knew he'd never played there and the festival founder Rod Kennedy wanted him to play there.

I was invited to play and got on the phone. I called Rod and said, "Rod, I'm grateful for you to ask me to play your festival, but what would it be like if I brought Mickey Newbury and gave him my spot and played with him?" Rod said something that people say he never would've said. "I'll kiss your ass if you bring Mickey Newbury, who I've tried to get here for seventeen years, to play my festival." Startled me. Rod didn't seem like a guy who used those words. Needless to say, I brought Mickey to the festival, and he said, "Aw, it's hot and dusty. All those hippies. I don't wanna be there." "Mickey, if we're gonna do this tour, you've gotta be there." Grumble, grumble, grumble.

I put him up in his hotel room, and word got around the festival grounds at Quiet Valley Ranch pretty soon that Mickey was playing. Great songwriters like Chuck Brodsky were coming up to me, "Any chance I can go up to the hotel and meet him?" "You know," I said, "he's very open to that." Chuck and the others came up to the Y O Ranch, sat at his feet, and paid homage. Mickey loved it. The day before the performance he sat out on the back deck where all the artists hang out. He was sitting there with Tish Hinojosa and Townes Van Zandt's son, J. T., who looked so much like Townes. Mickey had a tear in his eye when J. T. walked away. I said, "Wow, that was something to see Townes's son look so much like him." "No, that's not it," Mickey said. "He had liquor on his breath."

Anyway, Mickey was in hog heaven backstage. All these great songwriters like [Peter, Paul and Mary's] Peter Yarrow and Chris Smither were coming up to him and paying homage. Then he went out onstage with his oxygen for one of the first times ever. There were roughly eight thousand people in the audience that night. It was like Caesar came back to Rome with one of the greatest Texas songwriters coming back to the festival. Mickey was singing his ass off despite the fact that he needed to pump oxygen into himself. I watched him do things vocally on oxygen that people with emphysema weren't supposed to do. He had incredible breath control. I was in tears most of the time.

The audience was on its feet by the third song and in tears both because he was ailing and what they were hearing was so incredibly beautiful. They knew this was the only time they'd see him on the Kerrville stage. If you've ever been to the Kerrville festival, you know they have a box stage right with about a dozen seats for the VIPs. Sitting in there were Peter Yarrow, Tish Hinojosa, Chris Smither, several other notable songwriters. There wasn't a dry eye in the box, probably the most intense moment of my seven years singing and traveling with Mickey. He completely brought the house down and even joked about being on oxygen. He said, "I came out here with oxygen. Pretty soon everybody's gonna be doing it just to be like me."

He was pissed at me for booking Kerrville, but I knew he'd be in heaven. He was pissed at me for booking Houston, but I wanted him to see his mama. "Don't book me in Houston," he said. "Why?" I asked. "I've already booked Houston." He got really angry. "My mama's gonna show up," he said. "She's gonna be heartbroken to see me sick like this." "Man, that's your mama, Mickey," I said. He'd already told me tales about her and I'd met her. She was a delightfully free-spirited woman. "If anybody in the world needs to be around you when you're ailing and need help, it's your mama. You're gonna go play with me at the Houston Folk Society." "No," he said. "I ain't going." "Well, you get a fucking ride yourself." We were at each other's throats.

He rode back up to where his mother lived [near Houston] in New Caney after the show. His mama and his brother lived side by side. I stayed at her house and slept in the back in the rec room on a couch at the foot of her pool table. Mickey was still grumbling at me for bringing him to face his mother. I was over at his brother Jerry's one morning in the man cave, and Mickey was sitting there in his silk robe with a cigarette. In walks [Newbury's mother] Miss Mamie with a huge pan of steaming white biscuits with white gravy straight out of the oven. Mickey looked up at her with so much love in his eyes. Then he looked at me and growled, "Don't you say a goddamn thing."

Nevertheless, I was able to get him to go home to see his mama. I feel really good about that and getting him to play Kerrville. Then I was booked in Nashville at the Bluebird, and I asked him to play with me. "No way," he said. "I don't wanna be anywhere near that industry, those people." Well, by this time, I knew I could get my way. I booked the gig, and it was standing room only. The parking lot was full of people looking in the glass window to the venue. Harlan Howard was there in the crowd with all these old-time writers Mickey was friends with. They were there to see Mickey.

He was already getting pretty weak. I was there to look after him. "You okay to do this, man?" "Yeah, man." I basically was his care-taker. I did that the whole evening. The performance was probably five hours. He talked a lot and had a hard time breathing. I got two notes sent to me from Harlan Howard during the show. "Man, if I could do it over," the one for Mickey said, "I'd like to do what you're doing." He meant playing house concerts and not worrying about the industry. "When I get old and want to keep playing music," said the other note, meant for me, "I hope I have a friend like you." Touched me deeply. Mickey performed as best he could and nobody left. I've never seen the Bluebird so packed.

He eventually followed me to Florida when he was beginning to get really weak. I had us booked at the Unitarian Universalist Church concert series in Lakeland, Florida. Then we were going on to Orlando and other shows. Mickey performed for three and a half hours straight with no break in Lakeland. I had to excuse myself at least once to go pee. He just sat there and played. I don't know how his affliction works, but he would get clogged up somehow and had found out how to break that loose in order to sing. He would be backstage, get down on all fours, and force cough it out. He was getting clogged up during the concert and finally said, "I don't want to put you through this. Don't be worried or scared or weirded out, but rather than me leave and take a break, just wait." He got on all fours onstage, did his thing, and got back up and sang.

People were horrified. They didn't know what to think about this crazy guy, but they loved the concert. We didn't go backstage after the concert. We walked straight down to the merchandise table and had people showing up with fifteen, sixteen LPs to have signed. Mickey had just sung his brains out for three and a half hours, but he sat there with emphysema for another hour and a half with his fans. Mickey finally said, "I'm really tired, Jack." He got up, and I let him out the back door. He had respiratory failure right there. People were watching over him, so I ran over to get his nebulizer. A nurse called 911. I ran over to the van, drove straight across the Unitarian Universalist Church lawn, and jammed his nebulizer in. He finally started reviving. He looked at me and said, "Tell that goddamn nurse to cancel the 911 call. I have gigs to play." We were going to Orlando the next day. "Next time that happens," Mickey said, "let me go. Don't call the doctor. You do nothing. I want to go like that."[3]

Guitarist **Jack Williams** played with and cared for Mickey Newbury on tour during the songwriter's later years performing on the road.

Newbury cover.

Mickey Newbury's teenage doo-wop group, the Embers, in Houston, Texas. Newbury is pictured far right.

Mickey Newbury's graduation photo from Jefferson Davis High School, Houston, Texas.

Mickey Newbury during his tenure in the military. Newbury served in the air force for three years at RAF Croughton, Oxfordshire, England.

Mickey Newbury during his tenure in the military. Newbury spent many weekends at Swiss Cottage in London, which inspired his song "Swiss Cottage Place" on Frisco Mabel Joy (Elektra Records, 1971).

Mickey Newbury (bottom right) and his Global C&E Systems military class.

Mickey Newbury (center) with his father, Milton Newbury, and his mother, Mamie Newbury.

Mickey Newbury (left) and Paul Williams.

Mickey Newbury (center) and Paul Williams (right).

MICKEY NEWBURY

Exclusive Management:
ACUFF-ROSE ARTISTS CORP.
2510 Franklin Road
Nashville, Tenn. 31204
(615) 385-3031

Acuff-Rose promotional photograph of Mickey Newbury.

Mickey Newbury (right) receiving a songwriting award in the eighties.

Mickey Newbury relaxing at home. Friends say Newbury was always sharply dressed.

Mickey Newbury relaxing in the water outside his houseboat on Old Hickory Lake outside Nashville in the seventies.

Milton Newbury and Mamie Newbury (standing); Susan Newbury and Mickey Newbury on their houseboat outside Nashville.

*Acuff-Rose
promotional
photograph of
Mickey Newbury.*

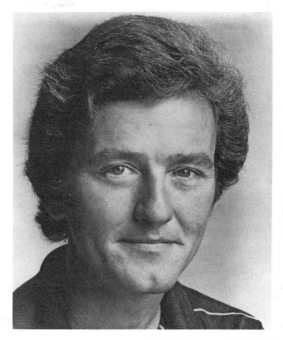

MICKEY NEWBURY

*EXCLUSIVE MANAGEMENT:
Acuff-Rose Artists Corp.
2510 Franklin Road
Nashville, Tenn. 37204
(615) 385-3031*

Mickey Newbury performing at the second annual Tokyo World Song Festival in 1973. Newbury won the Grand Prix for best song with "Heaven Help the Child."

Promotional photograph for the New Christy Minstrels. Susan Newbury is pictured second from the right in the second row.

THE NEW CHRISTY MINSTRELS

Mickey Newbury and Susan Newbury.

Left to right: Mimi Fariña, Mickey Newbury, unknown, Joan Baez performing together. Photo by Jim Marshall.

Mickey Newbury performing in the eighties.

Acuff-Rose promotional photograph of Mickey Newbury.

MICKEY NEWBURY

Exclusive Management:
ACUFF-ROSE ARTISTS CORP.
2510 Franklin Road
Nashville, Tenn. 31204
(615) 385-3031

Mickey Newbury (second from right) golfing with friends during his time at Acuff-Rose Music Publishing in Nashville.

Left to right: Milton Newbury, Mamie Newbury, Mickey Newbury, and Susan Newbury at Old Hickory Lake outside Nashville.

Mickey Newbury golfing in the nineties. Susan Newbury-Oakley says her husband would frequently play fifty-four holes of golf a day starting at five o'clock in the morning.

Mickey Newbury backstage.

Mickey Newbury with fans in the nineties.

Elektra Records' advertisement in Rolling Stone for Heaven Help the Child. Photo by Brian T. Atkinson.

Verse: I Came to Hear the Music

Juan Contreras

I met Mickey through Bob Beckham when I worked a theme park in Kentucky called Kaintuck Territory in 1968. We used to have these regional battles of the bands with Chet Atkins, Bobby Bare, Billy Sherrill, and Ray Stevens for judges. We'd put them up in a hotel and take them on a trail ride at Kaintuck in the morning after breakfast. We had a nice creek and chuck wagon. Then Mickey and I reacquainted ourselves when I started working at Acuff-Rose around 1980. We toured Australia at the same time Elton John and Kenny Rogers were touring over there. Mickey was friends with [longtime John lyricist] Bernie Taupin. Mickey was an unbelievable talent but always thought he was dying.

People were drawn to Mickey wherever he went. He was charismatic and hypnotic. His singing would knock you out. Mickey won the world singer-songwriter competition in Japan during that time with "Heaven Help the Child." I talked with Bob Beckham one time about *Looks Like Rain*. "I didn't know I was doing a drug album," he said. "What do you mean?" I asked. "People take drugs," he said, "and listen to them." I thought that was funny. Mickey was a hero, the absolute king at Acuff-Rose. He had humongous cuts and was regarded up there with legendary writers like Hank Cochran, Don Gibson, Harlan Howard. They were all peers and friends. Mickey was a top earner.

I asked Mickey if we should take concessions to Australia. "What do you mean 'concessions'?" he asked. "Well," I said, "we should take some albums to sell." "Ah," he said, "I don't wanna do that." I told him it would help offset expenses, but he didn't want to do it. He told me I could take concessions if I wanted, so I bought about five hundred copies of *Frisco Mabel Joy*. We sold them all for about twenty bucks apiece. I gave Mickey half the cash, and he bought gifts for his wife and kids. I thought it was unbelievable that we were somewhere he'd never been, but he didn't want to take records.[1]

Longtime Nashville music industry veteran **Juan Contreras** worked for Mickey Newbury's publishing company Acuff-Rose as well as Monument Records, where he promoted musicians such as Larry Gatlin, Kris Kristofferson, and Billy Swan.

TROY TOMLINSON

I started at Acuff-Rose when I was twenty-four years old. They had a vast catalog with giant songwriters. Roy Orbison, Don Gibson, John D. Loudermilk, and Mickey Newbury all would come by Acuff-Rose. They had already moved on to another season in life by 1988, but they'd come by to do business or get a check or see friends who worked there. There were a lot of long-term employees at Acuff-Rose. Then I actually met Mickey in 1988. He was in town and came into Acuff-Rose to say hello to his old friends. We were introduced, and he asked me if I had a small recorder. He wanted to lay down a few work tapes while he was in town.

We had a little Tascam four track that recorded to a cassette. Mickey laid down some guitar and vocal parts he'd written recently. I think for my benefit he laid down some acoustic versions of his hits. Then he did a song or two a cappella. I remember a piano covered in white-pleated leather in that writers' room. Mickey was telling me stories and talking about people who influenced him. He was a Stephen Foster freak and was telling me all these Stephen Foster stories. I was blown away. I was a twenty-four-year-old kid who had only been in the music business four years at that point. I went down into the Acuff-Rose vault when he left. They had a massive record collection with multiple copies of virtually every album that had ever been released with an Acuff-Rose song on it. I pulled Newbury's albums and then albums that had Newbury songs on them and took them home.

My wife and I were living in a shitty little duplex with an awesome stereo system. We'd just gotten married. I sat up after dinner and told her, "I'm gonna go through all of Mickey's albums and make notes on them." I did. I sat in a rocker and listened through the speakers for a long time. Then when she went to bed I put on headphones and listened. I would laugh, cry, write notes about each song. I read the liner notes while I was listening to the songs. My wife came in around three in the morning and said, "You've gotta go to bed. You have to work tomorrow." That night was the night I really began to respect Mickey Newbury's songwriting. It was cool sitting in the room with him singing the songs, but listening to those songs back to back on his albums that were so well written really gave me a respect and love for him. He was so genuine.

I was drawn to the vividness in the lyrics. He certainly used metaphor in ingenious ways in his songs, but the tangible nature did it more for me. The melodies were like the first time you hear Queen. There are all these melodic changes within a four-minute song that you've never heard before. Mickey's melodies took you places you weren't used to going to—particularly if you were just listening to the radio. The most practical example that moved me was "She Even Woke Me Up to Say Goodbye." He says, "Baby's packed her soft things and left me." I remember sitting in that rocking chair in front of the stereo that night, pulling the needle back and playing that over. Anybody could have said, "Baby packed her stuff and left." "Baby packed her clothes and left." "Baby packed all of her pajamas and left." He said, "Soft things." You know exactly what he's talking about. Little moments like that are Mickey's genius.

Country music today is more about the groove or hook line that everybody sings along with, but among a certain group of writers you still hear a real attention to really tangible, touchable lyrics. Tom Douglas and Allen Shamblin wrote a Miranda Lambert song called "The House That Built Me," one of the biggest songs of the last ten years. "The House That Built Me" has a beauty similar to Mickey Newbury. The song describes the house that she grew up in. She visits the people who now live in the house and says to the lady at the front door, "Up those stairs and in that little back bedroom is where I did my homework and learned to play guitar. I bet you didn't know that my favorite dog is buried in the yard." You're there. People would write us letters and say, "You know, I didn't have an upstairs bedroom. I never played guitar. I never had a dog, but that was my house." That's the ability Mickey had. He makes you feel like you're the guy who walked into the bedroom of your home and all your wife's soft things are gone. You felt like you were there. That's not typical for today's hit songs.

Changes over the past thirty or forty years in publishing probably simply are changes. We've certainly made gains in our genre with a broader audience than ever before. Our music is easier to access than ever. It's more economical to have music. I think many people would disagree with me, but I think we could use a little more focus on the songs, lyrics, and innovative melodies to make the genre healthier. The more we get toward track-based music you risk a sameness occurring. As opposed to when a writer like Mickey Newbury sits down in a room with an acoustic guitar and an idea that popped into his head when he woke up that morning and he's working through that melody that connects with the emotion of the lyric.

We don't have as much of that connection between lyric and melody as we did even twenty years ago. I think we'd be a healthier format if we had more connection. There's still an element of [songwriters playing their new songs to publishers], but we can't usually do all the walk-ins. We don't have the staff. There are fewer people knocking on your door wanting to play you a song and look for a publishing deal, but we still get new music every day from songwriters who have moved to town to get a deal. It usually comes through a referral from another writer, which happened back then as well. One writer tells you about another writer they met at a bar. They wrote a song together. My writer says, "Hey, man. We only wrote one song together, but I'm telling you this guy's got something. You ought to take a meeting."

People are more apt to learn more about your music and you as a person if a songwriter stays engaged in the community. They'll run into you at the Kroger or at a ball game. Certainly there's less connectivity over time if you remove yourself and go way outside town and don't have that many contacts in town. I think with Mickey, I don't doubt that story happened [about calling Acuff-Rose after he moved to Oregon and not being remembered]. If you get a new intern or a new kid out of college at your front desk, they don't know the biggest producers or songwriters in town. They're just learning. I never answered the phone, but I'm sure I said some silly shit to great writers over the years.

Mickey certainly did remove himself. He wanted his family to be in Oregon. I'm sure everybody respected that, but I'd focus more on what I saw as a young man. Royalty was in the building when he came back to town and walked into Acuff-Rose. Same with Don Gibson and John D. Loudermilk. Acuff-Rose was the pillar publishing company in Nashville for country music. People would come into my office and say, "Newbury's here. I just saw him pull into the parking lot. He just walked in the front door." I'd become a stalker and find a way to get myself into the hallway he was gonna go down so I could say how much the music meant to me. Mickey was revered.

He was in the top five percent of the earning, revered, revenue-creating, known writers for a twenty-year heat. You had all those other guys I mentioned in that rarified air also, but I think the mark in publishing as a heroic figure in a songwriter is: Do the songs stand the test of time? Mickey Newbury songs stand the test of time. People still cut them today around the world. They still hum them. People who don't even know it's a Mickey Newbury song know his songs. If a songwriter is to be judged about their impact on the breadth of the music industry and America, longevity of the songs is the measuring stick for me. Mickey certainly measures up.

I have a funny story from those days. The Acuff-Rose building on Franklin had its own print shop with a winding, circuitous route from the front door through the building. Sam Waldon was the runner in the mail room. Mr. Rose called on Sam for everything he needed. Sam also was the emergency phone number if the alarm system went off. Sam told me that he got a call in the middle of one night from the metro police saying that the alarm's going off in the Acuff-Rose building and they were there in the parking lot. They said all the exterior doors were secure, but the alarm's going off. There's been movement. Doors have been opened.

Sam opens the door for the police. He's the only one who knows all the doors in the building. He goes into each room and opens the door, and the cops are shining their lights with their guns drawn. He goes into someone's office where there's a couch. Of course, the office is dark. Sam flips on the light by the door out of habit and Mickey sits up on the couch. They all have their guns drawn on him. Sam said he kept going, "No, that's Mister Mickey. Mister Mickey. Don't bother Mister Mickey." I said, "What happened after that?" He said it shook up Mickey for a minute but then we told him we were sorry to interrupt his sleep. He'd probably gone out with some buddies and decided to crash at Acuff-Rose. Anyway, he lay back down on the couch, and I reckon he spent the night there. I always loved that human side of Mickey Newbury.[2]

Longtime Sony/ATV president and CEO **Troy Tomlinson** worked at Acuff-Rose when Mickey Newbury was writing for the publishing company. He's currently chair of Universal Music Publishing Group Nashville.

John Lomax III

I managed Townes Van Zandt from 1976 to 1978. Mickey Newbury really was Townes's discoverer. I found out that Mickey had arranged for Townes to audition for Wesley Rose. You can imagine how that must have gone. I don't think Wesley got it. Then Mickey brought Townes over to Cowboy Jack Clement, and that led to Townes's first publishing deal. I started to immerse myself in country music when I came to Nashville in 1973 and learned Mickey had written hits and was regarded as a fabulous songwriter. I also realized that he was a spectacularly good singer.

Fast-forward to the late eighties. We floated Airborne Records through a penny stock offering and ended up releasing Mickey's *In a New Age*. Everyone thought that New Age music was gonna be a viable commercial option. Of course, New Age never developed into anything other than something to put you to sleep. Anyway, we put that album out on Mickey. He came around to the office to get us to do various things, but we didn't have many resources. He wanted the things a major label would do with more advertising and tour support. He didn't tour much, and he didn't have a band. There wasn't much we could do.

Owsley Manier was his booking agent. Owsley would book him and never tell the label anything about the dates. Mickey would play somewhere and everyone would fuss at us that there weren't any records in the market. We hadn't known he was in the market to begin with. Everything petered out. There wasn't much we could do with country radio with that record. It was mostly instrumental and wasn't a typical Mickey record. We were at a loss and were trying to break Mickey Gilley at the time. He was let go from Epic Records. Airborne eventually crashed and burned after two and a half years. We weren't able to do much for Mickey other than put the album out.[3]

Nashville music industry veteran **John Lomax III** has worked as a country music journalist, music distributor, and manager with Kasey Chambers, Steve Earle, and Townes Van Zandt.

OWSLEY MANIER

Mickey was a middle-aged guy when I started really working with him. His voice had taken on even more power by then. He was always a great singer who sounded like a choir boy in the sixties, but his voice had more soul later. It was really powerful when you add age to that range. Being a ridiculously good singer separated him from the other writers. We ran into Mike Reid, who had some hits in the late eighties and early nineties, at the airport once. I was walking along with Mickey and went, "Mike Reid, this is Mickey Newbury." There was this long pause. "Mickey Newbury," he said. "You're the reason I write songs." That's Mickey in relation to songwriters in a nutshell.

I opened Nashville's Exit/In in 1971. The Exit/In was a listening room. We demanded silence. Mickey didn't play very often, so he would pack the place when he did. Mickey influenced all the songwriters, and they would come to the gigs: Kristofferson, Johnny Cash, Townes Van Zandt, Rodney Crowell, Guy Clark, everybody, a real songwriter's treat. I started managing Mickey in the late eighties, but he was unmanageable. I ran into Chet Atkins at the airport one time and said, "Hey, Chet. How's it going?" "Good, Owsley. What's going on?" "I'm managing Mickey," I said. "Owsley," Chet said. "God bless you." Mickey was Mickey.

I heard Mickey was in town one time and hanging out at Greg Humphrey's house. This indie label Airborne Records was gonna put out a bullshit tape of Mickey's demos. Terrible crap. Mickey was distraught. He took the cassette and crushed it with his boot. I said, "Damn, man." I said, "Mickey, I'll tell you what. Let me assist you in fixing this album that's fucked up." There was no formal agreement, but we shook on it. Airborne had all the printed material for the album, but they hadn't manufactured any records or discs. So, the order of the songs and the times were set. We went into a studio and in under twenty-four hours we recorded the whole album again, the same songs exactly in the same order. Mickey was a one-man band playing strings on his midi guitar with this incredible violinist named Marie Rhines accompanying him. We finished the whole thing, and I went to Airborne Records and made them take it. They released it as *In a New Age*.

I came up with some money when Winter Harvest Records started and made that *Live at the Hermitage* video with Mickey and guitarist Jack Williams in 1995. We did it on a wing and a prayer. Winter Harvest was a songwriter's label, but I had some bogus partners who were essentially stealing the money. We did Steve Earle's album *Train a Comin'* and a shitload of money was generated, but then it just vaporized, ten years of my life out the door again. Then Bob Rosemurgy started Mountain Retreat as Mickey's label after Winter Harvest. We went on to do about thirteen records like Jonell Mosser's [Townes Van Zandt tribute] *Around Townes*, Steve Earle's, Mark Germino's *Rank and File*. Mark's a great writer. I produced some and designed graphics on some including Mickey's.

Mickey was in his own category. We talked about songs all the time. I'd come up with a line that I thought was cool, and Mickey would have already written the song. We had fun with it, too. We made up goofy things like "Just Dropped In (To See What Condition My Transmission's In)." He said, "I'll never license that to a transmission company, but wouldn't that be funny?" Mickey had these really dark songs with amazing lines. There's nobody better than him at doing rhymes within a line and turning a phrase that has eight different meanings. Mickey told me one time, "Every now and again, I wrote something simple enough to be a hit." He never set out to do that. They just came from where they came from. Mickey said, "I wish I could write like Townes." I'm looking at Mickey and thinking, Townes is thinking the same fucking thing. Mickey was a huge advocate of songwriters.

Roger Miller recorded "Me and Bobby McGee" before Janis Joplin. Mickey told me that he went up to Roger, grabbed his lapels, and started shaking him. He went, "Busted flat in Baton Rouge . . ." He hammered the song on him so he would record it. Mickey was all about writers. Mickey could take a very simple line and make it mean five different things. I remember exactly where I was when I heard Kenny Rogers's "Just Dropped In." I went, "Oh my God. What is that?" Mickey was a little embarrassed by "Just Dropped In" because it was such a big hit. I couldn't get him to play it. "Mickey, you really should do 'Just Dropped In.'" "No, I'm not gonna do that. I don't wanna do that." "Mickey, come on." It was the lead track on *Nights When I Am Sane*. I finally convinced him to play it at Great American Music Hall in San Francisco and the place went fucking nuts. Guess what? He played it after that. Then this group Supergrass in England recorded it and the song was a hit there.

Mickey didn't really talk about favorite songs, but I know that "San Francisco Mabel Joy" was near to him. Mickey did a lot of three-quarter-time songs. He said, "I basically keep writing the same song with a different melody." He'd laugh and say, "Well, maybe not such a different melody." In terms of the process, he didn't really talk about it much, but what a word craftsman. We talked about lines all the time. We talked about songs from Nashville to Hawaii. Mickey was big in San Francisco. He had so many references like in "Frisco Depot" when he says, "Frisco's a long way from home if you can afford to fly / But it might as well be the moon when you're as broke as I."

Jack Williams was very instrumental in going around and taking Mickey to smaller venues much later in the nineties. Mickey called him "Cadillac Jack." He just didn't like playing live. I put together a whole fucking tour of Australia, and he blew it off. I put together a tour of England. He blew it off. "Fuck this," Mickey said. "I'm not doing these shows." So, we didn't go to Australia or England. I had everything organized and made it as easy as possible. We'd always rent a Town Car and have people wherever we could to make it simple so it could happen. I always asked for first-class tickets, and we usually got them. Of course, it pissed me off that he blew it off, but what are you gonna do? I don't really know why he didn't do the Australia tour. The guy over there was unhappy. I think Mickey might've had stage fright, but he was mesmerizing when he settled in.

I did get him to go to Poland once. He played this big, beautiful lakeside festival right on the border with Germany. The Berlin Wall was knocked down at that time. Things were very tense. Anyway, this woman called and asked if Mickey would be interested in playing at this festival in Poland. I said, "Sure. We'll require first-class tickets." She said, "No problem." It was sponsored by the US Information Agency, which I didn't know at the time was a huge CIA front. We were followed like spies the whole time. He and Marie played the gig at this huge amphitheater. It was pretty crazy to see Mickey and a violinist get in front of twenty thousand people. That would give me stage fright. I don't want any pats on the back, but I got him out there doing it again and more than he ever had. He did more gigs from 1987 on than he ever did in his life before.

Mickey always carried a derringer with him. He'd put it in the bottom of his golf bag and fly with it when we were going on planes. Obviously, this was pre–9/11. He always had that weapon in his boot. Anyway, we were in a hotel party room with a weird crowd in Nashville. Things got really out of hand, and there was getting ready to be a brawl. Probably drunk people bullshit. Mickey pulled out that derringer and popped a round in the ceiling. Everybody chilled out real fast. That took care of it, but that was the only time I saw anything like that happen with him. That was a Texas mentality. Houston can be rough and dangerous if you're on the wrong side of the tracks. Mickey grew up on the wrong side but told me that where he was was really good compared to where Kenny Rogers was. Mickey was a small guy growing up so people fucked with him.

Mickey was a sweetheart, but he would do stuff like blow off those tours. Imagine you're the record label. Mickey was fortunate enough to have a huge run of covers and hits early. He was making more than $100,000 a year with his Acuff-Rose catalog when we started working together in the late eighties, which would be easily $250,000 today. Mickey looked at Wesley Rose as a father figure, and it was a huge betrayal to him when Acuff-Rose ripped off him and everyone else. I remember going to Acuff to get him money one time. He was still getting advances in the late eighties, but there were strings. "Okay, we're gonna front you twenty, thirty thousand dollars, but you agree not to sue us." In reality, everyone from Orbison to Hank Williams who was big as a writer had sued them for being ripped off. Mickey never did. There was something up with that.[4]

Owsley Manier opened the famed Nashville club the Exit/In in 1971. Jimmy Buffett and Guy Clark performed at the venue regularly in the seventies. He helped run the Winter Harvest record label, which released albums by Steve Earle, Mark Germino, and Mickey Newbury.

LARRY MURRAY

I met Mickey Newbury through Kris Kristofferson. I had a suite with a living room and office at the Ramada Inn [in Nashville]. Mickey was always there. We were the core people that kept growing during the time I spent there working with Johnny Cash, pitching my own tunes, and writing for television. I think Mickey had just gotten out of the air force, but he had already had some success with songwriting and was writing great songs. Kris, Mickey, and I would sit around swapping songs and telling tall tales. I'd watch Kris and Mickey go at it, which was entertaining enough. Mickey was such a sweetheart, so loyal and generous.

Mickey and I would go to sessions when we had time off and pitch Kris's songs. In fact, we pitched "Me and Bobby McGee" in the same day to Gordon Lightfoot and Roger Miller, who both cut it within twenty-four hours. Mickey never played one of his tunes when we were pitching Kristofferson songs. I really appreciated that. That's the kind of guy he was. We spent a lot of nights partaking of forbidden fruits on his houseboat named *Sweet Memories* out on Old Hickory. Our Nashville bunch grew into Vince Matthews, Townes Van Zandt, Chris Gantry, Marijohn Wilkin. Nashville was rolling over with a new bunch of guys. We started getting our tunes cut.

Nashville was amazing at that time. We were all pretty shaggy looking. Townes Van Zandt was like Kris but on the periphery. His songs were ragged because he wasn't a crooner, but I was floored when I first heard them. You had to be a songwriter and really listen, but when you did you'd go, "That's a motherfucker." The established Nashville people were finally realizing that the tide had turned. You could smell it in the air. That was Nashville when Music Row was Music Row. I've seen Harlan Howard walking down the middle of Music Row with a gut-string guitar in his hand without a case going to pitch songs. You knew he was gonna get something cut. It was easier then. You could play songs for producers or drop off tapes. [That changing was] what drove me out of the songwriting business. I got tired of dealing with the suits and the attorneys and cowriters that want your publishing. "Give us your firstborn and get out of here."

Mickey had quirks. He always carried ChapStick. He'd smear it on every time he went to say something. We'd hide it from him and watch him go bananas. He'd say, "I have to go down and get some ChapStick." "Mickey, it's three o'clock in the morning. Nashville's closed." Marijohn Wilkin put up most of us shaggy guys. She supported and mothered us all. Her son Bucky Wilkin was in and out. He went out of town one time and just got back when Kris, Mickey, and I were holding our powwow at the Ramada. Kris says, "Mickey, Bucky's back in town. I saw him and he looks really good. He's lost a lot of weight." Mickey says, "Yeah, but Bucky's got a fat mind." I don't know what that meant, but it was apropos at the time.

I'm from Waycross, Georgia. Mickey thought Waycross was a great-sounding name for "San Francisco Mabel Joy." Waycross is a great and sneaky small town called the Gateway to the Okefenokee. You get past the swamp and go into the Barrier Islands with the cypress trees and Spanish moss and kudzu. Mickey threw in Waycross because we were talking about it, and he thought there was a ring to it. Everybody thinks Waycross has a ring. There are more people than I thought who came out of Waycross. Gram Parsons is the most famous.

I worked for the Smothers Brothers show and the Glen Campbell show. Johnny Cash was slated as a guest on the Glen Campbell show. Johnny loved Mickey's songs. Mickey would have had his own television show if things were different. John always wanted to know what was going on with Kris and Mickey because he knew we were all hanging out together. Kris was in and out. He had an Opal car with all his shit in it. He would drive that down from Nashville to New Orleans and fly workers out to the oil rigs by helicopter for three days and nights. Then he'd drive all the way back to Nashville to clean up studios at Columbia. So, Kris hadn't hit it yet, but John knew he was one of the best songwriters he'd heard. He agreed that Mickey was good company.

Mickey came from a pretty poor family. He had enough success with Acuff-Rose, and they liked Mickey because he was making them money. So, they'd actually give him money. I never got any money even though I was signed by several publishers. I'd hear my song on the radio and wonder where my fucking money was. I think Mickey was getting paid and started realizing that he could now do some things he couldn't before because he had the finances. Mickey was a real pioneer. He wasn't really underrated because he had success the traditional way, having tunes cut. He was a great singer. I learned how to play all of Mickey's tunes in ten minutes. He played everything in D with the same licks. My favorite Mickey songs are "She Even Woke Me Up to Say Goodbye" and "33rd of August."

Those songs were inside him. I love being a writer because you can make something out of thin air. You can create a character, a whole world out of nothing, which is still exciting and magical. Mickey had that knack of pulling stuff out of the air. He also had girlfriends and would lose them like everybody. Mickey was handy with words. I think he realized that being steeped in country music was all about tragedy. I think he figured when in Rome, do as the Romans do. I think songs are in the air and if your antenna's up, you're gonna pick them up. It's called parallel evolution. Jesse Winchester said he believed in parallel evolution, which means the song that you're writing is already out there.

Mickey was a dreamer who wrote blue-collar poetry. His songs hit the beer drinkers and Bible thumpers. Mickey just didn't put himself out there. Kris did. Kris was amazing. He had his whole career and life planned when he came to Nashville. Everything Kris does is well thought out. It worked for him. I would watch it happen over and over. He would advance his career, and I would say, "I totally understand how he got there." Mickey was just Mickey. He liked writing. You could tell that he loved his own songs when he sang them. Maybe it was a management situation. Mickey never had any management that was very aggressive. Kris fell into some very aggressive management right off. He was smart like that. He had people working behind him while he was out there drinking and throwing up onstage. Mickey never was a household name, but the people who met him and heard his music never forgot him.

Mickey would always sit up in the middle of the bed and expound on his stories and songs. Kris was enamored with Mickey because of his simplicity in looking at things, but there was a love-hate relationship between those two, although that's the wrong way to put it. Kris would always say, "Mickey, you don't know that." It would upset Mickey. He'd say, "I do." Kris would go, "How do you know?" "I read it." Kris would fall on the floor laughing. "You read it? Oh, excuse me." Kris would always knock a hole right in Mickey's stories. That was his hobby. It wasn't anything other than Kris loved playing with him like that.

Mickey was very superstitious. He was in the hospital for stomach problems at one point, and they had taken some X-rays that found this spot on his stomach. They said, "Tomorrow, we're gonna have to go a little further and look at that." Mickey was talking about the power of prayer, which Kris didn't believe in. Mickey said he prayed all night. He didn't sleep a wink. He just prayed, prayed, prayed all night. He went in for the X-rays the next morning, and there was nothing there. Kris says, "Wait a minute, Newbury. When you took those first X-rays, did you have a smock on?" Mickey said, "Well, yeah." "Did you have that smock on the next time you went in for more X-rays?" "No, I was on a table." Kris says, "Mickey, don't start with me. It was a knot in the smock." Newbury went crazy. "No it wasn't. It was the power of prayer." Kris really did love Mickey. I think if he hadn't, he wouldn't have been comfortable saying the things that he did. It was all out of love, but maybe Mickey internalized more of that than I thought. I never saw Mickey get mad at him, but you never know.[5]

Songwriter **Larry Murray** served as leader of Hearts and Flowers and released the acclaimed solo album *Sweet Country Suite* in the early seventies.

RANDY DODDS

I had been around Townes Van Zandt and Guy Clark when I was sixteen years old and they were playing Sand Mountain on Richmond Avenue in Houston. Mickey had a management deal with Townes, who was the first guy to have a label deal. There was also a lot of talk on the street about "San Francisco Mabel Joy." Mickey was a poet. No question. Townes was a different kind of writer. There are arguments that Townes is better than Dylan. There were so many different types of writers, but Mickey was accessible. Nobody could break your heart like Mickey. You identified with it if you ever experienced that heartache or growing up in honky-tonks or driving all night in the rain. The guys that Mickey genuinely touched back in the day, their lives were transformed.

I was working for ABC Records when RCA released "Sweet Memories" as a single. I remember going to an AM radio station back in the day and asking Joe Ford, "Why don't you play Mickey's song? He's a hometown boy." I'll never forget it because I was just a kid. Joe said in all sincerity, "No one wants to hear a song that goes, 'My world is like a river / as dark as it is deep.' Nobody does." I said, "You're wrong, man. One day." It was always an uphill battle getting airplay for Mickey. He was writing songs that weren't fitting a mold but were very accessible in many respects. Nobody was doing what he was doing in Nashville. No one.

Nashville historically only cut really commercial records. Mickey never did fit into any norm in Nashville. RCA didn't know what to do with him when they put out [Harlequin Melodies]. It was really overproduced. Mickey wasn't even happy with the cover. That Nehru jacket was a last-minute purchase. The guy doing the photo shoot had hay bales around thinking Mickey was a country artist. Mickey was never a country artist. He wasn't a singer-songwriter. He always said he was a songwriter-singer. He was a songwriter first. That's what he said distinguished him. Looks Like Rain was one of the finest records to ever come out of Nashville, but they certainly didn't know what to do with it. The Mercury president said it was one of the worst albums he'd heard in his life.

I've had that Rolling Stone magazine since 1973 with the full-page ad when he released Heaven Help the Child, and they compared him to the Robert Frost of music. He had critical acclaim everywhere he went. He always mesmerized the audience anywhere he went. Nashville just didn't know. I think he got disenchanted. A lot changed when Wesley sold Acuff-Rose [to Grand Ole Opry parent company Gaylord Entertainment Company in May 1985]. Mickey always believed that Wesley would take care of him. Mickey was Acuff-Rose's premier writer whether or not his own albums were doing good. His songs were doing amazingly well. That changed him.

Mickey was hurt like so many people with the [savings and loan] crash back in the day. He got caught up in that and lost about two million dollars. That was big money then. I mean, it still is, but it was bigger money then. By that time, royalties were still coming in, but I don't think he ever recovered from that. I talked with him the night before he died. He was like a brother to me. When Mickey was at his sickest, my birth father was really sick. Mickey and I had grown up with dads who were pretty tough. Milton was a pretty good guy, but Mickey would tell me stories. My dad was critically ill at the same time. We were in Austin and Mickey told me, "One of us is gonna go first. You have to be prepared."

I think Mickey knew that he was highly regarded as a songwriter. He was comfortable with his career. I've been in a room with Waylon and Willie, George Jones, Alex Harvey, Tony Joe White, Whitey Shafer, Bob McDill, anybody who was having the big hits in the seventies, and when Mickey picked up his guitar you could hear a pin drop. Nobody wanted to follow him. I think there was a disappointment in the business itself. I told Mickey before he died, someday after you're gone, some kid's gonna find a copy of *Looks Like Rain*. He's gonna be a brokenhearted kid like us. He's gonna connect with that album, and it's gonna be just as fresh in twenty-five, fifty years as the day it was released. That record has its little flaws, but it's the most timeless record you'll hear.

I think Mickey will be rediscovered, but the record business is really funny. Mickey wrote a song called "Lie to Me Darling" toward the end of his life that I really tried to get to George Strait. Mickey was still writing good records. He didn't necessarily write country hits, but he could've written the standard hook song. A lot of great artists cut his stuff. He was writing hits toward the end. Needless to say, we were unable to get through to Strait at the time. I told Mickey, "Man, 'you can lie to me darlin' / but come lie in my bed?' That's a hit song." The hook was "I'll keep hanging on / Until I'm hanging on by a thread / Lie to me darlin' but come lie in my bed." I thought that was a perfect George Strait song.

Townes crossed over into Europe and everywhere. He's still revered. He created his own mystique. Townes didn't self-promote.

Townes was Townes and that was good enough. Mickey didn't self-promote either, but it was a different style. You couldn't get Townes or Mickey to do that. They wanted no part of it. Their business was to create and write. Mickey's songs were like if you had a girl and you broke up and you hit the road this morning at dawn, rolled into town, and had coffee at your motel. Mickey could write about a broken heart better than anybody. DJ Tom Donahue at KSAN, who was one of the godfathers of progressive radio, used to say nobody could write a song like Mickey, but get out your razor blades. He'll break your heart and make you want to cut your wrists.

He mesmerized. I mean, he would take your breath away. I saw him do it time and time again. Mickey didn't have a thesaurus when he wrote those songs. He wrote them from the heart. I heard *A Long Road Home* over the phone a cappella. You know that opening line, "I was from a shotgun shack"? He was. He was very conscious of everything he wrote and it all had a real-life foundation. There were a lot of guys who were extraordinarily jealous of him and envied his success, but they were small in comparison. Thousands admired him as a writer and an artist. Nobody in Nashville had written lines up to that point like "Winter's in labor / And soon will give birth to the spring / Sprinkled the meadow / with flowers for my Angeline" [from "Angeline"]. If you went to a guitar pull and caught him with the lights low and the mood right, some of these guys were in tears. It was a heavy time in Nashville, but I was in Texas for the most part.

Really listen to *A Long Road Home*. Mickey was around sixty when he recorded it, and that's probably the finest autobiographical album you'll ever hear. Listen and you'll go all the way back to Houston to Nashville to Springfield. It really charts his life. The stories will break your heart. "So Sad" is a true story: "I waited all that morning to hear you say 'I love you.'" Mickey's breathing was so incapacitated, he couldn't walk sometimes. He was so vulnerable. You know that line, "I am dead in Tennessee / They buried me alive"? The way that evolved was that Mickey called Acuff-Rose one day around 2001. A young intern in all his innocence said, "I'm sorry, sir, but can you tell us who you're with?" Mickey said, "That's okay, son. Forget it."[6]

Randy Dodds worked for ABC Records when RCA Records released Mickey Newbury's "Sweet Memories" as a single. The friends remained close through Newbury's final years.

MARTY HALL

I met Mickey at his home upriver in Vida, Oregon. Mickey couldn't have been more welcoming or unassuming. We found ourselves in his recording studio at some point. Mickey set up two desk chairs facing one another not more than a foot or so apart. He took an Ovation guitar, tuned differently than I had heard before, then pitched his head back, closed his eyes, and started singing "Wish I Was," a song I'd never heard. I still have not recovered from that moment. Words fail me in adequately describing the experience. I have been in awe of Mickey—both for his mastery of songwriting and his heart—from that moment to this. Hearing him sing "Wish I Was" directly to me melted me.

"Just Dropped In (To See What Condition My Condition Was In)" was the very first Mickey song I'd heard when I was in high school. I didn't know who wrote it at the time, but I do remember being struck by the lyrical sparseness. Most lyrics in commercial music then and now were more splattering syllables to fill every musical crevice in time rather than to thoughtfully and concisely tell a story. Most people tell me they focus on the psychedelic lyrics, but what stood out to me was the excellent play on words for the hook and how deliberate and concise the lyrics were. I was also struck by the arrangement, specifically running the backing vocals through a Leslie.

Mickey's songwriting started with a chord progression on guitar or keyboard from what I observed. The melodic part was far more effortless than his lyrical work. He didn't generally rely on a groove to carry the song but rather an interesting and engaging melody and a story told simply and elegantly. Mickey would use a yellow legal tablet to start writing the lyrics and would start what he called his editing once there was a basic structure. This is when the bloodletting commenced. He would unforgivingly work and reword and rework every word and phrase. Entire verses would be written, edited, discarded. His editing was never complete.

Mickey was a genuine wordsmith. He considered the words, what they convey, how they sound, how they fall on your ear, how they can be either graceful or graceless. He often worked seemingly incongruous words and meanings into new light. He was unafraid of creating new words. Occasionally, he used words or phrases that reflected reference to culture or the arts outside popular music for effect. His palette was vast, but his brushstrokes as a lyricist were very deliberate, considered, necessarily sparse. He knew that every element should be essential or it should not be there at all. He held himself to that standard. This principle also applied to Mickey's melodies. You will notice that they are most often deliberate, not overly complicated, and interesting.

His song "Little Blue Robin" from *Blue to This Day* illustrates Mickey's lyrical prowess. I lament greatly that I failed to press Mickey to explain this song, for it clearly invites questions. Jonmark Stone feels the same. On a personal note, I promised Mickey's mother, Mamie, before she passed that I would decorate Mickey's grave on Christmas, Easter, and his birthday so long as I was able. I have "Little Blue Robin" set to start playing at a particular place in the route when I go so it finishes just as I arrive at his resting place. There is a happy and transcendent feeling as I listen to him tell the story of the little blue robin and the characters Mickey imagined into our consciousness.

Mickey would audition his latest work-in-progress song to those around him, which he would do with his instrument of choice or just by thumping on his chest with one hand and singing the lyrics to the thumping. He would look the listener dead in the eye between glances at the lyrics on the yellow tablet. Then he would press the listener for brutally honest feedback when he was through. He truly wanted to improve his craft and definitely wasn't looking to be puffed. He considered and occasionally incorporated suggestions the listeners might offer. Songwriting was art to Mickey and not about creating a commercial song. It wasn't to please anyone. It was about his being true to his craft of songwriting. He knew that if he were true to that he would be true to the art and likely have written something worthy.

Mickey apparently had studied the word "amen." He traced its
origins back through time to what was an essential chant slurring
the letters together, a tone. He was interested in this and it reflects
his care with the words. He was always seeking perfect meter and
perfect rhyme and did not like contractions. He said they are graceless. He preferred "once" to "used to." He preferred "for" instead
of "because." He was careful in the use of the word "that," for he
correctly understood it often is superfluous and unnecessary clut-
ter. These subtleties likely escape most listeners but not Mickey.
He often chose words because of their touch upon other cultural
meanings, thereby expanding or offering an invitation to expand
the meaning of the word and song. Mickey wasn't only a student
of language, though. He was interested in and thirsted for knowl-
edge about virtually everything. He was constantly eager to learn
about something so that he could apply a new synergy in creating
something new.

Mickey had an idea for an entire album exploring the relationship between a Vietnam veteran who returned home to his lady
but was never really all there psychologically. *The Ballad of Maggie & Jessie* was metered to match the cadence of helicopter blades
huffing and thumping. Mickey had in mind to ask Bonnie Raitt
to sing Maggie's parts and he would sing Jessie's parts. The lyrics
were gloomy like the subject matter, but the project was effectively
abandoned when Bonnie's [landmark 1989 album] *Nick of Time*
was released and created a life of its own for her. Mickey couldn't
hear any other female voice for the project, and it died with that
so far as I know. Mickey and Bonnie were together at the Bread
and Roses festival at the Greek Theatre in Berkeley in November
1989, but *The Ballad of Maggie & Jessie* didn't come up.

Mickey was a dear friend, and I tried to be as good a friend.
He loved playing with ideas of all kinds. We related that way. He
was always available to me, as he was to everyone. His telephone
number and name were always published in the phone book. He
was as inclusive and unassuming as any person I have known. He
didn't overlook any kindness given to him. He made me laugh at
least once in every telephone conversation, and every conversation
would end with "I love you." Many, including me, encouraged him
to leverage his talent more aggressively, but talent and potential

held less value to him than his family and friends. He was definitely less motivated by fame or money than he was by love, affection, being true to his art, and doing the right thing.

Mickey knew I was intrigued by songwriting, and he gave me
the gift of many hours of constructive criticism and mentoring.
That must have been a burden to him, but he would never have
let me know. He was unwilling to overlook anyone. He was playing
at the Venetian Room at the Fairmont Hotel in San Francisco one
time. I was staying at another hotel. Early in the morning I came
to find Mickey at the Fairmont, and he was in the kitchen having
coffee and gabbing with the staff. He was inclusive to a fault and
attracted kind-hearted people. He enjoyed bringing together his
extended family of friends. Many of us he joined together remain
close.

Mickey would be golfing instead of writing songs when the sun
was shining in Oregon. I have heard others wonder if that might
be why [he wrote so many] sad songs. There was no way to know
what Mickey might bring up when we hung out. He had theories
and ideas about nearly everything. Some were well informed. Some
were imaginative. We would most often play with ideas, which in
our minds seemed elevated above shooting the breeze. He was com-
passionately curious about everything and particularly interested
in left-field applications of things. A typical evening talking with
Mickey might run from him being concerned about New Orleans's
vulnerability from a deadly flood years before Hurricane Katrina,
to Ireland being more aware of the cultural value of artists, to how
hypnosis works.

Mickey asked to stay with me for several weeks in 1999. He
needed to complete recording several tracks he had recorded earlier in Nashville as well as finish writing more than a dozen new
songs he'd been working on. The ultimate objective was to have
Mickey record his guitar and vocals on the best new material he
would be working on and then the rest of the production could be
completed in Nashville. My role on *Stories from the Silver Moon
Cafe* was to support Mickey, which included providing the environs
but more important to just be available to him as much as possible.
Mickey liked my place with the separate apartment attached with
a recording area, rough cedar walls, and skylights like his studio in

Vida. He brought his beloved "Susie" guitar. His eldest son, Chris, was there for a time.

Mickey insisted that I wake him around six o'clock every morning to have coffee and talk with him. He would work on songs during the day and share the results with me when I returned home from work. Sometimes he would pick up his Susie guitar and sing. Bob Rosemurgy and Paula Wolak arrived once the songs were ready to record. Bob stepped up in many ways to facilitate Mickey and his music. His touch is on everything Mickey produced from the mid-nineties until his death. Mickey loved Bob immensely, and I am not alone in still loving Bob. He has more than earned our respect and affection. He was a very positive addition to the loving energy present during this project. Paula was credited with engineering. She kept Mickey and me laughing yet focused and captured in one day around eight hours of Mickey playing his new songs. They would become *A Long Road Home* and *Blue to This Day* and some pieces on *Stories from the Silver Moon Cafe*.

Mickey continued to work at my home on recording and editing with Michael Charles McDonald. Mickey especially loved what Michael was able to do with the audio transitions between tracks. He somehow read Mickey's mind and delivered what he wanted. We who were there often remember that time as being quite special, even magical. Mickey invited us into his personal creative space, and we experienced the very best of who Mickey was. The silence was deafening for quite a time after he left. Mickey's work stands for itself, which is the sign of genuinely good art. That reason is why his material—much of which was originally published forty years ago and much of which has never been widely distributed—is still being covered by many diverse artists.

I was decidedly ignorant about Nashville and country music, which seemed just fine with Mickey. His style wasn't to circle back to his heyday in Nashville. I probably learned more about that from Susie. His time as a songwriter in Nashville would surface when someone famous would call while we were together, or he would have me contact someone from Nashville. Sometimes he would introduce me to someone famous where we were. I know his guitar pulls on his boat at Old Hickory Lake were legendary, as were his friendships with many music stars. I can tell you that many of those friendships endured through the years, judging by those who would call Mickey or make an effort to connect with him when in the same town. Mickey clearly made an intentional decision to put his family in Oregon as a top priority. He knew what was at stake and so far as I can recall he never lamented the decision.[7]

Oregon resident **Marty Hall** was instrumental in recording much of Mickey Newbury's music after Newbury and his wife, Susan, moved to the Beaver State.

JONMARK STONE

I had been vaguely aware of the name Mickey Newbury. "An American Trilogy" was probably the first song I'd heard. They had begun to start listing writers and musicians on the back of LPs in the seventies. I was always gonna be a musician from the time I was a young guy, so I absorbed who the writer and players were on any record. I got to Nashville at the end of 1979. I came to town to be a performer and was pretty quickly informed that everybody at least had to try to write. We were going through the singer-songwriter period in Nashville. I immediately went to work with a publishing company and began to write. Mickey was like God then. Mickey would be on the list if you asked any writer in Nashville their top five songwriters at the time.

I met a really sweet lady named Judy Mehessey when I moved to Nashville in 1979. She was a friend of Mickey's. Judy knew that I wasn't necessarily writing what they were trying to write in Nashville. I had come up listening to really poetic people like Paul Simon, Jackson Browne, and James Taylor. Judy encouraged me to continue down that road. She walked into the office one day with a stack of Mickey's albums and plopped them down. She said, "Here's your assignment." She had all the classics like *Looks Like Rain* and *I Came to Hear the Music*, etcetera. They blew me away. Mickey was already gone by then but came back to town a lot and usually for long periods of time. He came through town a month or so later and got in touch with Judy. She took me over to the Holiday Inn in Franklin, Tennessee, where he was staying. We sat and visited for a while and really hit it off.

Mickey wasn't a father figure. He was more like a rambunctious older brother to me because there were twenty years between our ages. He immediately gave me his phone number. Mickey was a notorious phone talker. He loved to get to know people that way. We started to communicate, and every time he came to town I was company for him. We'd play golf in tournaments, and he started using me on some recording sessions. He even had me go over to Acuff-Rose and do alternative demos on his own stuff. He was so well known. He was hoping that a different voice on his materials might get the song listened to quicker. His voice intimidated the hell out of people. Mickey sang like an angel and country music was a different style.

Mickey was a smart man and gave me a real education. He was respected on many different levels and was so well known because of the number and variety of artists who were cutting his songs. There were a lot of guys in Nashville at the time who only got country cuts. They made a good career out of writing simplistic things. Mickey had friendships through Acuff-Rose with Roy Orbison, Joan Baez, and friends like Dylan through the folk world. He had a literary style. Listen to those first albums. They were so different from what was going on in Nashville. You would have thought for all the world he was cutting in Los Angeles with all the weird arrangements and how there were interludes and tracks that never really ended. They were true albums.

Mickey was revered, and the young writers who came from my background couldn't believe he wasn't a superstar. He maneuvered in subculture circles in a way that most Nashville songwriters didn't. He was very much an enigma. Graham Nash was a real good friend, but I don't think Mickey wanted to be more famous. He famously said he didn't want to tour, but he spent a lot of time away from home. He would play in really cool places like the Boarding House and other counterculture places, which was odd because Mickey was very conservative even though his friends were not. He and Joan Baez were like brother and sister. Politics were discussed, but not in the same hyper environment like they are now. He hung out with a lot of hippies.

I love depressing music, which is a real strain among people who are his fans. He wrote some really, really sad songs. I think he shot himself in the foot on purpose. I think everybody would like to have that level of income that a superstar gets, but I don't think he wanted to be there. He was so cool. That probably would have separated him from the people who would come to his shows when he played the Bluebird in Nashville and places like that. Mickey would come out after the show and sit down with whoever and talk until nobody wanted to talk anymore. He was so personable. Peers who were superstars certainly recorded his stuff and contributed to his comfort level. Mickey bridged worlds. He hung out with Harlan Howard and Joni Mitchell at the same time.

I wanted to be a performer. I love standing in front of people and playing more than anything else in the world. I could go the rest of my life not writing another song, but I wouldn't want to think about not playing live for people. Mickey was the opposite. He was so prolific. He lived to get up in the morning, take out that yellow legal pad, and just write, write, write. Some songwriters did that, toured, were superstars, and could do that. Don Henley, Jackson Browne, Paul Simon have been able to keep the two separate but connected. I'm not sure Mickey could. I use those names because that's the level of writer where I put Mickey.

Johnny Cash, Waylon, and those guys would come in whenever we were doing recording sessions to watch Mickey work. Absolutely amazing to see someone as famous as John Cash show up just to stand there and watch Mickey do what he did. They were huge fans. Waylon could tell you album by album, track by track what was on Mickey's albums. I don't think there were many people who recorded more of Mickey's songs than Waylon. Orbison and Ray Charles did quite a few. I know it was a real surprise to the folks at Acuff-Rose to get cuts by Tom Jones and Kenny Rogers when he was a rock and roller. That's not what Acuff-Rose was founded on. Mickey famously told a story about going to see Wesley Rose after he wrote "Just Dropped In." Wes was like, "I don't know what the hell I'm gonna do with this." Then Kenny hits it and it's a monster rock-and-roll hit.

Mickey's songs were meticulously written. He didn't inject passable lines to finish the songs. He labored over each and every line. His great songs literally turned Acuff-Rose into a mouthpiece. People were coming after his tunes. He had massive success. Kris and Orbison probably had something to do with getting those songs outside Nashville. It didn't hurt to have Ray Charles cut his songs and give him a wider audience. The list of people who have cut his tunes is pretty cool.

Larry Butler, who wrote big records outside Nashville like "Raindrops Keep Falling on My Head" had been a driving force in Kenny Rogers's second career and produced all those monster country hits. He had agreed to do spec sessions with Mickey at his own studio on 17th Avenue in Nashville in 1984. Waylon's favorite thing to say at the time was that you're not American if you haven't heard Newbury sing. He put it a lot of ways, but the phrase hit me. I went home and wrote "When I Heard Newbury Sing." I came back to the studio and played it for Mickey and Waylon that night. Then I never touched it again. I put it away and never recorded it.

Fast-forward. We were working on another album called *Lulled by the Moonlight* around 1995. Mickey's health was really failing at that point. He smoked those stubby nonfilter Camels and was beginning to have all the associated problems with congestive heart failure and emphysema. He was on oxygen. We drove from Perdido Key on the border of Florida and Alabama to Nashville to do that session, and he's smoking, on oxygen, and coughing and scaring me to death. He was talking about dying a lot. Anyway, I got that song out, polished it, and changed quite a bit when we got back and recorded it in my own home studio. They played it at Mickey's funeral.[8]

Singer-songwriter and guitarist **Jonmark Stone** wrote the song "When I Heard Newbury Sing" about Mickey Newbury and has released albums such as *Etched in Stone* and *Folk at the Cannery*.

BOB ROSEMURGY

I had been a Mickey Newbury fan since buying *Frisco Mabel Joy* in 1970. I did civil trial work as a lawyer back then and traveled all over the country but never had an opportunity to see him perform. I saw a reference to his manager Owsley Manier in *Billboard* magazine and called on a whim. "I'm a big fan, and I travel," I said. "Where can I see Mickey play?" He wasn't performing at the time, but Owsley and I talked a couple of times. He called me in early 1994 and said he and another fellow were thinking of starting a new label in Nashville for singer-songwriters called Winter Harvest. Mickey was gonna be their flagship artist.

I knew my investment in Winter Harvest in all likelihood would not succeed. However, it was a hoot for me and an opportunity to see Mickey. So I said, "Sure." [My investment] in essence paid for *Nights When I Am Sane*, which was recorded at Nashville's Hermitage Hotel ballroom. My wife, daughter, and I went down for it. Mickey came in the ballroom, and I knew who he was. He said, "You must be the lawyer." "Yes, I am." There wasn't sufficient cash for Mickey to do the next recording because they had other artists. Owsley and Steve Roberts did an acoustic bluegrass recording on Steve Earle called *Train a Comin'* as soon as he got out of his prison sentence, and several other albums. Mickey talked to me and Joe Gilchrist, and I got involved in finding his fans who knew his music and would be interested in buying his albums. I asked Mickey if he had any letters from fans. He did. We started a website around 1995 that was part of songs.com, which had numerous artists and survived for a period of time.

Then Mickey got enough money together and did *Lulled by the Moonlight*, which came out the day Mickey was gonna start a mini half-moon-shaped tour that I put together. I got dates for him in the Detroit area, Traverse City, my hometown Escanaba, Milwaukee, and Chicago. I met Mickey in Detroit and simultaneously got a shipment of five hundred CDs, put a bunch in my trunk, and went down to Detroit to start the tour. We got this idea that it would help sales if he would sign and number them and decided there would be two thousand numbered and signed. Mickey used a gold permanent marker. He signed the CD itself on some of them because Joe Gilchrist liked that, and he signed the cover on some because that's what I liked.

Then we started Mountain Retreat, which went all the way with Mickey. We released *Lulled by the Moonlight*, then *Live in England* from his touring overseas with Don Williams. Mickey had been dormant for a while, but now he was in creative mode. He was writing because he knew he was ill and wanted to get things down while he could still sing. We worked diligently on getting brand-new things that he was writing at home and went to Nashville to record. We went to Marty Hall's when that got to be too much of a struggle. Marty had a very good studio in his home. Mickey would move in, sleep, and record there. He maintained odd hours there. We always had to be ready for when he was up to it and could record. I went out there several times.

Mickey wasn't really an early morning person because his health was deteriorating. He didn't have much energy or time when he was at his best at Marty's. We worked when Mickey felt like working at Marty's house. We would basically hang around and Mickey would say, "Okay, I feel better now and think I can do it." We were right there, plugged in, and away we go in minutes. Mickey couldn't use oxygen while he sang in a recording studio because microphones were so sensitive. So, he'd build up his air supply and sing and was exhausted by the time he was done with a song. You might get one or two songs a day recorded. He was on oxygen twenty-four-seven by then.

Mickey was a creative person and had many thoughts, songs he wished he'd have written. He had bits and pieces in his head that he wanted to finish. We went into Marty's garage studio once, and Mickey had this electric piano and a big pile of stuff in the corner. He went over to the piano and started to play. Mickey was self-taught and not a great pianist. He reached over into this metal Woolworth's wastebasket that you'd buy for two dollars and ninety-nine cents. He had these sheets in there—Mickey said he could only write on yellow legal sheets with a blue ballpoint pen—with lyrics to incomplete songs.

He'd sit there and pull lyrics out of the trash can and put them up. He'd look at them for a few seconds and start to play. "I haven't thought of that song for years," he'd say. "When you pick up that piece of paper with the lyrics," I asked him, "how do you know the melody?" "The melody comes out of the words," he said. "I know the melody when I look at them." There were a lot of songs that he never finished that stayed in that wastebasket, but that's how he worked. He'd sit on his bed and write lyrics on the legal pad. Mickey had great skill as a writer with words that were so simple but powerful. He used basic words and his great strength was editing.

He would be brutal on himself and take out words that he felt weren't essential to the song's intent and meaning. "Good Morning Dear" is a good example. "Were the nights any sweeter / were the mornings any cooler when she was here / or was a mind grown accustomed / to hearing, 'Good morning, dear.'" It wasn't "a mind grown accustomed to hearing her say, 'Good morning, dear.'" He would edit like that, which made his songs so powerful. The editing was so clear and good that there wasn't any wasted motion in the songs.

Mickey flew from Portland to Detroit to do the tour I booked. The trip exhausted him. He was in good spirits but tired when he arrived. Mickey was apprehensive about the tour. He hadn't performed much for a while. Mickey had been playing big places like Wembley Stadium in his prime, and that had disappeared over the years because of the music scene and Mickey had retreated. His last commercial recording was 1981, and he didn't issue another commercial recording until 1988 with *In the New Age*, which had very limited distribution. The label had gone broke. Mickey had fans, but they were all older. Young people had no idea who he was. The people who did still had his LPs, but they didn't have anywhere to see him.

The first place we played on that tour in 1994 was at a Unitarian church in Detroit. Mickey was apprehensive, but the people there knew his music. They knew "Heaven Help the Child," which really broke the ice and fired him up. These were devoted fans who had never seen him. They were in tears. Then we played a date at a recording studio in Traverse City. People requested songs and said they'd been waiting for this all their life. We had a good crowd in Milwaukee. Those were middle-aged people who knew his music and knew him. Mickey got energy from that tour. He was surprised and gratified by his reception and how important he was to those people.

He played the Flora-Bama songwriters' festival for years. We came up with an idea in 1999. Mickey was going to Flora-Bama again in November, but that year we decided to have a special Mickey Newbury concert night. We were on the internet then. I was getting requests and emails from people in Australia, England, Japan, Germany, all over the world. They wanted to see Mickey Newbury play. We had his website by then, and we posted that there will be this concert where you'll be able to meet Mickey in a room and sit and talk and then at night he's gonna give the concert. People came from all those countries to see him.

There was a bar across from the Flora-Bama with a big room, and we had Mickey show up there at one o'clock in the afternoon and sit at a table. People came over and told him how much his music meant to them, which was good for him. He was blown away. He was really suffering from COPD and didn't live much longer, but he gave a great concert that night. He put on a show for these people, and they loved it. Many were friends online and were looking forward to meeting each other. Seeing Mickey finally realize how important he was to these people was very rewarding. I'm sure it was gratifying to walk into one of those bigger old halls like he used to, but here he was face to face with someone who had flown from Australia to see him, which was very, very emotional.[9]

Former Michigan-based lawyer **Bob Rosemurgy** was instrumental in supporting Mickey Newbury's later career after the singer-songwriter moved from Nashville to Oregon.

CHRIS CAMPION

Mickey's voice is an absolute wonder. He was an extraordinary emotive singer who hooks you right away. I'd previously only heard "An American Trilogy" as the showstopper that Elvis had done with the epic production, but all of *Frisco Mabel Joy* has very tasteful production with the rain and atmospheric noises. Mickey had the full package. I think anyone who's exposed to his music hears that. There are very few people that I've played the albums for who have not really taken to them. The response typically is the same as the one I had: "Why have I not heard of this guy before? How is it that this guy who has written these phenomenal songs hasn't been recognized as one of the great songwriters in the American songbook?"

Mickey was very aware of the history of American song. He took these historic songs and recontextualized them into "An American Trilogy," not making a political commentary as much as a humanistic commentary on what was going on at the time. There was a lot of controversy about playing "Dixie" at college football games because they said it harked back to troubling times in American history. Mickey's feeling was that whatever political commentary you want to apply to it is your own thing. The song shouldn't be corrupted in that way. "American Trilogy" is just masterful. It's ironic that Mickey's probably best known and has made the most money from a song he technically didn't write. He'd made enough changes harmonically and melodically to claim songwriting on a new and brilliant work.

The *American Trilogy* box set was my idea. He referred to *Frisco Mabel Joy*, *Looks Like Rain*, and *Heaven Help the Child* as a trilogy, and they felt connected to me. They were all recorded at Wayne Moss's Cinderella studio, and they had the same sound with pretty much the same musicians. They seemed like a cycle of records, which I found quite unusual. *Frisco Mabel Joy* connects *Looks Like Rain* and *Heaven Help the Child*. Mickey was already established as a songwriter, but he was establishing himself as an artist over a period of time. Also, he was single when he started *Looks Like Rain*. Then he got married and had a child by the time *Heaven Help the Child* came out, with the title track looking toward the future.

The records after he moved to Oregon seemed connected, but they also spoke to a certain period in Mickey's life where he had achieved a certain amount of success as a songwriter and had grown significantly in the space of a very short period of time over three records. Some people write Mickey off because he didn't stay in Nashville. They think maybe he didn't have the ambition to make it as a successful songwriter. I think that's totally wrong. He had to balance his personal and professional life. Songs that he wrote after those three albums were just as compelling. Mickey never lost it. His songwriting and musicianship just matured very gracefully over the years. His last records are phenomenal. His last record, *Blue to This Day* [2003], is bare bones but remarkable. He was the songwriter's songwriter. His peers all received counsel and inspiration from Mickey.

Townes Van Zandt really changed Mickey's approach to song-writing. He became a wordsmith and a poet. He became the guy people were looking up to. He mentored songwriters over the years including Townes, Kristofferson, and Larry Gatlin. The name on their lips was Mickey Newbury in terms of the artistry he was investing in his songwriting. His songs were so beautiful and well constructed. There are those two songs he cowrote with Townes called "The Queen" and "Mister Can't You See," a wonderful, beautiful, powerful song. "The Queen" was especially a turning point for Mickey with the flowery language he hadn't had before. I date Mickey's turning as a songwriter to those cowrites with Townes. Kristofferson referred to him as William Blake, and he got his poetic sense from Townes.

I searched a long time for the master tapes before we put out the box sets. Mickey believed that they had been destroyed in a fire. That was the story when Hickory was absorbed by ABC Dunhill. There was a fire in a warehouse somewhere and a lot of masters were destroyed. In actual fact, ABC Dunhill's notorious because they taped over or destroyed masters in the seventies because they didn't think they were of any use. Mickey believed that *Looks Like Rain, Frisco Mabel Joy*, and *Heaven Help the Child* were all gone as well as most of his masters. I set about trying to find them. I wanted to make every effort to put the best-quality audio out there. It ended up I was working with a lawyer at the time who had a connection to Rhino and put in a request. The masters were in the Rhino vault, but someone had spelled Mickey's name Newberry, so they'd basically been lost.

The thing that really spoke to me in his songs is what he went through personally and what songwriting served for him. He was bipolar and spoke of the songs as a catharsis to get through the down periods in his life. He said he wrote his sadness. There's his quote, "I found that life on this planet is just not meant to be utopia because sorrow is always there and something everyone understands. In music, I began to strive to reach people on this emotional level because then I knew I would be reaching them eternally and if anyone had calloused himself over then I wanted like hell to break through and make them hurt again." That really hit me and speaks to what informs Mickey's sad songs. They weren't meant to make people sad. They were there to help people.[10]

Chris Campion runs the boutique record label Saint Cecilia Knows, which has reissued Mickey Newbury albums including *Frisco Mabel Joy*, *Heaven Help the Child*, and *Looks Like Rain*.

JOE GILCHRIST

I had come back from teaching school on the West Coast and ended up with a bar in Pensacola and then ended up at the Flora-Bama in 1978. Several musicians there were familiar with Mickey and played his music. I encouraged that and thought they were exceptionally special songs. A singer-songwriter friend eventually called me from Nashville and said, "Joe, I know you like Mickey. Here he is." We talked about him coming down and playing for a couple of days. I made arrangements. He was very upset at the music industry. He got here the day before I was back and already had started making friends. He fit right in with all the characters. He could have stayed a couple of days and never come back east of the Mississippi again, but he stayed for a month. We became really great friends. He came back another time and spent six months with me. The environment was delightful. It was very important to me that there was a connection between the singer-songwriters and the audience.

We ended up with many eccentric characters down here at the Flora-Bama. I think Mickey was comfortable here. Mickey felt less threatened and more appreciated here than most places. He felt like he had been betrayed again by the structure of the music industry. He was supposed to have a deal with Red Man tobacco and a publishing company, and he had a lot of great writers ready to go. It all fell through at the last minute. We would have fairly intellectual discussions and hear great music and have incredible guitar pulls with three or four world-class writers at my beach house about seven hundred feet from the Flora-Bama. Mickey didn't like to hang around the beach too much, so one time we got ahold of his slacks and made him cutoff shorts.

Mickey described railroad tracks as "threads of silver" in "East Kentucky." They're worn. He had ways of talking about things without actually saying it. He stated things in a way that made sense even though most people wouldn't say it that way. People who can transmit their feelings through music have an incredible skill. "San Francisco Mabel Joy" is a story song where you have to fill in the blanks. You know that the song keeps going along but it skips a few years. How did he get from the present back to San Francisco? Mickey rewrote songs to reduce the number of words but increased the emotion. Mickey had some anger issues sometimes that I tried to get him to quit. I tried to get him to dwell on the happy parts of life.

Mickey was going back to Oregon one time and asked, "Why don't you ride with me, at least partway? You can fly back." I thought that sounded interesting. We stopped in New Orleans on the way. I was just planning on getting out in Houston, but then we ended up at Willie Nelson's place in Pedernales outside Austin. I played golf with Willie Nelson and Mickey Newbury. These are things you don't expect to have happen to you much in life. It was a very good day. I sat in the cart watching them play as I became somewhat confused by the company in my presence. Mickey didn't smoke pot. He thought it diminished your brain capabilities.

We ended up in Las Vegas for two days and stayed at the MGM, which was the Hilton at the time. We ran into Don Williams there. That's when Don asked him to go on tour with him in England. I had mentioned to Don that Mickey would be receptive to an adventure like that, and Don contacted him a month or so later and took him to England. Mickey's *Live in England* album came from that tour. I think it was fun for Mickey. He was well received. I like that he was shown respect there because as a songwriter Mickey wasn't always appreciated by the entertainment part of the business as much as he was by the singer-songwriters who realized what great songs he was writing. Anyway, I didn't escape until we got to Reno, when he did the last leg to Eugene. He loved to play golf and played some of the top golf courses. He worked at golf like music until he got better at it. He was a perfectionist. Mickey developed a real skill.

He started playing one night around eight o'clock and went straight through until three in the morning. You never knew what he wanted to do. He played and played and tried to not repeat any songs for seven hours straight. I think the poets make the world a better place by letting us know each other a little better. I think Mickey made a positive impact on my life and others in general. Music that helps you think is a good thing. These songwriters have had hard lives in many cases, but they're able to say things to make other people's lives better.[11]

Joe Gilchrist runs the Flora-Bama Lounge, Package Store, and Oyster Bar. Additionally, he curates the Frank Brown Songwriters Festival, which hosted Mickey Newbury several times in his later years.

VERSE: SWEET MEMORIES

CHRIS SMITHER

I'm sure Mickey Newbury would have been influenced by Lightnin' Hopkins growing up in Houston. Lightnin' was my first venture into blues when I was seventeen. I was down in Mexico City, and my roommate in college really liked the way I played guitar, but he kept saying, "You need to hear this guy. I've got a record." He pulled out Lightnin's *Blues in My Bottle* on Prestige Bluesville Records. I was totally blown away. He sounded like two or three guys playing. That was my first introduction to any fingerpicking guitar. Lightnin' was huge in my life. I asked my roommate, "What is this guy?" He said, "Blues." Well, obviously I didn't know anything about blues. I started digging and found my other great love, Mississippi John Hurt. Mississippi John Hurt led me to Mance Lipscomb. They were more songsters than blues guys. They were into the song itself.

Mickey was someone I'd heard about for a long time, but the only time I ever saw him at all was at the Kerrville Folk Festival in the Hill Country in Texas. Everyone was all excited for him to play. I thought, I finally have a chance to hear this guy. He came on hooked up to an oxygen tank and played with Jack Williams on guitar. There's a side-stage seating area for performers at Kerrville, and I sat there for the better part of an hour and was totally transfixed. It was an amazing performance. He held my attention the whole time. He threw off his oxygen mask about two-thirds of the way through and drove the crowd wild. They were cheering like crazy.

Mickey was everything I like in songwriting. He delivered the songs, had the ability to sell them, and totally convinced people that they had to listen. He had all that in spades. The arrangements and his guitar playing were great. I don't remember if it was particularly technically brilliant, but it was perfect. He sang melodies that suited me. I don't even remember anything about the songs, which is infuriating in a way. I've never dug deeply into his music since, but he was mesmerizing that night. His was a very impactful performance. I loved it.

The important part telling stories playing solo is making sure the audience can hear the words. The song has to have something to say and you have to hook people when you only have about three minutes to get the whole thing across. My rule of thumb is that you're a big winner if people can walk about remembering one line from each song. You need to hook them early with a good entry line and then don't disappoint the listener. Don't get too obtuse or involved. That's one reason that country songs work so well. I've heard Mickey Newbury described as country, but I don't think of him that way. The songs were more involved and captivated my imagination more than standard country fare.

Let me know if you find out why some people aren't better known. I'd like to know why I'm not outside certain circles. You don't have any trouble finding people who know who Townes Van Zandt was, and Mickey and he came out of the same thing. Everybody knows Townes. He was the reason I ended up on Poppy Records. He was on the label at the time. I thought, If they like him, they like me. They did. I made my first two records with Kevin Eggers, the guy I learned to hate, for Poppy. I think everybody hated him. I'll never figure out how he stayed out of prison. Michael Cuscuna really wanted to produce me something awful. He suggested I go to Poppy. He said, "They have this guy Townes. Let's get them a tape. They'll probably like you." I said, "I know Townes."[1]

Celebrated acoustic blues singer-songwriter and guitarist **Chris Smither** shared a label with Mickey Newbury's favorite songwriter Townes Van Zandt for his first two records on Poppy Records, *I'm a Stranger Too!* (1971) and *Don't It Drag On* (1972).

RODNEY CROWELL

Guy Clark consistently would say, "You gotta know about Mickey Newbury and his work." Guy gave me Mickey's *Live at Montezuma Hall* record after we got friendly. I listened to that constantly. All the poets—Guy, Kris Kristofferson, Townes Van Zandt, even Willie Nelson—had more of a baritone delivery in their voice that lent more gravitas to the poetry they wrote, but I'm a natural tenor. Newbury

was writing "Cortelia Clark" and "Heaven Help the Child" and singing as a tenor. I went, "Yeah. I can do it with a tenor voice." Mickey
was a huge influence on me. He wasn't a self-promoter, but he was
every bit the artist. I was absorbed in his work in 1972, 1973, 1974.

Mickey wasn't sticking with the first chorus, second chorus,
bridge structure. He would have long verses, B verses, then something that resembled a chorus but wasn't. Look at "Heaven Help
the Child." You don't get Guy Clark's "Desperados Waiting for a
Train" without that song. The chorus structure and how he sings
the line "heaven help the child" is "desperados waiting for a train."
Newbury was influencing folks deeply. Guy [thought Mickey was]
everything you aspire to be as a writer, the quality of the narrative, the songs inching toward literature. He liked Mickey's guitar
playing. Mickey used Drop D a lot on his gut-string guitar, which
created a drone that gave him a real solid platform to use his voice
the way he did. He could make things get really still and yet the
rhythm was moving the song along. That influenced my guitar playing. The incredibly nuanced performance on *Live at Montezuma
Hall* drew me to it, but he was incredibly charming, too. He was a
little shy and reticent.

I found out early on that he's from the Denver Harbor area in
Houston. I'm from East End, which is real working class. Denver
Harbor is even deeper. I was impressed. "Man, you're from Denver Harbor, and you're up here writing songs? Whoa." He had my
full attention. I might have heard his name in Houston, but I didn't
know him. Kristofferson was the guy in Nashville, the Dylan, the
poet. I realized that Newbury and Kristofferson were hand in hand
on the street when I got to Nashville. Maybe Newbury was second
in command because Kristofferson was so huge and had become a
big star. Mickey wasn't gonna be a big star. He was a shy, taciturn
fellow, but he was really open and funny.

Guy, Townes, Mickey, and I did three shows together in Texas,
the first time I performed with Mickey. I watched him battle [stage
fright]. He'd have to smoke some cigarettes and drink some whiskey to calm his nerves down. Watching him onstage was like,
"Oh, man, that's so good. What am I gonna do?" I'd follow Townes,
and we all know that's impossible, but I was more intimidated by
Mickey. Mickey was very well regarded in Nashville. Everybody in

Nashville at that time knew Mickey Newbury and respected him. I talked with Bobby Bare a lot about Mickey.

Not everybody could handle his songs. Jerry Lee Lewis took all the nuance out of "She Even Woke Me Up to Say Goodbye." That's why people who really study early Americana, Nashville outsider, outlaw songwriting consider *Live at Montezuma Hall* the holy grail. Even an up-tempo song like "1×1 Ain't 2" with a word tumble like [Bob Dylan's] "Subterranean Homesick Blues" is really nuanced. Mickey was a rare dude. He was dazzling one on one, but taking it out to a bigger scale wasn't his nature. He performed solo. He wasn't gonna be in front of a band. He never really grew his hair out. He was still wearing slacks, rayon shirts, and loafers. He was conservative in style, but he was really into the Beatles. Their harmonics and chord structures influenced his writing for sure. He was taken up by the currents of the sixties and what it all meant even though he wasn't stylish.

People covering his songs never reached me because he was reaching me. Listen to him play "Just Dropped In (To See What Condition My Condition Was In)." He played it entirely different, like a soul ballad instead of this psychedelic rave up. "An American Trilogy" did play right into Elvis's real broad stroke bravura, though. Elvis got it. In my case, I think Bob Seger did such a great job on my song "Shame on the Moon," that song belongs to him, not me anymore. I can't point to one of Mickey's that someone took away from Mickey. I never heard anyone outdistance his versions.

I do a pretty good job of "She Even Woke Me Up to Say Goodbye," but I've never recorded it. I should. I know what that song is inside and out. I probably listened to it five hundred times when I first heard it. That's the thing about Newbury. I'm still influenced by wanting to capture that kind of nuance to this day. Guy Clark's "She Ain't Goin' Nowhere" is very much torn from Newbury's pages. I used Drop D for the guitar playing and really adapted Newbury's almost Spanish style of rhythm for my song "Until I Gain Control Again." That song probably was more influenced lyrically by Kris Kristofferson, but my approach and melody definitely were torn from the pages of Mickey Newbury's notebook.

You can get anecdotes about Townes like giving money to waitresses, falling out windows, being an alcoholic, being sweet and a

snake at the same time. You don't get all that color with Newbury.
He was very contained. They'd send young writers around to write
with me for a while, and they'd have no idea who Newbury was.
You say, "Look, man, go to school. Get *Live at Montezuma Hall.*"
They wouldn't bother, but if people would bother to look at songs
like literature in a hundred years, "Cortelia Clark," "San Francisco
Mabel Joy," and "Heaven Help the Child" have to be alongside the
great narrative songs like [Clark's] "Let Him Roll," [Van Zandt's]
"Pancho and Lefty," and [Marty Robbins's] "El Paso." How much
better can characters be profiled in a song?[2]

Rodney Crowell topped mainstream country music charts a quarter century ago, but he's always been a workaday songwriter. His
writing earned a Grammy Award for "After All This Time" (1990)
and notched ASCAP and Americana Music Association lifetime
achievement awards in 2003 and 2006.

STEVE EARLE

I knew who Mickey Newbury was almost as soon as I started playing because I'm from Texas. I didn't instantly know that Mickey
wrote "Just Dropped In" when I heard it on the radio, but I learned
that by the time I started playing guitar and going to coffeehouses
when I was underage. I was very aware of who Mickey Newbury
was by the time I got to Houston. There was a mural on the back
wall at Sand Mountain in Houston that was Mickey Newbury, Guy
Clark, Townes Van Zandt, Jerry Jeff Walker, and Don Sanders, a local
folkie who never quite broke out. I was listening to Kris Kristofferson then and the kind of country music that connected to Bob
Dylan records and folk music that I listened to. I actually bought
his records. Mickey's were ambitious concept records that made
sense alongside *Sgt. Pepper's Lonely Hearts Club Band.*

I had a direct connection because Mickey was Townes's first publisher. He signed Townes to a publishing contract and gave him a
record deal, but Kevin Eggers approached Townes and wanted his
publishing. Kevin had started the Poppy label. Newbury called me
the day after Townes died and was in tears. He was sick himself

by that time, so he was a little overly emotional. He was trying to blame himself for Townes being the way Townes was. He was wondering how things might've been different if he hadn't released Townes from his contract to sign with Poppy and Kevin Eggers, which is bullshit. Townes was his own worst enemy, a master of self-sabotage.

Mickey called Guy one time and said he was in town. I was at Guy's house making tapes to take to publishers. Guy said, "You wanna meet Mickey Newbury?" I said, "Fuck yeah, I wanna meet Mickey Newbury." By then Guy and Susanna were out at the lake in the house where Townes later died, so we drove into town and probably got there around eleven o'clock at night. Not only Mickey was there, but Roger Miller and Grant Boatwright were there, and the guitar started going around. While we were sitting there, Roger and Grant went to Wartrace, Tennessee, which is about ninety miles southeast, woke J. W. Gallagher up in the middle of the night and ordered a guitar, and came back while we were sitting there, an all-night thing.

I probably didn't see Mickey for a year after that. This was long before I ever made a record. I had just gotten a publishing deal, and I was hanging out with Guy and that crowd when Mickey walked up to me at an ASCAP party that I'd crashed for free booze and shrimp. He recited half a verse from a song I'd played only one time the night we met. He was super, super smart. We were all post–Bob Dylan songwriters, but Mickey really wasn't. Most of us were doing what we were doing because of Bob Dylan and thought it was all right to do it in Nashville because of Kris Kristofferson. Kris was there largely because of Mickey. Mickey was already writing songs by the time Bob Dylan came along, but he understood how important he was. Mickey was just so smart that there was no way to contain him in the confines of commercial country music, or any other music, really. He was ahead of his time. He was making these records that were too smart for people when you get right down to it.

Mickey commuted between Houston and Nashville in a Cadillac and slept in it most of the time to get his career going. He saw bus stations and bowery bars. One of the last conversations we had was about this bar right next to where CBGB ended up in the

Bowery in New York. He had this photographic memory for things that he saw and people who he saw that he didn't know or even have a conversation with. He watched them struggle, empathized with them, and lent them a voice, like the whole concept and idea of "San Francisco Mabel Joy." That song's like Steinbeck. He gave them a really beautiful setting in his songs, which gave them some dignity. That's what made me want to write some songs that I went on to write and some of the things I emulated the most.

Mickey was one of the best solo performers I've ever seen. Newbury and his guitar was your money's worth any way you look at it. I think Townes emulated him the most. He would sit perfectly still and close his eyes. He was not a shoe gazer. His head was back and you could always see his face. He would make eye contact from time to time, but it was almost like you were intruding on something private. It was like he was meditating and then that voice would come out of him. He could get audiences to be quiet just by being quiet himself. That's a great skill to learn. Sing softer, not louder, when the crowd gets rowdy. He had dynamic range and used a lot of different colors on the palette. He could hit those notes no matter how loud he was singing.

I think he was one of the best songwriters around. There was a quality to his lyrics. In some ways, he was a bridge between Bob Dylan and the people who followed directly in Bob's footsteps and people in country music like Johnny Cash. Dylan was listening to translations of the French poets and the Beats, but Townes and Newbury were more about Shakespeare and Robert Frost and more traditional poets. I think that's why Newbury latched onto Townes so much. That makes their stuff unique among people who were writing songs at that time. Newbury was coming from being a songwriter who got songs covered. He was a staff writer, and we all learned from that because we didn't necessarily want to be that. We all wanted to make records, and so did Mickey. People knew that there were great songs there. He came along in a moment in the late sixties when there were some country and pop artists that were just looking for higher-quality material. Dylan had raised the bar.

I think songwriters in Nashville [regarded him highly], but Nashville was and is very anti-singer-songwriter because it upsets the balance. They didn't want artists to write their own songs. Publishers controlled the town, and it was the last Tin Pan Alley. They wanted an artist who stayed out on the road making money for themselves touring and then would come in and record songs that they published by their staff writers. They figured out that the best songs came from people who were smart like John D. Loudermilk, Willie Nelson, and Hank Cochran. Not all those guys were the best-looking guys in the world or great singers. Bob Beckham knew that to get "Help Me Make It Through the Night," he had to let Kris Kristofferson write "The Silver-Tongued Devil and I."

That died out, but Newbury was what established it in the first place. People in Los Angeles had recorded his material, and he was one of the reasons that people on either coast started looking to Nashville for material. At the end of his life, I'd just come back to the world after almost dying and Newbury had been diagnosed with emphysema and wasn't touring. We were on the same record label called Winter Harvest in the midnineties for a second and got back in touch. That's why he called me after Townes died. He had my number. I've always been lucky in that I do know the history in what I do, and I know who came before me and why I do what I do.[3]

Steve Earle broke into public consciousness with his seamless debut, *Guitar Town* (MCA Records, 1986). The San Antonio area native might be his generation's most diverse songwriter, with classic country (*Exit 0*), rock (*I Feel Alright*), and bluegrass (*The Mountain*) albums under his belt.

BUDDY MILLER

I was fascinated with Nashville and songwriters when I was in high school and was drawn to storytellers and deeper songs. I would hunt down songwriter records. Each Mickey Newbury record was pretty important to me. I discovered him through *Frisco Mabel Joy* and then backtracked to *Looks Like Rain*. They came at a very formative time in my life. Pop music on the radio was great at that time with the Beatles and country and R&B, but for what was coming up later in my life as a songwriter and musician and producer, hearing *Looks Like Rain* was different than anything I'd ever heard with the production value and rain between every song.

Birds, cicadas, and noises go through my whole SiriusXM show. They're a nod to Mickey Newbury, the production on *Looks Like Rain* and his other records. *Live at Montezuma Hall* and *Lovers* were huge for me. So was the way he weaved together "Apples Dipped in Candy." Mickey was a very soulful, smart, torn person who I was very moved by. I listened to everything he did. Mickey was an incredible guitar player. You hear a nylon-string guitar and the first thing you think is Willie Nelson. I've played on a record with Willie sitting four feet away for a few days. He's amazing, but with Mickey that sound becomes part of the song. He was a great, soulful player. I recorded "Please Send Me Someone to Love" on a record due to Mickey's recording his version of the Percy Mayfield song. Mickey wasn't doing a cover song. It belongs to him. I forgot that I was so influenced by Mickey Newbury until recently.

I think the outlaw country thing looked like a cartoon to Mickey. I don't think he minded not being part of it. Mickey wasn't trying to play the game. I think he was glad to get cuts when other people covered his songs, but that's not what he strived for. Nashville is so different now. I live right near Music Row. When we moved here from Austin twenty-five years ago, there was a sign out front of a house that said something like, "Mickey Newbury Appreciation Society." I never got a picture of it, and it's not there anymore. This town has moved on. Commerce is always the thing here, but there was such deep art there with him. I think Mickey's had more influence than people know. I've heard Kristofferson say things backstage. He's credited Mickey with starting things.

Mickey's been overlooked because he didn't want to be that cartoon character. It's cool that there's an outlaw movement. I'm not putting it down, but even to me it's a little [much]. I'm on a station called Outlaw Country. That just seems at times cartoonish. "Just do the music." I don't feel like Mickey felt like he needed to play that game. He wrote songs, and his records were beautiful. They are meant to be listened to one side at a time. Everything down to the artwork on his Elektra records was gorgeous. They had expensive cutouts on the front.

As commercial and money driven as it is, I think Nashville back then especially had respect for the songwriter and creative powers like Mickey Newbury. They didn't give them huge budgets, but they let those guys make their records. Cats like Dallas Frazier, Troy Seals, Mentor Williams were writing and producing for Dobie Gray, which was a different thing than Mickey, but there were songwriters like Bob McDill who did a record for Cowboy Jack Clement's label. There's always a respect for deep talent. They knew the songs weren't gonna be hits, but they let the writers express themselves. That still goes on now to a certain extent.

I wish I knew Mickey. It's incredible how he's been overlooked. I'm gonna do a two-hour radio spot with Jim Lauderdale soon on Mickey for our Sirius show. His records were big deals to me. The rain factored in, but it's not just that. *Lovers* flowed and told a story. Mickey was a storyteller like Tom T. Hall. I like hearing him tell the stories like Cortelia Clark's on the live record. The songs were connected, artful, and poetic. I wasn't just a country freak. I loved the Grateful Dead and old-time music. You listen to *Anthem of the Sun* and everything flows together, a crazy hybrid live record with weird studio stuff in there. Mickey fits on the same dinner plate as far as I'm concerned, though he's much more musical.[4]

Nashville-based songwriter **Buddy Miller** has performed with such Americana stalwarts as Larry Campbell, Shawn Colvin, and Jim Lauderdale. Lauderdale and Miller currently host the popular *Buddy and Jim Show* on SiriusXM's Outlaw Country channel.

MATRACA BERG

My mom [Icie Calloway] and aunt [Sudie Calloway] were backup singers in Nashville in the sixties. Mom had Mickey Newbury records and would play [*Harlequin Melodies*] with "Sweet Memories." I thought Mickey was really handsome, and his voice was beautiful. Mickey really was my first taste of great songwriters when she would play his records in our little bungalow on Blair Boulevard. Mom was drawn to different music than mainstream. I think he signed to Acuff-Rose the year I was born. So, this comes from a pretty early place, but his influence can't be measured. Mickey, Kris Kristofferson, Billy Swan, and a different breed of songwriter were coming to town. There was a lot of bar raising going on, which had a trickle-down effect on music.

Mickey's lyrics are so simple, but they're classic in the great songwriting tradition, which is the hardest songwriting. I appreciated that style more in my thirties. My challenge to myself in my thirties was to achieve more economy of language with more air between the thoughts and emotions so people can have time to absorb the song. Mickey's classic melodies also really influenced me. There's really no category. Anybody can record it. I'm not quite there yet, but that's something I've aspired to be. I aspire to write songs that an R & B, rock-and-roll, or country artist could record, a lofty place to shoot, but Mickey got there probably more than any other songwriter. No small feat. Not many people can do that. Maybe one percent. Mickey's songwriting will last forever. We can only aspire. I think the closest we have to Mickey right now would be Rodney Crowell.

I was successful on a few songs, but it's a challenge to write [at the same level as] Mickey Newbury, Harlan Howard, some Kristofferson songs. They were my template, but I'm still trying. I wrote a song called "Back When We Were Beautiful" that Rodney and Emmylou Harris recorded that I feel was successful at that particular style. I wrote a song with Jim Collins called "I Don't Feel Like Loving You Today" that Gretchen Wilson recorded, and it was nominated for a Grammy even though it wasn't a huge hit. I think "Strawberry Wine" goes there. I went through a phase writing everything in Drop D like Mickey. There are a lot of great songwriters who stick with that. It works. Having that low note gives it a warmth. Also, there's the [high] E that you can move around to other chords and still have the constant drop note.

Mickey wasn't an extrovert. He was a recording artist but not a showbiz guy. There's such a big part of his life that's a big blank when he moved to Oregon with his wife. They forget about you pretty quickly here when you're not around. You don't hear names thrown around anymore. People are out of sight, out of mind. Mickey had that quiet time later on when he made records, but there was space between them. He wasn't big on self-promotion.

I can completely identify. I love making records, but I don't really care about the other part as much as I probably should. I just wanna write songs. You've gotta be careful. I told Harlan Howard once that I was thinking about taking a year off. "Kid, I took a year off once," he said. "I realized that no one missed me when I came back to work."[5]

Three-time Grammy-nominated singer-songwriter **Matraca Berg** has written songs recorded by Deana Carter ("Strawberry Wine"), the Nitty Gritty Dirt Band ("Oh, Cumberland"), and Gretchen Wilson ("I Don't Feel Like Loving You Today"). She lives in Nashville.

LESLIE SATCHER

Mickey Newbury was a huge influence on me as a singer-songwriter growing up in Texas. Willie, Waylon, and all those guys really turned me on to his music. Then I was writing with a guy once I got to Nashville who was really dear friends with Mickey and introduced me to him in the studio. That was a turning point, a real touchstone for me as a singer-songwriter. Mickey was amazing. We were talking about doing what you have to do to make it in the music business, and he told me a funny story about when he started out singing in Houston as a kid. He worked at this Italian restaurant, and they wanted him to be a strolling balladeer with a guitar. They wanted him to sing in Italian, but he didn't know any Italian. "The guy goes, 'You're gonna sing.'" I said, "What did you do?" He said, "I just started making up stuff—*oh sol mio*, jibber jabber. I made great money for six months. You know what, it was one of my best jobs. You do what you gotta do."

Mickey was already pretty old and having a hard time breathing the day we met. He was cutting demos for a new project at that studio in Berry Hill [southwest of Nashville]. He couldn't work for a long stretch of time, but he was feeling good. My friend hadn't told me he was taking me to meet Mickey, but I knew who it was right away. I had seen him in concert before and had worked at different places where he was working. Man, it was so amazing to spend fifteen or twenty minutes with him. Then he got back on his oxygen, went back in the studio, and sang again.

The soulfulness of his music is what really drew me to him. I thought his songs were just so poignant and soul stirring. I saw him live at a club here called the Exit/In one time. He walked out onstage and there was just an ashtray, a little stool, and maybe a whiskey drink in the dark. He had an electric guitar, and the place was jammed, a tiny club with two hundred people in there. He sat down for two hours. Nobody said a word. Nobody moved. Riveting. I remember thinking, If you can move your audience like that with just your voice and a guitar, that's where it is. He was such a great influence on us.

Mickey was spectacular in concert because he was real and coming from his heart. He sang so soulfully. It's like you're sitting in the living room conversing when you're being real and playing great songs with those great vocals. Mickey was like that that onstage. People love it because it's so intimate. He was a master at capturing the intimacy of a venue and laying it out there for the audience. They felt like they were his friends, which is a very rare thing to do. Dolly Parton and Willie Nelson do that. Mickey had the same endearing quality.

All the older songwriters knew who Mickey was when I got to Nashville and would bow down. He used to play this songwriters festival at the Flora-Bama called the Frank Brown Songwriters Festival. He would play late in the evening and people would scramble over from whatever club they were playing just to see him and that riveting presence. He didn't need a band. He laid out those songs, talked, and smoked. It was really cool. He really understood women. His songs are very sensuous. There's a line [in "She Even Woke Me Up to Say Goodbye"], "Baby's packed her soft things, and she left me." I heard that as a young songwriter and was like, "Oh my gosh." I knew exactly what he's talking about. You can see this lady packing up her lingerie drawer and leaving. He was dealing with things men don't normally. He saw that leaving moment and recorded it.

Mickey was a master storyteller. He made little movies in three minutes. When you're a young songwriter and you see a guy condense a story into a three-minute movie like he did with "San Francisco Mabel Joy," that's a mark to try to reach. Oh my gosh, what a killer song. He was like Kristofferson. The young songwriters were drawn to Kristofferson when I got to Nashville in the late eighties because of his mastery. "Sweet Memories" is my favorite. It's so mournful and really, really timeless. Not a lot of singers attempt that song [anymore] because of all the great singers who have attempted and landed it. It's so iconic. You have to be a singer's singer to do that song.

I was with Sony for fourteen years. Now, I'm with Notting Hill Music out of London. Normally, if you're with a publishing company, you'd take your song into a meeting with the song pluggers. They know all the acts and they take them and run with them to a producer, act, or management company. They're the middleman, but when you've been in town as long as I have, you can just call the producer or artist yourself. The way we get songs to an artist is a little different, more complicated than it used to be when Mickey was doing songs. Melba Montgomery told me that when she and George Jones would be recording, they would get a hotel in Nashville and put the word out to the songwriters: "Hey, we're recording an album on Friday." All the songwriters would show up Tuesday and play their songs live, and they'd pick. Then they'd record them on Friday. That's old-school right there.

Prayer is important to making it in Nashville. If you don't have faith, I don't know how you can stay in this town. Everything that happens is a miracle—a miracle that a song gets cut, that you get noticed by a publisher in a town with a zillion songwriters who are landing here every minute, that a song makes the final album. The biggest miracle of all is when a song gets to radio. My faith has kept me here and literally seen me through. I came here with two hundred bucks and that was it. I got an apartment and a job. I went to work trying to figure out how to make a living in the music business. It was two years before I was actually in the music business, which is the norm.

It makes it all worth it when Willie Nelson grabs you at an award show, which he did to me four or five years back, when they were honoring him with the BMI Icon Award. I was just gonna touch him on the shoulder and say hello, but he turned around in front of all my friends and said, "Your song is my favorite song I've ever recorded." I wish I had a tape recorder. Willie Nelson. He recorded a song of mine called "You Remain" [the closing track on Nelson's 2002 album *The Great Divide*] with Bonnie Raitt. I couldn't believe

it. George Strait has been recording my stuff for years. I just got a
Sheryl Crow and Stevie Nicks cut. When you start getting icons from
your childhood like Stevie Nicks recording your songs? Dadgum.
There is a God in heaven.

I wrote "You Remain" with my friend and great songwriter Don
Poythress. He asked me one day, "If you could write a song for anyone, who would it be?" "Willie Nelson." He said, "We can't get a song
to Willie." "Man, you said, 'Who would we write it for?'" Well, I was
in the middle of recording my first record for Warner Bros. at the
time and [longtime Nelson harmonica player] Mickey Raphael was
playing on my album. We wrote that song about Willie for Willie,
and I recorded it at a demo session the next week in one pass. We
took it to Mickey. He took it out to play for Willie in Hawaii. Willie
called me on the phone and said, "I wanna cut your song." I said,
"Man, it's your song. We wrote it for you." He went into the studio
at midnight and recorded it in one pass. Then Bonnie Raitt came
in and sang on it. It was one of those rare times where everything
lined up.

Mickey was a songwriter's songwriter like Kristofferson, Willie,
and Dolly Parton. When you're that person your legacy spiderwebs.
Think about country writers who were influenced by Mickey Newbury. They also write rock and pop songs. Mickey's legacy is huge. I
would say that about the first two-thirds of my writing career was
inspired by Mickey Newbury. I wasn't a really great guitar player.
I only knew two or three chords. I was listening to a Mickey Newbury record, and I asked my friend, "How does Mickey get his guitar
to sound like that with the big, bassy sound?" "Well, he drops that
low string down into D and he gets an open tuning." He showed
me how to do that and—boom—my career took off. I learned to
play like that and make up original-sounding melodies, which was
huge for me. So much of the first part of my career was influenced
by learning how to play in that tuning. I simply wanted to sound
like Mickey Newbury.[6]

Leslie Satcher has recorded two albums (*Love Letters*, 2000, and
Creation, 2005) and has had her songs recorded by Vince Gill, Mar-
tina McBride, Willie Nelson, George Strait, Pam Tillis, and Gretchen
Wilson. She's a native of Paris, Texas.

JENNIFER WARNES

Mickey Newbury was like Bob Dylan. Dylan had visions, wrote them, and the world received them no matter how strange or odd they were. Mickey was in that echelon. So was Leonard Cohen. The small group of songwriters who have very specific visions should be left alone. Mickey was belligerent about refusing to do things someone else's way. You run into trouble whenever you take a person's spirit or soul and turn it into a commodity. Mickey was all about spirit, soul, great singing. There was truth in his voice. Putting business into that mix and people wanting to control you is one of the most painful transactions that can happen. His God-given tenor was like Roy Orbison. Mickey was way before his time.

I met Mickey when I was on *The Smothers Brothers Comedy Hour* and *The Glen Campbell Goodtime Hour* in the late sixties and early seventies. The Smothers Brothers went on hiatus every summer, and they put John Hartford and Glen Campbell in the summer slot while they reassembled a plan for the coming season. [Campbell] had great comedy writers, but he didn't have that many musicians. He'd come off a successful season and brought with him Mickey Newbury, Kris Kristofferson, and Larry Murray to advise us on the music for *The Glen Campbell Goodtime Hour*, which was like a repertory group where everybody filled in for everybody else in many ways. I did a lot of singing and comedy work and met both Kristofferson and Mickey then.

Mickey was a songwriter for Kenny Rogers and the First Edition and Elvis Presley then, but it was clearer than a bell that he was better than everybody else when he sang. Meanwhile, Kris was on the verge of breaking out with the Monument record [*Kristofferson*, 1970]. I was the first female to perform [Kristofferson's hit song] "Help Me Make It Through the Night" on national television [on *The Smothers Brothers Comedy Hour* on September 2, 1970]. He was probably so excited that it was going national when I sang it that he called his friends and told them to watch on Sunday night. I knew I could turn the gender like I did with a lot of Leonard Cohen stuff, but no one ever credited me with being the first to leap on "Help Me Make It Through the Night," not even Kris. Kris's friend Connie Smith recorded it in Nashville the next week, and I think they liked that it became popular from a Nashville artist.

Mickey and I admired each other from afar during that time, hung out with all the same people and hobnobbed at CBS, but I didn't get close to him until years later when Randy Dodds, who was in San Antonio with Arista Records and pushing [Warnes's 1977 hit] "Right Time of the Night" up the charts in Nashville, reached out and said that Mickey was ill. Apparently, Mickey really loved [Leonard Cohen's] "Famous Blue Raincoat." Randy sent me Mickey's record *A Long Road Home*, and it knocked me out. I called Mickey. Our lives were well known to each other through the passing of the years. He went on and on and on about "Raincoat."

I said I was deeply affected by the nature sounds on his records. They were atmospheric, big, emotional, rhapsodic. He created great highs and lows in his songs. Mickey was an emotional guy. We were on the phone for hours. I was inclined to talk more because I knew that he had health issues. Finally, I said, "I'm gonna record [one of your songs]." He said, "Well, I'll never hear it." "Of course you will." That was when I think I had maybe four or five nice conversations with him. He told me about this animated film about a little bird in his head. He was probably influenced by Harry Nilsson. He wanted to make this movie about a little bird. Of course, the little bird was Mickey.

Mickey fills my emotional needs in song. He puts me in a genuine, complex, beautiful emotional position. I could have recorded any of his songs, but I liked the disappointment and sadness of "So Sad" [on Warnes's 2018 album *Another Time, Another Place*]. Mickey felt too much, like Leonard Cohen did. The music business puts a sensitive person through so much. People who become elaborately disappointed in art have high hopes. Mickey had very, very high hopes for his life and work. His visions for his work were higher and brighter than everyone else. They were sky high, so he suffered a lot just like Leonard Cohen. He was very disappointed.

Mickey's [rebellion against the music industry] wasn't belligerence. His rebellion was a feeling that he had a right to manifest music [the way he wanted]. It wasn't, "I hate you. I'm gonna do it another way." It was, "I hear it, see it, feel it this way. It's a little different than you feel. As the artist, I have the right to paint the painting the way I want." He's absolutely right. Other artists have had the same mission in their heart with the vision of how to do something. He was an artist, a great singer, and his visions were very particular. He deserved the right to manifest them, but the publishers don't want people [with a unique vision]. They just want you to sing their songs and get on with it. Mickey was emotionally attuned. He saw the proper way to execute a song, and he felt he had the right. Of course, the industry doesn't want to pay for that in a recording studio.

An artist like Mickey Newbury can start their own record company today. Then they don't have to answer to anybody. They do whatever they want to, and their visions are very particular and unique. Mickey was right. He just took a very hard-line stand in a very conservative time. No one would question him if he were doing right now what he did then. Artists have these ideas about what we're supposed to do with our lives, and it's kind of silly for companies to stand in the way of that. Imagine somebody telling Willie Nelson to do it a different way. Not gonna happen. Mickey suffered because he had strong visions that were true and good and he made records like *A Long Road Home*. I think the industry is starting to figure out that they'd better step back when there's soul involved, but they didn't know that back then. So, Mickey went to Oregon.[7]

Singer-songwriter and arranger **Jennifer Warnes** was a close friend and collaborator with legendary songwriter Leonard Cohen. She and famed British singer Joe Cocker had a hit song with "Up Where We Belong," cowritten by Buffy Sainte-Marie. Warnes recently recorded Mickey Newbury's "So Sad."

GRETCHEN PETERS

I discovered Mickey Newbury in my late teens when I was living in Boulder, Colorado, during the late seventies. The country hippie thing was happening in the Colorado music scene with the Nitty Gritty Dirt Band, Flying Burrito Brothers, and everything that grew up from that branch of the tree. I hadn't been exposed to that when I was a kid, but I found a guy who owned a little record shop in Boulder. He figured out I was interested in learning about this. I'd go in there once a week, we'd go in the back room, and he'd throw records into my hand. "You need to learn about the songwriters. Check out Linda Hargrove." Mickey Newbury's records came into my possession in that process.

Mickey was a link between the folk music I'd grown up with and the country music I had completely fallen head over heels for. This may sound like a cliché, but the first thing that drew me into his songs was his deep well of sadness. There was something deeply moving and sad about his songs, and I've always been very attracted to those qualities. I identified with him on a very cellular level. I'm sure I couldn't put it into words then, but I've spent time thinking about it the past couple of years as I've been doing this record [of Newbury songs]. I think he had this vision of himself as an artist. Even though he was a songwriter and he was far more successful as a songwriter than an artist in his own right, his vision of himself was purely as an artist. That really attracted me.

People who know about Mickey know how great he was, but I feel sad that he's not really given his due in Nashville outside a small coterie of songwriters and musicians. Honestly, they're from an older generation now. I'm sure a lot is that Mickey left Nashville. Also, Mickey rejected what Nashville was about, and I don't think that sat well with a lot of people. However, everybody who knows anything about country music will acknowledge what a brilliant songwriter he was. He's in the Nashville Songwriters Hall of Fame, but there are plenty of young songwriters on Music Row who don't know who Rodney Crowell is and certainly don't know Mickey Newbury. He's not even as well known as Harlan Howard. I hate to say it, but Mickey is much more in danger of being forgotten than someone like Townes Van Zandt.

I had been thinking about doing an album of Mickey's songs for about fifteen years. I just said, "It's now or never." I realized concurrently that Cinderella Sound Studio, which is the studio where Mickey recorded all those great records from the late sixties and early seventies, is still a working, operating studio run by the owner, Wayne Moss. Wayne played on those Mickey records and has all the Mickey Newbury stories that you want. Also, he's a renowned guitar player who played the famous guitar riff on Roy Orbison's "Pretty Woman." I've taken people in to Cinderella who I know would appreciate what went on in there, which is like a living, working museum. Anyway, that held a fire under me. I thought, What if we go in and record in that studio?

We went in blind, and it was magic. The place basically hasn't changed since 1969. The studio itself is in a converted garage in Madison, Tennessee. Linda Ronstadt recorded her first album there. Steve Miller recorded there. The list of people will blow your mind. There's gear and memorabilia from all those eras. In fact, Linda Ronstadt used the bathroom as a vocal booth, which I did on this album. It was the best room to get isolation on the vocals. I'm a big believer that places—especially studios—hold magic in their walls. Once I figured out that we could do that and we cut three tracks there and got something really great, I thought, We gotta do this. We went in every couple of months and cut songs, and by the end of the year we had a record.

I had to feel my way around interpreting Mickey's songs. I wanted permission to play around with the song structures a little bit when I needed to, and I talked with several people who know Mickey. I knew that he fooled around with his songs all the time because I listened to all kinds of bootleg recordings. He would take lines from one song and put them into another. He would change titles. Sometimes his songs structurally were strange once you got down in there and looked, partly because he would produce a song on his own records more like a pastiche. There would be a couple of verses and then an orchestral musical interlude that went somewhere else. I knew I needed to get in there and adjust the structure. I talked with old friends and touring partners and said, "I'm doing this record and what do you think Mickey would have thought about somebody rearranging his songs?" Pretty much everyone said, "Oh my God. He did that himself. Go for it."

He was such an operatic singer with an incredible voice. I had to get away from his records and sit down with my guitar and go, "Okay. If I had written this song, how would I have recorded it? How would I sing it?" Some songs were easier than others. I didn't lay down any parameters as far as which songs to do. They didn't have to be hits or songs that were even covered. I cut some of the later, folkier ones that he wrote. I found the songs that I identified deeply with and went with those. I have to admit that some of the more straight-ahead country songs definitely were a challenge but turned out the best. My God, his singing was every bit as genius as his writing.

Jennifer Warnes just recorded "So Sad" on [*Another Time, Another Place*, 2018]. That woman really knows a song. I listened to her recording this morning. That's not one that we cut for my album, but the lyrics to that song absolutely devastate me. You know, after diving so deep into him for my record, I think of Mickey as the country version of Leonard Cohen. He has very Cohenesque verses in his songs. Those are the ones that really drew me to them for this record that I made. One of the first we recorded was "The Sailor." There's something about that song. I felt it so deep in my bones. You always have the track that's the blueprint for where you're going next on a record, and "The Sailor" was definitely one of those.

My album's mostly me with my husband, Barry Walsh, on piano and Will Kimbrough on guitar. We also recorded "Just Dropped In (To See What Condition My Condition Was In)" during that first session. I was on the fence about recording that song, but it turned out to be one of my favorite things on the record. We recorded "Saint Cecilia," which a lot of people don't know because he wrote it later. I think the title track to the record will be "The Night You Wrote That Song," a song I've always loved. The lyrics are really pointedly about Nashville. We also recorded a couple of wild cards like his later song "Three Bells for Stephen," a tribute to Stephen Foster. We also did "Frisco Depot," which is a favorite.

I think Mickey's in the top three purely genius songwriters in country music history. The thing that initially drew me to country music in general was the deep reservoir of sadness that I mentioned before. Mickey's melodies are gorgeous, but his lyrics are devastating. He could take a song from sad to devastating simply by the power of his lyric writing. He's one of the very best we have. A great country song has very simple, straightforward lyrics with no trickery. There's some ambiguity in a great song, but maybe not to the extent that a great rock song would have. Country is simple and honest, so the choice of words is hugely important.

For example, "She Even Woke Me Up to Say Goodbye" is simple, but I'd defy you to find another songwriter that would write: "It's not her heart, lord, it's her mind / She didn't mean to be unkind / She even woke me up to say goodbye." There's nothing obscure about that, but it goes straight from sad to devastating. I guess it's maintaining empathy in his understanding of what's going on between both characters in his songs. He's aching for himself, but he's empathizing with her, too. That's what makes you feel it so much. His writing is not one dimensional.[8]

Nashville-based singer-songwriter **Gretchen Peters** has released several albums including *Dancing with the Beast* (2018), *Blackbirds* (2015), and *The Secret of Life* (1996), as well as the all-Newbury covers *The Night You Wrote That Song* (2020). She frequently tours with fellow songwriters Mary Gauthier and Eliza Gilkyson billed as the Three Women and the Truth tour.

WILL KIMBROUGH

I was in Sweden on tour. My booking agent set me up with some people I didn't know from Adam on my night off. They were gonna come pick me up at my hotel, which was gonna cost me like four hundred dollars that night. A fellow named Martin and his son came to pick me up and took me to a house on the largest lake in northern Sweden, which was frozen over. They cooked dinner for me that night and played Mickey Newbury's *Live at Montezuma Hall*. I knew Mickey was singing, but I didn't know that record for some reason. I was also playing twenty nights in a row on tour in a rental car and was exhausted. I said, "What is this record?" They looked at me like I was crazy. "This is Mickey Newbury's *Montezuma Hall*." They said it like the record was *Meet the Beatles*. I thought it was cool that somebody somewhere thinks this record is something that everybody should just know.

People either want to hear the string section, the background singers, and the drummer, or they just want to hear the person sing. Mickey was a great singer and could write these great songs, and his guitar, timing, phrasing are all beautiful. *Live at Montezuma Hall* is like listening to Nina Simone, Nick Drake, Robert Johnson, Hank Williams, or John Lennon singing solo—or Bob Marley doing "Redemption Song." Mickey's in that league regarding singing, songwriting, playing, timing, tone, phrasing, everything. Newbury was the whole magical deal wrapped into one playing solo. His solo performance was magic that sucks the listener in.

You can't discount that there's something about the unadorned but beautiful guitar in the space of the room he was in that creates something very special. Mickey wasn't self-conscious on his studio records, but there's a real unselfconsciousness to *Live at Montezuma Hall*. He had a way of speaking poetically but also being direct, which is something unique that John Prine has as well. The cover versions are great, but there's something about the way he sings when he's singing the songs. I like it best when it's just him singing and not superproduced—with all due respect to Wayne Moss and all the cool recordings they did at Cinderella. I would always pick *Montezuma Hall* first. Everything you need is there already. He could sing "Heaven Help the Child" and "How I Love Them Old Songs" a cappella, and I would listen.

He wrote the saddest songs like "Cortelia Clark" and "San Francisco Mabel Joy" that you wanna listen to over and over again. They're desperately sad, but you listen to them over and over the same way you read a great novel or short story that's very sad. At the same time, he wrote some songs that were downright psychedelic or funny. I'm a songwriter, but it's hard to describe exactly why a song is so great. Maybe an English or literature teacher could say it better, but there's something intangible that touches you. I wish I knew a better way to put it.

Gretchen Peters and I have a lot in common as far as what we do and how long we've been in Nashville. When Gretchen and Berry called me and asked me to be on her album of Mickey songs they said, "Would you be interested in working on this? We're not going in for a week to record. We're doing it whenever we have a day or two." Of course, I said, "Absolutely." I wasn't given the music ahead of time, which is typically the way we work with her and most people in Nashville. I think most people know that you want to get a first emotional impression with particular session players before it becomes rote. I don't think she wanted me to listen to Mickey Newbury records and get stuck on the parts that were there originally. She wanted to sing the songs pretty true but also interpret what key works for her and what tempo works for the phrasing.

Playing Mickey songs with Gretchen at Cinderella Studios was like something from the seventies. Linda Ronstadt did her vocals for [her 1970 Capitol Records debut album] *Silk Purse* in the bathroom. There's still the brown shag carpet in there. You can picture her in there barefooted singing "Long, Long Time." [Legendary drummer] Kenny Buttrey's drums are there. He played on "Lay Lady Lay" and "Heart of Gold" and a million other things. I played a different session there where they said, "These are Buttrey's drums." Then they set them up on the spot. "Holy shit. I wanna play these drums." The piano there is the one Ray Charles demanded when he played the Opry. They sat him down at a baby grand. He said, "No, no, no. This is a baby grand." "That's what we have." "I'm not playing that." They had a grand piano and had it delivered and Wayne got it somehow.

There's always the Texas-versus-Nashville or Memphis-versus-Nashville debate. I played Memphis the other night and one of my favorite music fans was sitting in the front row. I was telling some old story about Nashville related to the era when I met Guy and Newbury. She said, "Why would you ever write anything good about Nashville?" I told her why. It's still true. I've been here thirty-one years. The first people I saw in Nashville when I got here and was performing were John Prine and Townes Van Zandt sitting at the bar at the Bluebird. Of course, I was totally overwhelmed and intimidated. They weren't being intimidating, but they just were. I was like, "Well, they live here." Then I met Steve Earle and John Hiatt. "Well, they live here." There's an energy between the musicians and writers that still exists. I'm proud of what we do. I think the cruelty of show business isn't Nashville's fault.

Mickey and I shared a publisher in the late eighties. I moved to Nashville and was signed to EMI Publishing in 1988. I knew Newbury's songs like "Just Dropped In (To See What Condition My Condition Was In)," but like a lot of people I didn't know they were his. I went to the EMI Christmas party that year and Guy Clark and Mickey Newbury were there. I was twenty-three then when I met him. I don't think he was in particularly good shape then. I remember having a drink with Mickey and Guy and thinking I was out of my league as far as drinking and needed to go home. Mickey was the old-fashioned songwriter and was totally sweet and funny. I can picture his face right now smiling and laughing with Guy Clark at everything, but I could look at his face and tell that he drank too much. I come from a human family with alcoholics and saw those broken blood vessels across his nose. Guy and Mickey looked like the faces on Mount Rushmore.[9]

Americana Music Association instrumentalist of the year **Will Kimbrough** (2004) has performed with Todd Snider and the Nervous Wrecks as well as being a solo performer for years. Kimbrough served as guitarist for Gretchen Peters's Newbury covers album *The Night You Wrote That Song*.

BOB DIPIERO

I discovered Mickey Newbury and his music around 1979 when I moved to Nashville from Northeast Ohio. I was a rock-and-roll guitarist and really didn't have much grasp on who Mickey Newbury was, but then I jumped into the whole vibe and history of country music in Nashville and followed songs back to where they came from. Of course, Mickey was a major touchpoint for songwriters at that point. He was a songwriter's songwriter and had a mythical image. I was at Columbine Music where Kris Kristofferson and the Gatlin Brothers were, and Mickey was friends with Kris and other folks who worked at Columbine like the publisher Bob Beckham. Mickey would come in and have this aura. You knew he was in the building before he was in the building.

His songs mixed Dylanesque folk with iconic country songwriting and were American music bigger than any genre. He crossed genres with his ability to write and connect with people. I've always wanted to write songs that weren't necessarily timely as much as timeless. Mickey's songs were timeless with universal themes. The coin of the realm is to write a song that means something to somebody in Canada, Texas, all over the map. Mickey's use of language was aimed at communicating with people. He wasn't writing down or up. He was writing at them. Mickey was top tier in Nashville and looked upon as an artist of Kristofferson's caliber. He was maybe more of a songwriter's songwriter than Kris. Waylon Jennings would drop by Columbine and treat Mickey as a friend and equal. That's how he was treated on Music Row.

[The title track to and number one hit from the Oak Ridge Boys'

1983 album] "American Made" was the second song I ever had recorded. I was just another guy who came to Nashville to figure out if he was a guitar player, songwriter, or singer. "American Made" was my ticket into the game, like Kenny Rogers and First Edition recording Newbury's "Just Dropped In (To See What Condition My Condition Was In)." The song made the community ask, "Who's this guy Bob DiPiero who wrote 'American Made'? This is bigger than a country song and is on the pop charts. They turned it into a beer commercial." The song gave me more face time with people. I would like to say I had more lofty ambitions, but I was just trying to make a living and keep my contract.

I was feverishly writing every day and sometimes twice a day. I know when I wrote "American Made," I didn't remember someone saying these things quite this way. I said we have all this foreign-made stuff, but my baby's here. She's American made. I love her. I thought, That's a pretty interesting way to write, but I certainly didn't think it would do what it did. I've written songs since then that I thought would cure cancer and nobody cared. I was just doing the work in that moment. I wasn't looking for any kind of brass ring. I'm a commercial songwriter making a living and I wanted to continue. I get input from my publisher, the general public, and my fans about what they are turning on to. "Okay, I get this. I see what they're responding to. I think I can serve something up that good."

Two or three number ones under my belt gave me more confidence. I was thinking I figured it out, but even now I'm still figuring it out. I'm always a student, always learning. I had to figure out language and lyrical content that people wanted. I've always said that country music is deceptively simple and subtle. Speaking in the language of the people listening to the song is important. The music is like primary colors. Keith Richards talks about being an antenna in his book. You get out of the way of the idea and bring it into the real world. Mickey struck the universal vein of gold in how to communicate with people. Great songwriters are great communicators, and Mickey was an iconic communicator. All the songs he wrote being recorded is amazing. I've had a thousand songs recorded, and I think that's ridiculous. Mickey was the king. He spoke to our heart.[10]

Bob DiPiero has written hit songs for several top country stars including John Anderson, Vince Gill, Faith Hill, Tim McGraw, the Oak Ridge Boys, Restless Heart, Tanya Tucker, and dozens more.

DARRELL SCOTT

Nashville's daily paper the *Tennessean* wrote about Mickey when he died, as they do when someone in the industry dies. They said two things: "Newbury will be best known for his mention in the song 'Luckenbach, Texas,' where it says 'Newbury's train songs,' and the Elvis cut of 'An American Trilogy.'" I was immediately infuriated and have been ever since. That may be true for the ignorant public, but for someone like me who was intimate with his music that doesn't even begin to describe Mickey Newbury. Although, I guess if you're a writer for the *Tennessean* and you're writing something overnight for tomorrow's paper, that's probably the scramble of words you're gonna come up with. You're writing to tell somebody who doesn't know who Newbury is. That's criminal in Mickey Newbury's case.

He was mountains ahead of that description. Here's what I've noticed being in Nashville: anyone who was around during that time like Guy Clark, Townes Van Zandt, Steve Earle, and Rodney Crowell talk about what a large place he held in their imagination. Also, Guy bought his house on the lake from Mickey, and when Townes needed a place that's the place he got from Guy. I've been in the company of all those people, and there's no question of the impact and quiet place they have for Mickey Newbury. I certainly witnessed Guy having it. The Nashville-Texas connection is largely attributed to Willie Nelson, but I think as much if not more might be attributed to Mickey. There may have been people who predated Mickey, but I haven't seen anyone who was a singer-songwriter, a true artist, and had a publishing deal trying to get cuts. I don't think anyone handled that better than Mickey Newbury and stayed true to himself while doing it.

My first exposure to Mickey was probably people covering his songs but me not knowing it. I probably discovered Mickey doing his own songs on the *American Trilogy* records. I was definitely

seeking out the singer-songwriters who wrote the hits in Nashville and the California version with Jackson Browne, the Canadian version with Joni Mitchell, and eventually the Texas versions.
I found that Mickey was fitting in within every camp possible. He
was getting Nashville cuts, Joan Baez and Elvis were cutting his
songs. He had my attention from the age of sixteen on because
he was crossing genres. Mickey had an integrity at all levels that
shook hands completely with his writing, his singing, his vibe. He
seemed like he wasn't about compromise.

Mickey doing his own songs and other folks cutting them was
distinctly different. Same goes for all of us singer-songwriters as
far as us doing our own tunes and having people record them in
the marketplace. The real catch wasn't his songs done by Ronnie
Milsap. It was Mickey singing his own songs.

He had an artistic purity doing his own songs because he wasn't
swinging for the fences of the industry big time. Mickey Newbury
was very much an artist intact, first and foremost. I could hear that
in his songwriting and arrangements. He wasn't just someone who
has a record deal and is called an artist. His writing, voice, and performance showed he was like a painter, a playwright, a poet.

Mickey always had this otherworldliness that really stood out
when I was younger. I was looking for something that felt a little
more true than the puffed-up industry stuff when I was sixteen,
and he stood out as an individual among an industry that tries to
squeeze out artists like sausage. Those were artists with a small
a. Mickey was an artist with a capital *A*. The emotional truth that
he would discover and talk about in his songs stood out. It's hard
to put into words why he stood out in those ways, but I could tell
it from a lyric point of view. He wasn't just going for clever, tight-
knit songwriting, although he could and would do that sometimes.
He was drawing from a larger emotional palette and not just going
for hit making only.

Mickey went against the industry as an artist and not so much
as an outlaw "fuck you." He was a complete artistic individual and
didn't have to say it. His "fuck you" was in the songs, the music, in
him playing a gut-string guitar. Mickey was from another planet
for his time. His attitude was in the work as opposed to the ver-
biage. He didn't have a PR company talking about how much of

an outlaw he was. Mickey wasn't raving, "Hey, look at me. I'm an outlaw." He just was an outlaw. His work had a purity as opposed to a strategy that had my respect very early on. From my vantage point, when I found Mickey I found a quiet, artistic outlaw who was original and unique.

I don't think Mickey's contemporaries would question his importance, but now you race through the decades and come to modern times. The last person I was able to talk Mickey Newbury with was Buddy Miller. Buddy and me were on the bus touring with Robert Plant, and it was just us awake one night. We got into a Mickey jag playing jukebox on the iPad as we drove down the road. We picked out Mickey Newbury songs all night for each other, but it's not often that I get a chance to talk about Mickey. Folks who know, really know. Folks who don't, really don't. I connect with that, a guy who gets cut and is maybe a greater artist than anybody who cuts his songs.

Mickey was on the short list when I was doing [Scott's 2008 album] *Modern Hymns*, a record of songs by folks who had been huge inspirations to me through their writing and artistry. I had my heroes like Mickey, Gordon Lightfoot, Paul Simon, Guy Clark, John Hartford on there. I knew "Frisco Depot" from an old Waylon Jennings album [*Ladies Love Outlaws*, 1972]. The song struck me as killer. You can't describe that forlornness of being stuck at a train station without the money to get anywhere. San Francisco was supposed to be all love and peace and Haight-Ashbury, but [it's depressing] to someone who doesn't have enough money to even eat. I had to have a Mickey song on that record since it was me declaring, "These are the folks who meant the world to me." I called it *Modern Hymns* because of how I saw that collection and those people.

I didn't see interpreting a Mickey Newbury song as a challenge. Sing it with heart and soul, and it will take care of itself. Mickey did the work. You sing it. At the same time, you don't want to suck because the integrity must be there. I cast that song very simply when I did it. All the harmonies and instrumentation are live. I wanted a real clear, direct, honest read. I was looking for that Texas-Nashville connection. I wanted to bring Mickey to folks' attention because I think it needs to happen. I've wanted to make a tribute album to Mickey for fifteen years or longer—pretty much since I read that *Tennessean* article. I was like, "Fuck you. He was huge."[11]

Nashville-based songwriter **Darrell Scott** has written songs for Sara Evans ("Born to Fly"), Patty Loveless ("You'll Never Leave Harlan Alive"), and Travis Tritt ("It's a Great Day to Be Alive"). He frequently worked with the late legendary singer-songwriter Guy Clark.

WALT WILKINS

My friend Frank Patterson was writing a film script in 1987. His dad was a musician who had grown up in Houston and ran into his old friend Mickey Newbury at an airport during the same period. Frank's dad called to say that Newbury offered to write a song for the movie. Frank thought maybe he could write a small role for him, too. This led Frank and I to go see Newbury play in a club in Houston called the Backstage. Frank had arranged to meet Mickey that afternoon at a club before sound check. I wanted to meet Newbury, and Frank was kind enough to let me go with him on a miserable August day outside in Houston. We met Newbury in the green room where it was cool and dark. He had been golfing that day with an old Houston friend he called his "doctor." He had lived in Oregon for years by then, but we got the sense he was having a good homecoming back in Houston.

Newbury was drinking a black Russian. Then he had a white Russian and another black Russian. He said the doctor had given him something for his back pain, which we learned later was a real ongoing curse to him. Newbury couldn't have been kinder or more open. I know now in a way I didn't then that we were guests in a sacred part of the day: the rest and gathering of energies before a show. Newbury pulled out his little Martin guitar. He was small himself and a little fragile for a man still in his forties. He picked around on the guitar and we talked a bit, but not much about the movie. Then he sat down and played a Luke the Drifter song I had not heard before. I was mesmerized totally and completely. I pulled a chair up in front of him, and he smiled. "Do you know who Luke the Drifter is?" he asked. "Yessir," I said. He smiled again. I will never forget how kind his eyes were. He went on to sound check and said we should come back for the show that night.

A few nights change your life. This did for Frank and me. We sat on the club's second level right at the railing. Newbury was a little drunk when he started, but I had never heard anything that sounded like his guitar playing and voice. My heroes at the time were Steven Fromholz, Willis Alan Ramsey, J. D. Souther, and Jackson Browne, all geniuses in their own way, but this was another level of expression. I was twenty-four and had written a few songs. I knew that's what I wanted to do more than anything, but these songs reached into me at a place that had not been reached yet. I was crying by the fourth song, "Ramblin' Blues." I'm sure that was the first time I had been moved to cry by beauty.

Frank and I could not fathom how a man and a guitar could sound the way he did. He sang himself sober in front of fans, family, and old friends in the audience. It felt like we had stolen into a side gate of heaven, like somehow we'd been gifted something that maybe we didn't deserve. When I was in high school, playing in a band and already trying to write songs, my friend and mentor Roger Paynter had loaned me a couple of Newbury records, saying, "You've got to hear this." I wasn't ready. Newbury requires maturity, being knocked around a bit, losing some things, maybe having a broken heart. I guess I was finally ready that night.

As it turned out, that show was recorded for the purpose of a live record. The record never came out, but he had a new one that came out soon after called *In a New Age*. It was atmospheric and otherworldly like all his records. The album was recorded in a studio live with two sets with just him and a violin player named Marie Rhines. The guitar on that record had been built for him, and he used bass pedals to make this full and eerily compelling wall of sound. Frank and I listened to that record over and over. The production sounds dated now, but the songs and delivery are first-rate Newbury, and maybe that was the last great record he made.

I got to see him a couple of years later at the Cactus Cafe in Austin. He did two shows, and I bought a forty-dollar ticket to each show, which was a fortune at the time. I'm sure I ate beans and toast for a month to pull that off. We visited between shows, and I helped him and Marie find a lost contact. He asked if I liked the guitar and how I was. He had such a sweet countenance in my time with him. He didn't have to be that kind. After all, he was the greatest songwriter alive, but I learned something very important from him. Modesty is compelling. Modesty is compelling not because it makes him "nice," but because that's how he was in the world and the place he wrote from. Listen to "Willow Tree."

The shows were both great. Newbury sang "Ramblin' Blues" at my request, a song that I do now when I feel particularly brave. My favorite Newbury songs require the whole being to even begin to deliver. Ron Flynt and I recently started preproduction on a daunting record of Newbury songs. We speak of Townes Van Zandt and Guy Clark in our world of songs, but for me—and I love Guy as much as anyone—Newbury is the third in that holy triumvirate. Mickey Newbury: True humility. True artist. True poet.[12]

Walt Wilkins has had his songs recorded by Pat Green ("If It Weren't for You," "Rain in Lafayette"), Kenny Rogers and Pam Tillis (both cut "Someone Somewhere Tonight"), and Ricky Skaggs ("Seven Hillsides"). The longtime Nashville resident currently lives in the Austin, Texas, area.

FRED EAGLESMITH

I discovered Mickey Newbury on [CBS Records' 1972 release *One Hand Clapping: Big Sur Festival*] with Mickey, Joan Baez, Taj Mahal, and a bunch of others. I remember hearing "San Francisco Mabel Joy" and maybe "33rd of August" on there. I'd never heard his songs and couldn't believe how good the writing was. Mickey blew my mind. I was about fifteen or sixteen years old and was into stories and songwriting. That was exactly the right age to hear "San Francisco Mabel Joy." I left home at fifteen, hitchhiked, and hopped freights across Canada so that song really resonated.

Mickey was tough. I played a concert in Atlanta at Eddie's Attic one time, and [venue founder and former owner] Eddie [Owen] told me a story about having trouble with some guys who were renting the place downstairs. Mickey went down with a gun and knocked on the door. Mickey got in big trouble for that, but he wasn't fooling around. He wasn't just talking about being a bad guy [in his songs]. I couldn't believe it. Mickey hadn't seemed that way the few times I talked with him, but he was the real deal. He was an outlaw in that he made those records that didn't sound like [the mainstream]. He was thumbing his nose at Nashville. I especially hated Nashville in the eighties when they were trying to use synthesizers.

Mickey was having none of it. I heard people criticize his records, but I thought they were real art. There's mainstream music in country, but then there are guys out there like Mickey who are making art. He was on top with that. I always thought *Looks Like Rain* was brilliant and wore out lots of vinyl copies. I used to have this guy Willie P. Bennett in my band. He'd bring his wife over to my farm, drink, and play *Looks Like Rain* until dawn. I was always about Mickey's overproduction. He was so far out, so precious and not pretending not to be. Mickey was just going, "Here's more production and more production. This will be sadder than it should be."

He could twist lyrically like nobody could. He made up his own vernacular like "33rd of August." New vernacular has always been important to me as a songwriter, and down the line it became very important. "It's the 33rd of August and eight days from Sunday." There aren't eight days. He made up his own story and his own language. That's what songwriters don't do much. Tom Waits can do it a bit. They make up a word or use a new word. You don't know what it is, but you believe it anyway. Mickey forgot the rules. People hate the production because he threw out the rules for that, too. I love it. I could hear those guys in Nashville saying, "You can't put horns on a country record and you can't say those words."

I've had people say that same thing to me in Nashville. I would write a twist, and they would say, "How can you say that? That doesn't even make sense." "Listen," I'd say. "Just listen." They would and then they'd go, "Aww. Yeah. That totally makes sense. I never thought of it that way." I wrote a little ditty once that went, "If you've got something to say, why don't you say it now / While I wait for this train that I missed anyhow." That makes perfect sense to me, but the song plugger was like, "That doesn't make any sense. How can he be waiting for a train he missed?" That's the stuff that I learned from Newbury. I was waiting for a train I missed. Newbury would have done it exactly that way.

I made a record called *Things Is Changing* back in 1993 that had a lot of Mickey's influence, and I was aware of it. By [Eaglesmith's 2004 album] *Dusty*, I had probably forgotten that, but his influence was probably ingrained in me. That's what we're supposed to do: we learn from people, then forget it, then do our own thing. I would say that *Dusty* had a bit of Newbury, and to be fair, I lost about half my fans when I made that record because of the production. I learned well from Mickey. I don't think he ever played the game until his *Lovers* record. You gotta play the game. I know this from experience. You don't move to Nashville and not play the game. I lived in Nashville in the nineties, and there was a hipster world there even then.

I remember Mickey coming into Nashville around 1996 to do a show at Douglas Corner Cafe. Everybody was like, "Wow, Mickey's coming to play a show." He [recently] had done an interview and talked about how bad the songs were in Nashville at that point. Half the songwriters wouldn't go see him that night. "I'm not gonna go see him if he's gonna be that kind of prick." Mickey just said what he thought. Nobody will say anything negative like that today. There was some pretty good country music happening in the nineties, and he could have turned what he said a little differently. You have to play the game, whether you look like you are or not.

He called me a couple of times later in his life when he was dying. I guess he had read something I'd said about him in a newspaper article or he heard something. He wasn't totally coherent, and it sounded like he was hurting financially, although that's hard to believe. He was promoting himself too much. "Check out my website." I said, "Mickey, it's great to hear from you. I was just a kid then, and now I'm pretty established. Things are going well for me. You did all this." He didn't want to hear much about that. He just wanted to talk about his career. It was really weird and hard to hear from him.[13]

Widely popular Canadian singer-songwriter **Fred Eaglesmith** has released more than twenty albums including *The Boy That Just*

Went Wrong (1983), *Dusty* (2004), and *Standard* (2017). His vibrant vignettes frequently feature working-class narrators struggling for purchase on better days.

TOM RUSSELL

I became familiar with the outlaw movement when I moved to Austin in 1974. I think I heard Townes Van Zandt and Willie [Nelson] talking about Mickey. Then I was hanging out with Guy Clark one night back in 1980, and substances were being imbibed and snorted abundantly. Guy started talking about Mickey. I respected Guy so much I went out, bought whatever stuff I could find that had a Newbury song, and wasn't disappointed. His stuff has a sad intimacy that draws you toward the sadness the man is feeling but at the same time illuminates you. His songs had that "thing" that great songs, poems, and paintings have.

Mickey certainly listened to his own deep muse. Sugar Ray Robinson was once approached by the young Cassius Clay for some pointers on boxing, and Sugar Ray said he learned something from Jean Cocteau—believe it or not—in Paris: "The muse opens the door and points the way to the tightrope." You gotta have the guts to walk out on the high wire, and Newbury certainly made the journey and took the risk. He cut to the core and bone in an intimate way without a worry as to how deep the sadness goes and without resorting to cliché. He's telling us stories that don't leave out life's sad details like "San Francisco Mabel Joy" or "She Even Woke Me Up to Say Goodbye." They remind me of Raymond Carver stories, but Mickey was also able to turn around and write a hit song on occasion. He also drew on a deep well of old folk songs like "All My Trials" and "Down in the Valley." He suddenly blended his songs into an old song or melody, thus keeping the folk process alive.

A lawyer named Robert Rosemurgy or his daughter gave Mickey my folk opera *The Man from God Knows Where*, a record with Dave Van Ronk, Dolores Keane, Iris DeMent about my ancestors coming from Norway and Ireland, songs using their own words mostly from their journals. It was recorded in an old farmhouse on the west coast of Norway, where one of my great-grandfathers came from. Mickey was deeply intrigued by it and wrote me a lot of emails about how much he liked the record. At the same time, the leader of Kronos Quartet wanted to do something with me because of that record. There was interest from Broadway, but nothing eventually happened there.

Mickey had that CD by his bedside when he passed. His daughter told me he listened to it a lot, which really moved me. It was akin to a moment like when I picked up [Grateful Dead lyricist] Robert Hunter in New York City when I was driving cab, and he got me back into the music business. These magic moments mean so much to you, but the general public would not be aware of their meaning, a secret admiration among musicians. The more I listen to Mickey, the more I realize that in most of his songs he was writing mini folk operas, and he sang with a big, folk-operatic voice. Legitimacy is not granted by the critics, the magazines, the radio, the Grammy committee, or what is left of journalism but by the song catalog, whether it's one song or a thousand. Did van Gogh get legitimacy as a living artist? Legitimacy is in the work.

Mickey and I chatted about old folk songs [in our emails], and we both had a yen for writing folk operas that had a theme running throughout. He was really an opera singer in a way, and his use of train sounds, rain, and reverb added a big theatrical vibe to his music. His wife, Susan, and I talked about her being a singer in the New Christy Minstrels because I know Randy Sparks, who started that group. We also chatted about Nashville and our shared dislike for the phoniness of that business scene. I'm not much interested in what's come from Nashville since the nineties. Nor was Mickey. Mickey was warm, literate, musical, soulful, poetic. No bullshit.

A few of my favorite Mickey songs are "So Sad," "She Even Woke Me Up to Say Goodbye," and "Nights When I Am Sane." "So Sad" has a great verse that suddenly appears in a love song, a verse about Bill Haley, Elvis, and Frank Sinatra, mostly intimating how the music business chewed them up. Then that verse ends with Mickey saying: "I am dead in Tennessee / They buried me alive." In "Nights When I Am Sane," he says that Nashville is a place "where a man sells his soul for a song." I don't know the specifics of what happened to Newbury in Nashville. I only know what I feel about the backslapping, phony nature of the place and what my friends have gone through, great writers like Dave Alvin and Ian Tyson fleeing the scene quickly.

Guy Clark recorded a fragment of "Desperados Waiting for a Train" for my folk opera *The Rose of Roscrae* before he passed on. Guy and I were sitting in his kitchen, and he was staring a long time out at the Nashville suburbs. I said, "Do you miss West Texas, Guy?" He turned back to me and pulled the cigarette out of his mouth and snarled, "Hell, yes. I should have left this shithole a long time ago." Of course, you won't see him ever quoted as saying stuff like that. Every song Mickey's singing is the "National Anthem" of deep hurt. He was a big-time balladeer and an honest singer with a grand sense of dynamics. We've lost that sense of honest dynamics in the *American Idol* generation. Everything is overwrought in a fake way. Mickey's voice was real. He wasn't so much an *influence* as an *inspiration* to go deeper. I mean, I'm a huge Bob Dylan fan, but no one is able to write like he has. Same way, really, with Newbury. You've got to be inspired by it and find your own path into the woods.

You can't figure out why he wasn't better known during his lifetime. I don't think Mickey had the bullshit soul it takes to sell out. You'll stand in a long line if you're willing to sell out in Nashville. I don't think Mickey wasted his time aiming at a Grammy. Listen to that verse in "So Sad" and you know Mickey knew what the business can do to you, even if you achieve huge fame. Mickey also wrote: "I'm just one man / Sometimes I wish I was three / I could take a forty-four pistol to me / Put one in my brain just for her memory, one more for my heart / And I would be free" [from "Nights When I Am Sane"]. Who would have the guts to write these lines? Maybe Haggard, Dylan, Johnny Cash, Billy Joe Shaver, Tom T. Hall, John Prine, Leonard Cohen, Steve Young. You absorb Mickey's legacy in every line in every song.[14]

Iconic folksinger **Tom Russell** has had his songs recorded by Johnny Cash ("Veteran's Day"), Suzy Bogguss ("Outbound Plane"), Nanci Griffith ("Canadian Whiskey"), Joe Ely ("Gallo del Cielo"), and legendary Texas songwriter Doug Sahm ("St. Olav's Gate").

Chorus: A Long Road Home

CHUCK PROPHET

I specifically remember somebody having a cassette tape of [*Frisco Mabel Joy*, 1971] with "The Future's Not What It Used to Be" in the Green on Red van. Nothing sounded better in that van. We were knocked out. What a weird narrative. I know that record was a gift from someone because we were all surprised with that sixties Gothic housewife production. We were way off into Lee Hazlewood, and [Newbury's] production was very dramatic and something we all agreed was cool. It was a big thing for us, but trying to explain [what makes the album good] is like trying to explain what makes "Me and Bobby McGee" good. The answer's probably in the details, which make stuff believable. Mickey's songs are believable.

I think the thing that made him particularly cool was that you had these singing groups in the sixties like the Fifth Dimension, the Association, and bands who gave life to those Jimmy Webb songs. That was a rarity in the post-Beatles era. I really admired that Mickey Newbury wrote "Just Dropped In (To See What Condition My Condition Was In)," which is an inspired song. At the same time, you could look at the song as some square having a copy of *Life* magazine on Music Row and saying, "Look at the Jefferson Airplane and what's going on in San Francisco. Let's write a song in a minor key with a reference to Alice in Wonderland." Mickey probably was just trying to keep his publishing deal when he wrote "Just Dropped In," which was killer and had that Partridge family thing.

[The 2000 Newbury tribute *Frisco Mabel Joy Revisited*] was a real shoestring labor of love. I was assigned ["You're Not My Same Sweet Baby"], but I'm not even sure I got the chords right. I did it with a drum machine and overdubbed the best I could. I don't remember being in a position to hire a group, which is the way I like to work. Tim Mooney engineered and played drums. He was the drummer in the Sleepers, who were like the first great postpunk San Francisco band and our answer to Joy Division. Tim passed away a few years ago and was a very beloved dude. I remember saying there was no budget and him saying, "We can do that. That'll be cool."

["You're Not My Same Sweet Baby"] is a very simple song with three major chords, but sometimes those are the hardest. You always think it's going to the other chord. You need two things when you're inventing a song: something to say and a way to say it. If you're John Lee Hooker, it's generally an E chord and you can go sing about the great flood of Tupelo, Mississippi. Mickey Newbury had his signature thing, but it's the inspiration, the magic that's the hard part, not the nuts and bolts. I guess he could show somebody the nuts and bolts of a Mickey Newbury song pretty quick, but good luck writing songs like his.

David Shepherd Grossman, a friend of mine who was a damaged guy but well liked within the neofolk underground, does. He's like a James Taylor with a light touch on the guitar. He was our age but always seemed more advanced. He's a big Mickey Newbury guy who befriended him. He's the kind of guy who will walk into a restaurant with a guitar and a list of songs on a piece of paper and if people come and give him a dollar he'll sing something. He lives in a trailer, a pretty gifted guy. We had long talks about Mickey Newbury.

I wrote on Music Row a little around 1997, which was the tail end of the Garth Brooks years. I was getting per diems and a hotel room, which was keeping me off the street. I would get in a room [for a cowriting session] and have nothing in common with this person at all, but there didn't necessarily have to be blood on the floor when we were done. There's a level of professionalism in Nashville. Nobody knew about Mickey by then. Green on Red played in Nashville in the eighties, but it was always pretty dead, a dystopian science fiction movie with a city where they had killed all the young people. We made a record there in 1991 at the Sound Emporium. We were still partying pretty hard and crazy. We would try to find a writers' night somewhere and we'd find a guy with a beard and an Ovation and he'd say, "This is a song Eddie Rabbitt cut, and it did well for me." It was a strange era.

Mickey was a singer-songwriter. His songs were well known, but I don't know that his body of work penetrated pop culture. I don't know how many people know about Mickey Newbury. Why wasn't Mickey a well-known, major star? Well, why wasn't Dan Penn? I love all of Mickey's music. Certainly his legacy will be entwined with Elvis's greatest vocal performance on "An American Trilogy" if you're a guy who likes the mid- to late-period Elvis as much as I do. Think about that performance. Christ.[1]

Chuck Prophet entered public consciousness with his band Green on Red (*Gas Food Lodging*, 1985, through *Too Much Fun*, 1992) in the eighties. He has gone on to become a critically acclaimed solo singer-songwriter (most recently *Bobby Fuller Died for Your Sins*, 2017) and producer.

CHARLIE WORSHAM

[Country Music Hall of Fame museum editor and longtime *Tennessean* music writer] Peter Cooper asked me, "Man, have you ever heard Mickey Newbury's *Live at Montezuma Hall*? If you were to ask Guy Clark, he would say that's the good shit right there." Indeed, it is the good shit. I put that record on and felt like I was in [the legendary Nashville bluegrass venue] the Station Inn, my favorite room for music in the world. I wish I could have been in that moment at Montezuma Hall. The song and the singer transport me to a timeless place. Songs like "Cortelia Clark" are like movies, but if they made a movie it would ruin the song.

I've spent a good deal of time on stages with nothing but my acoustic guitar, and I'm in awe of Mickey's ability to transcend the moment and pull people into an alternate reality with just his voice and playing and nothing else. Easier said than done. Mickey's made tons of great records over the years, but I believe in my heart of hearts that to get to see him with no reverb or arrangement behind him is the real magic. No production in the studio can enhance that raw ability. He gives me hope and inspires me. I'm in a place right now where that's what I have to rely on. If that was a part of the journey for him, maybe it's okay that it's part of my journey, too. Maybe I'll end up in a good spot after all.

[Performing solo] is literally creating a volume dynamic. You can't tell the drummer to wait until the chorus to chime in. You have to get into fifth gear with what you're playing, what you're singing, and how you're doing it. Most people hire an eight-piece band, a lighting director, and video screens to help them hit fifth gear. Our homeboy Mickey Newbury does it with six strings and two vocal cords. Come on. That's talent. I don't care what it is. You can't sit for an hour and a half or two hours and stay engaged if someone doesn't provide all five gears. I don't know many people who can do that with so few tools at their disposal. It's crazy.

Mickey Newbury created a basket weave of both lyrics and melody. People call songs cinematic, but his really are like movies. They take you somewhere. They move you the way an orchestra at the end of a dramatic film does. He had vibrato and an almost operatic tone. I can't listen to most people who do that. Somehow singing in an operatic way with soaring melodies and vibrato like that takes you out of the moment, but he does it in a way that brings you into the moment. The only way I can compare it is it's like when you're watching a guitar player and you know that what they're doing is technically insane, but it doesn't hit you like, "Oh, shit, that's Eddie Van Halen finger tapping." You're just like, "Oh, my God, my heartstrings." His superior technical ability doesn't impede the primary goal of reaching straight for your heart and squeezing it.

I will say that I don't think that his name comes up often enough in the writing rooms. Just today we were writing and we pulled up "Same Old Lang Syne" by Dan Fogelberg. That's a great tune, but I wish that we would have pulled up "Cortelia Clark" and been like, "Let's do it like this." I do wish his name came up more often and that I knew more about him. He gets straight to the emotion on songs like "She Even Woke Me Up to Say Goodbye." Especially today people feel like the more pyrotechnics they create the bigger deal it is. Having a deeper emotional impact with less is a lost art today. [Newbury did] "Danny Boy." Who does that? "Danny Boy" is a song you hear in an Irish pub. Not a lot of people can do that.

Mickey lives and resonates for me in *Live at Montezuma Hall*. I connect the most with him when I hear someone playing to a room that doesn't sound like a big room. It's not like you're listening to someone win over an arena with already tailor-made hits. He's winning over and feeding his flock of a couple of hundred people his life, stories, songs, and ability to sing and play in a way that nobody else can. When I go play the UK and Europe, ninety-nine percent of the time it's just me and a guitar playing to two hundred people. The only tools I have to work with are my singing, playing, stories, and charisma. It's inspiring to hear someone who has been there and done it and reached through the top of the mountain to the status of being a legend. He did it with those same tools.[2]

Charlie Worsham has released two albums for Warner Bros. (*Rubberband*, 2013, and *Beginning of Things*, 2017). Worsham charted the singles "Could It Be" and "Want Me Too" in 2013. He's currently a member of Old Crow Medicine Show.

ANDREW COMBS

I discovered Mickey Newbury while researching Townes Van Zandt and Guy Clark and how they got to Nashville. I admired Mickey's commitment to his vision, his writing, production, and recording his albums. His sense of melody's amazing. His lyrics are off the charts, but there's something thought out with a singular vision that runs through everything, a certain beauty and melancholy that's very attractive to me. His lyrics are abstract enough, but there's always something to grab on to. That's how all my favorite writers, painters, poets, and fiction writers are. There's something so accessible in their writing, but it's abstract at the same time. It's not formulaic like country writing is these days.

I talk more to journalists than songwriters about Mickey Newbury. Songwriters who really love Townes, Guy, and Kristofferson don't really seem to know Mickey. It boggles my mind. I guess he was a little bit older, but without Mickey I don't know how far those guys would have come in Nashville. I'm sure they would have flourished somewhere else. Mickey played a huge role in what they did. Kristofferson said he wouldn't have written "Sunday Morning Coming Down" if not for Mickey.

I think the production on his albums turns people off. I love it, but I send people to *Live at Montezuma Hall* before anything else so they can just hear the songs. Josh Hedley's a big fan. I had a big bonding with Jonny Fritz, who used to go by Jonny Corndawg, over Mickey Newbury. Joe Henry's an older guy who lives out in Colorado, but he was one of the few people Mickey cowrote with on an older record. He has good stories about going out to his house on Old Hickory.

I always send people new to Mickey to *Live at Montezuma Hall*, but I love the studio records like *Heaven Help the Child*, the *Better Days* rerelease through Drag City, *Rusty Tracks*, and *Harlequin Melodies*. "Leavin' Kentucky" is amazing. I can't get enough of his weird nineties stuff. I'm trying to incorporate his sense of melody and beautiful chord structures [in my own songwriting]. They sound really complicated, but they're not once you dissect them. Most songs don't seem standard writing with verse-chorus or A section and B section. I find his vision with production and incorporating rain very interesting, but that's probably something most people don't like. He stuck to his vision and nixed what the labels wanted him to do.

Joe always tells me that Mickey was ticked off that he wasn't more famous near the end of his life. I don't think he wanted a bunch of money, but I found that interesting because he never struck me as someone who would yearn for that. He has so many songs recorded by other people. I'm not sure why he's not at least in the Townes category. I think Townes's lifestyle helped him appeal to younger hipsters. Mickey wasn't as hard living. He'll be remembered as one of the greats from that era, though, as far as country or folk music. Mickey, Kristofferson, and Guy Clark are my gods.[3]

Andrew Combs has released four albums (*Worried Man*, 2012, through *Ideal Man*, 2019) and an EP (*5 Covers and a Song*, 2018). The current Nashville resident was born and raised in Dallas, Texas.

JONNY FRITZ

I'm obsessed with Mickey Newbury. I read that part in Billy Joe Shaver's autobiography where Billy was suicidal and put a gun in his mouth. He damn near pulled the trigger but was like, "Fuck, no, I'm gonna go to talk with somebody." He lived on this street in Nashville, and the only other light that was on was in Mickey Newbury's house. He went over and knocked on the door. Mickey came to the door really scared, and he had a shotgun himself. He was like, "Who's there? Who is that?" Billy Joe was like, "Hey, man, it's Billy Joe. Can I come in? Can we talk?" He said, "Billy Joe, thank God you're here. I was just about to kill myself." Holy shit. Those two guys are heroes.

Andrew Combs was really heavy into Mickey Newbury when we first talked about him seven, eight years ago. I really love the sadness. I can't get enough. I'm a pretty light and fun guy. I have a hard time with too much sadness, but I can listen to tons and tons of Mickey Newbury to access some sadness. He's my gateway. Otherwise, it'd just be all jokes with me. Also, I'm a pretty anxious and wound-up person, and all my music's fast, loud, and wordy. Mickey's is the opposite. It's so mellow and poetic without any million-dollar words, slow and quiet. If you focus on those arrangements, there's something like a keyboard or synth keeping the bass and maybe plucking some violin strings and a loud, hot vocal right in your face. He has a hell of a powerful voice. I'm always so inspired by him.

His lyrics are so honest and uniquely his own experience. His quiet and calmness carry so much weight and power. I listen to him and get chilled the fuck out. Unfortunately, I don't think people know Mickey out here in Los Angeles like they should. You know, Townes Van Zandt pisses me off. People are like, "Has there ever been a better writer than Townes Van Zandt?" "Well, yeah, there are lots of them." I feel like everybody says Townes is the underground guy nobody knows about, but I think everybody knows Townes. I'm spreading the gospel of Mickey Newbury. I think when people do catch on to Mickey, they're just like, "Holy shit."

My friends and I were always passing his records around when I lived in Nashville. I really like Mickey's later stuff like "Four Ladies," which is also called "Winter Winds," depending on which record you have. The song's about these four women who were very impactful in his life. Each chorus is this confession about why it didn't work out: "I've been trying to deal with my sadness / But there are times when I can't tell when I'm happy or it's madness." It's such a powerful plea, probably my favorite song. He does this Native American–like chant for the chorus. I listen to that record a lot, but I love "Are My Thoughts with You?" from *Harlequin Mel-odies*, too. Although I'm not as crazy about the early records as I am with the ones in the middle and the end.

I love him putting rain on all the songs. This was before there were samples. I imagine him wheeling out the two-inch tape and marching outside to capture the rain sounds. I love the idea of Mickey Newbury sitting around writing and somebody going, "You written anything lately?" "Well, yeah, I have this one. It's pretty good." "Is it gonna be a rain song?" "Aw, I don't know if it'll be a rain song. It's good, but I'm not sure if it's good enough to be a rain song." My favorites are rain songs.

I feel like that was his way of going, "Okay, I'm gonna get you guys into this. Here's the rain track to get you in the mood. Now, here's some powerful shit coming your way." There are so many songs like "Mobile Blue" and "T. Total Tommy" where it's fully twenty seconds of rain before anything comes in. "Let Me Stay Awhile" destroys me: "I'm just one man / Sometimes I wish I was three / I could take a forty-four pistol to me / Put one in my brain just for her memory / One more for my heart and I would be free." "Poison Red Berries" is up there, too. I had a chance to talk with Guy Clark a couple of times when I was in the depths of my Mickey obsession. I was like, "What do you think of Mickey Newbury?" He said, "I loved that first record, *Harlequin Melodies*, but it really bugged me that he started putting that rain shit on there." Well, that bugged me. "Really? Why do you care? Why are you getting so conservative about what people do on their recordings?"

The songs are so much more important than whether you like the production value. Guy's comment always struck me as odd. I wonder if the whole world felt that way, and that's why Mickey New-bury didn't really get the exposure he deserved. Part might be how conservative he was. There was an interview around 1968 during the hippie movement when people were playing these songs that were outlawed. He's like, "Well, here's a song that's been outlawed. This wasn't allowed in America." He was like, "Fuck yeah. This is my hippie movement. This is what I'm protesting." I was like, "Oh yeah, he's a Texan."

I've emailed with Mickey's son Chris a bunch. My parents live in Oregon so whenever I visit them I wonder if I'll stumble across

any Mickey Newbury stuff, but my parents are up in Central Oregon and he was near Salem. I've reached out to his family a couple
of times and just said, "Man, can I take you out for a cup of coffee
and talk about your dad? Is there anything I can see, any kind of
statue, his grave, whatever?" That's when I was living in Nashville.
He was like, "Nah, there's probably more stuff in Nashville than
there is in Oregon. I don't think anybody knew about him here." I
wonder if he did that just to get away from there. I would love to
know why he moved to Oregon. It's funny to be obsessed with the
rain so much and then to move there. It's like, "Finally, here's the
rain."[4]

Jonny Fritz (formerly known as Jonny Corndawg) has released
four albums, including *I'm Not Ready to Be a Daddy* (2008) through
Sweet Creep (2016). Fritz has played a large role in spreading word
about Mickey Newbury to the current crop of Nashville-based
songwriters.

JOSHUA HEDLEY

I discovered Mickey Newbury through Jonny Fritz. He would play
the shit out of *Live at Montezuma Hall* when we were touring
together. It was all over when I found out "Sweet Memories" was a
Newbury song. I became obsessed with the way that he writes. He
was such a good writer, such a fantastic singer who wrote incredible songs. Take "She Even Woke Me Up to Say Goodbye," a song
presumably about a man who's been left by his wife or girlfriend.
The narrator's defending her still, which is such a crazy concept
in country music. You're usually talking about hurting songs when
someone has left. "They could never understand it's her sorrow,
it's not a man / No matter what they say we know she tried." That's
insane, a sentiment that's not expressed in a song very much.

I'm pretty far removed from the songwriter community in Nashville, so I'm not sure what they're listening to down there on Music
Row today. I'm about eighty-five percent sure it's not Newbury,
though. He's pretty highly respected in the Americana and singer-
songwriter community in Nashville. Everybody loves and respects

Newbury in the circles I run in. He's influenced a lot of people in the Americana world lately, but he wouldn't survive on Music Row today. I mean, he barely survived when he was writing those songs. He had cuts and hits, but it was difficult for him when it came down to having a solo career. He didn't fit into a mold. It's crazy to hear his songs reimagined as popular songs of the era production-wise and then to hear his original recordings because they're totally different. You hear Jerry Lee Lewis do "She Even Woke Me Up," and it's a different song than when you hear Mickey singing it.

I think country music just wants to categorize you. Even I get it today. They want to call me everything but country music. They really were trying to do it then, and I think Mickey had a difficult time with that because the music itself was nontraditional. Jesus, by today's standards, he'd be really nontraditional. The craziest part about Mickey Newbury to me was that he had commercial success in country music as a songwriter, but he was also getting cut by Elvis, Solomon Burke, Andy Williams. He spanned genres. I think that's a testament to the songwriting. "American Trilogy" was probably his biggest success as a writer even though he didn't write those tunes. It's big when Elvis cuts your song, but I don't wanna listen to Elvis do "American Trilogy" anymore. Newbury's live version is the only one I want to listen to now.

"Sweet Memories" is the saddest shit I've ever heard. Dawn Sears would do it with the Time Jumpers before she passed away. Incredible. Moving. I started listening to Newbury do his original and I started covering "Sweet Memories" and I also do "She Even Woke Me Up to Say Goodbye." I did "The Future's Not What It's Supposed to Be" one time. It's difficult to match his voice or the guitar playing and the way he phrases chords. I think anytime you're trying to interpret a song by a writer, singer, and player of that caliber, you can't even try to replicate it. You just grit your teeth and hope for the best, which is what I did.

Mickey's certainly influential as a motivator and as someone to look up to as a songwriter. I feel like I'm getting an energy from him. I get a vibe and an energy when I listen to him that inspires me to write. I'm not gonna say there's any correlation between his songs and mine. I would never be so bold as to make that declaration, but he's definitely been an inspiration for me as far as writing and singing go. I'm the same way [as Newbury], being pretty happy-go-lucky, but I pour out my feelings in the sad songs. Writing sad songs gets rid of the sad feelings. I love horrifically sad songs. I feel like I've lived through those situations Mickey was singing about.[5]

Joshua Hedley's debut album, *Broken Jukebox* (2018), was released by iconic rock star Jack White's Third Man Records. Hedley has toured with Jonny Fritz, Justin Townes Earle, and former Old Crow Medicine Show member Willie Watson. Hedley appeared in *Heart-worn Highways Revisited* (2015).

WILL OLDHAM

I discovered Mickey Newbury through my friend Todd Brashear burning *Frisco Mabel Joy* and *Looks Like Rain* for me. I initially felt like there were some fairly obvious signifiers that I should like this music, but I couldn't get into it. The songs felt really heavy without any light, humor, or positivity, but I don't feel that way about them now. That initial feeling might be why he remains relatively unknown. He's not easy to begin with, but once you break through you find a world that does include so much humor, light, and positivity. Listen to the pace and sparseness. I used to shut everybody up in the band van with his record *Live at Montezuma Hall*. "She Even Woke Me Up to Say Goodbye" on *Montezuma* might be the most devastating thing I've ever heard on a record.

I started listening to *Rusty Tracks*, *The Sailor*, and other later records and discovered more upbeat numbers. Those later seventies records can be off-putting after you've gotten into the early records that are so spare and deliberate. You think, I'm not sure if I'm welcome or wanted here. I've already gotten used to a certain pace, and now he's fucking with the whole program. There's more to sink your teeth into right up front up-tempo. Then you realize it becomes a single body of work. *Harlequin Melodies* seems like the first Cat Stevens record [*Matthew and Son*, 1967], as if he hasn't quite fully taken the reins yet. He obviously took the reins after that and never seemed to give them to anyone else.

Newbury was very deliberate with his moves and recordings

from *Looks Like Rain* on. I started to love his music probably fifteen, twenty years ago, which could be an age thing. His music is beautiful, complex, mature. I think the really rewarding parts are even more rewarding after enduring a few things in life. I don't think there would have been much of a chance of me listening to his music in my teens and getting much out of it. His music demands patience that we're not trained to have and aren't evolved enough to have when we're twenty-five or even thirty.

I greatly admire a phenomenal Egyptian woman named Umm Kulthum, who's probably the biggest name in classical Arabic music. She uses her voice in ways that Newbury shares with her. I don't usually like a singer who sticks to a single timbre, but there are a handful of exceptions that blow my mind. You don't hear Mickey Newbury doing many different things with his voice dynamically. He has one sound whether loud or quiet: constricted, controlled, very emotional, throaty. He always knows where he is with his voice and is incredibly fluent with its use and power. He gets from one part to the next with precision and emotion.

Newbury and Tim O'Brien probably couldn't take a false step. Tim's sometimes too insanely precise, but I saw him on New Year's Eve one year at a small bar in Nashville. He was absolutely plastered and went up onstage. He's the best because he's like the world's greatest unicyclist. Put the world's greatest unicyclist on a tightrope and get them completely wasted, and they still wouldn't fall off. Watching that would be seeing the most interesting unicycle ride ever. Tim O'Brien performed like that that night. He was so far gone he probably wouldn't even remember the night, but he couldn't hit a wrong note, which made the expressiveness all the more beautiful. He was going places, but he wasn't messing up. He was just hitting a different set of perfect notes.

I can't say "deliberate" enough when it comes to Newbury. He conveyed various emotional states with his nylon-string guitar. He opens a toolbox: "Here's the part about memory. Here's the part about despair. Here's the part about joyful release." He's working with wood and not some esoteric, abstract concept. I think it would be interesting to hear people discuss this. Some people are compelled to change their approach to things throughout their life, but

he's somebody who didn't feel compelled. Also, people like Newbury, David Allan Coe, and R. Kelly are very self-referential in their
music.

Newbury would pull actual melodies from earlier songs like he's
composing one long concerto, one huge work that's of a piece. I
don't know if he ever addressed that and said, "Yeah, I wish I could
write outside of that," or, "No, no, this is the thing for me. I'm not
done exploring it, and I won't be done." Did he consider it a limita-
tion or was it exactly how he wanted to work? The strong aspects
of his rhymes and melodies in his later records are the same as
his earlier records. I know it's the worst time in the world to refer
to R. Kelly, but I have great awe for his music. He's constantly putting in lyric and melodic references from other songs of his in an
interesting way. He's not waking up and starting fresh every day.
He's waking up and jumping back in the same river he got out of
yesterday musically. Newbury seemed to do the same.

I recorded [the title track on Newbury's 1974 album] "I Came to
Hear the Music" [on Bonnie "Prince" Billy's 2007 EP *Ask Forgive-
ness*] when I wanted to make a record with Greg Weeks and Meg
Baird from the Philadelphia-area folk group Espers. I wanted to
share musical ideas. I thought an interesting concept would be to
record other people's songs that are very specifically solipsistic,
addressing the self, and make a self-obsessed record written by
other people. I thought that "I Came to Hear the Music" is a great
"to be or not to be"–like soliloquy moment, like taking a really high
dose of LSD and waking up the next day, looking around and saying, "This is where I am in my life right now." I was hoping all the
songs would be like that. "I Came to Hear the Music" is a great song
like that.

A friend asked if I would do a split seven-inch single where
we would each do a David Allan Coe song. I liked Coe's beautiful
song "In My Mind" and did it for the split single. We recorded that
in the mid to late nineties. Then I heard the *I Came to Hear the
Music* album in the 2000s when I started to listen to Mickey Newbury. He has a song on there called "If You See Her" that David
Allan Coe took almost completely for "In My Mind." I think David
Allan Coe has a mind-blowing body of work, but I never had any

illusions about his sanity or integrity. I didn't think, Well, that ass-
hole. I was more like, What a smooth con man. Listen to those two
songs. Ridiculous. I felt conned.

I figured I should perform the Mickey Newbury song live for the
next couple of years, but my version of the David Allan Coe song
was a fan favorite. I thought, Oh, this is terrible. The wool's been
pulled over my eyes, and now I've been pulling the wool over other
people's eyes. I had a lot of work to do to right the situation. David
Allan Coe seemed to have a particular fascination with [ripping off]
Newbury. The first time I heard "33rd of August" was David Allan
Coe's cover. I wonder if they were friends. I wonder if anyone was
friends with David Allan Coe.

Newbury's background noises were second nature. I don't like
recording studios because there's no life there, and I don't know
why you want to cut the world out. Newbury's music's clinical
sounding, so I like that he was compelled to include some real
world. The box set [*American Trilogy*, 2002] is one of the coolest, awesomest commercially available releases of all time and
impresses me to no end. This beautiful music needs to come out,
one of the best testaments to a human's work, so economically
done, beautifully presented, and worth exploring. It's not, "Now,
finally, remastered with bonus tracks." I don't need remastered or
bonus tracks. I only need the music to be available. Please.

You wonder when the moment comes when everybody in the
world finds out who Mickey Newbury was. You can't get out once
you're into him, but the problem might be that it's hard to get in
as well. Nick Drake has a Volkswagen commercial. I wonder why
Mickey Newbury doesn't. Did somebody ask, and Mickey's family
said, "No, Mickey left strict orders that we're not supposed to license
his music to movies or commercials"? Maybe nobody's asked. The
right music supervisor could use Newbury's music for ten years
without getting anywhere near running dry. I was just thinking his
song "I Don't Love You" might be the saddest song ever. You could
destroy someone in a movie with Newbury's "His Eye Is on the
Sparrow." Put that in and there wouldn't be a dry eye in the house.[6]

Multifaceted singer-songwriter and actor **Will Oldham** released
several albums billed as Palace in the nineties before assuming

his well-known stage name Bonnie "Prince" Billy. Legendary country star Johnny Cash recorded Oldham's high-water mark "I See a Darkness."

BILL CALLAHAN

I probably first heard of Mickey Newbury through the song "Luckenbach, Texas." Then he started appearing on mix tapes that were passed around. His cerebral songs always stood out from anything. They were so contained, individual, and from the heart's true voice. The words and the way the songs were produced, arranged, and presented [make] the type of music where everything stops to listen. I'd never considered covering "Heaven Help the Child" before [the record label] Drag City asked me to do that as a favor to help promote their reissues. His arrangements are so evocative and precise that it feels like trying to re-create a scene from a perfect movie using only chimps.

"Heaven Help the Child" was difficult [to interpret] because it has turns of phrase that don't roll off my tongue, like "quaff some brew," and references to Fitzgerald. Newbury grew up singing in church. I just saw the Aretha Franklin performance film *Amazing Grace*, and you have to start singing in choirs at age five to have a really good voice. "Poison Red Berries" always bowls me over with its horseshoe shape. That kind of song taught me to have patience with and to trust the listener. No one knows who Newbury is, and that's a real mystery to me. I think maybe he never wrote for the lowest common denominator. His songs were all pretty heady.

I'm always surprised when I listen to a Mickey Newbury record and how encompassing they are. They're whole worlds within themselves, galaxies or minds. The music takes you there and holds you. Few things have the power to do something so big and [exhibit] the calmness he shows within the grips of such power. From what I've read, it seems like some of the people around him at the time would hear his music and be worried for him. Messing with this stuff is beyond most men and women, but he always said, "I write my sadness." He puts all our sadness, joy, and the rest of it there. The songs are lifeblood.[7]

Bill Callahan released several albums billed as Smog (from *Sewn to the Sky*, 1990, through *A River Ain't Too Much to Love*, 2005) before branching out as a solo performer under his own name (*Woke on a Whaleheart*, 2007, through *Shepherd in a Sheepskin Vest*, 2019).

ROBERT ELLIS

I kept hearing the name Mickey Newbury. My friend Jonny Fritz is super into him. Bill Callahan has mentioned him in interviews. I knew some songs, but I didn't really dig into him until about five years ago. I was coming down from an intense mushroom trip on a waterfall, and Jonny put on "An American Trilogy" as I was coming down. I was completely in love after that. I have [*Frisco Mabel Joy*] on vinyl and probably listen to that record more than any other depending on my mood. Mickey Newbury can put me in a catatonic state. The songs are so fucking good. His voice is unbelievable, straightforward, and direct.

Mickey doesn't get bogged down in rewriting every line. Being straightforward allows the really great lines to jump out. He also turns phrases like "sunshine standing quietly at my door" [from "She Even Woke Me Up to Say Goodbye"]. Nobody talks like that. You hear that in a song and go, "Well, that's Mickey Newbury." I could hear someone else doing his song and know he wrote that. I find storytelling most effective when you know what's going on. I think that's lost in other genres. People hide out in metaphors and analogies. Mickey Newbury gets from Point A to Point B effectively. He has really good pacing.

Country music and short story writing have a common focus on minute details in the scenery rather than the big picture, which makes songs more powerful. Mickey talks about the way the sunshine is hitting him when he's waking up hungover, which is more effective than saying he doesn't want to be with this person anymore. My favorite Newbury song is "The Future's Not What It Used to Be." Fucking unbelievable. The time changes and slows the song down at the end. He talks about how he used to be alone and bummed out. Then he meets her and the future's not what it used to be. He turns the phrase three different ways, and by the third time, the music changes in this really amazing way.

I love "Sweet Memories." I used to go see the Time Jumpers when I first moved to Nashville and Dawn Sears would always sing that song. She's a singer's singer. There's not a time that I heard her sing that song when I didn't cry, and I probably saw her sing it twenty times. The song never lost its effect. The writing is like a Cole Porter jazz tune with the chord changes. I would be surprised if Willie Nelson wouldn't say he took a lot of inspiration from Mickey as far as writing with chord changes not standard for country music.

I love the production on his albums, his lonesome voice, and the reverb he uses. He was a wildly creative dude and definitely a square peg. The production sets his albums apart in many ways. The production and presentation are lyrical tools to establish a setting. Overwrought production can be very meaningful to the lyric if you're talking about feeling lost or sadness or aloneness. It makes sense to have a really far away–sounding guitar, which is a weird choice on paper. You want every instrument to be heard, but he made cool choices on those records to make them sound far away. That adds to the depth and makes his points so much louder.

Everything I write is influenced by Mickey Newbury. I was thinking about him when I was writing and recording the song "Lullaby" on my last album. He's really been an inspiration to me with his confidence and how he would stick to his ideas. He was very much himself as a writer. He wasn't trying to please everybody. He was trying to please himself. Some people like me really love his songs because of it, but they're not for everybody. He's fairly obscure compared to someone like Waylon Jennings. Waylon made big music for everybody. Also, Mickey didn't portray himself as the hero all the time, which is a common syndrome in pop music. He painted himself as complex and not always a good character. I relate to that.

Mickey's an outlaw if an outlaw is someone who does something differently. I've always thought that label for music was silly anyway. They're not fucking outlaws. They travel around making money by playing music. Mickey was definitely an outlier, though. The genre should be called Outlier Country music. I do think it was easier back then to have unique, weird songs and find a potential audience. I think listeners and record labels both took more risks. They weren't so strictly tied to genre. There's nothing wrong with that, but Mickey had a rock-and-roll hit with "Just Dropped In" even though he was considered a country singer and writer. Things are much more rigid now. I don't think you even have potential to end up in the right room today to have cuts in different genres. There are so many gatekeepers today. That's how people get in power and stay there.

Mickey Newbury doesn't get credit like Townes Van Zandt. Townes is a phenomenon. Some people like Townes just so they can say they like Townes. Everyone wants to name their dog Townes now, but Mickey's definitely a hard sell. I've played him for people who don't get it. Sometimes the timing is right when I play him for someone. I was with my drummer in the [South Dakota] Black Hills one time when he was coming off an acid trip. We listened to a whole Newbury record and he was like, "This is the best record I've ever heard." I think in order to really fall in love with his music you need to be open minded because the music isn't easily digestible. You're not just gonna put on a Mickey Newbury record at a party. He means so much more to me personally than Townes. I guess everybody finds their guy. I'm probably not more successful because I'm more influenced by Mickey Newbury than more popular artists like Townes Van Zandt.[8]

Robert Ellis's diverse commercial debut, *Photographs* (2013), accents timeless folk ("Friends Like Those") with buoyant country ("Comin' Home") and smooth soul ("What's in It for Me?"). Ellis switched from acoustic guitar to piano for his recent album *Piano Man* (2019).

JOE PUG

Everyone has moved to Nashville right now to make it as songwriters. I feel like once a quarter the songwriters in that circle find someone who history has passed by and venerate them. Mickey Newbury's definitely someone who comes up in those scenes as someone who deserves more veneration, but outside Nashville I never hear his name. I love Newbury's song "Willow Tree": "I wish I was a willow tree / leaning on a lazy breeze / I wish I was a grain of sand / Playing in a baby's hands / Falling like a diamond chain into the ocean." I'm a sucker for amazing imagery, and that struck me as powerful as anything on the early Dylan records, which is the gold standard for evocative imagery. I've loved that song ever since. I can see wanting to be that grain of sand given how tempestuous life can be. Newbury's songs are so compelling and lyrically forward.

The music business is brutal and fickle. There's only so much time and attention, but I think that's changing with the internet. Our medium is much broader. You had very narrow mediums back then like radio, where it was a zero-sum game. If one song was playing at a given time, someone else's song wasn't playing. The same with music media on television. If one band was playing on *Saturday Night Live*, that means another one wasn't. The internet makes that a much broader medium. Somebody can be listening to Kenny Rogers, but they can also be on their device listening to a Mickey Newbury song. Hopefully, we're heading toward an age where more people like Mickey Newbury get their due.[9]

Joe Pug (born Joe Pugliese) earned his first significant break opening for legendary outlaw country figure Steve Earle as Earle toured behind his album *Townes* (2009). Pug's debut, *The Messenger* (2010), and the following *The Great Despiser* (2012) connected the dots between.

CODA

MATT HARLAN

Mickey Newbury's "Willow Tree" sounds like a Townes Van Zandt song with all imagery and no clear story or resolution. I like the weirder songs Newbury wrote. He came up with new ways to say things. Some people say he coined the word "tripping." Go backward from Kenny Rogers's "Just Dropped In" to Newbury's. "Wow, how did they take that song and envision it as this weird, full-on psychedelic deal?" They just heard the words and were like, "Whoa." They could really trip the song out and use the underlying gems. Nobody could do them like Newbury could, but that leaves the songs very open for people to do them a million different ways. He made them accessible by making his versions impossible to duplicate.

Songwriters in Houston still talk about him at Anderson Fair, but more in relation with Guy and Townes. I don't hear a lot of, "I hung out with Newbury back in the day." He hit a good streak, helped other songwriters, and was removed from tour of duty. Everybody starts with hard-won success, sleeping on couches, and getting drunk. They love that myth. Mickey probably did a fair amount of that early on, but it paid off. Then he helped people. He didn't necessarily have to be languishing around on the folk circuit. I think he's been eclipsed by folks that he helped facilitate when they were younger, but he seemed real content not being the center of attention.[1]

Houston-based songwriter **Matt Harlan** crafts sociopolitical narratives with an artist's eye ("What We Saw") and a poet's elegance ("Mountain Pose"). His sixth and latest album, *Best Beasts* (Eight 30 Records, 2019), might spotlight his narrative songwriting best.

NOTES

FOREWORD

1. Larry Gatlin, interview with Brian T. Atkinson, July 18, 2019; Gatlin was inducted into the Nashville Songwriters Hall of Fame not long after this interview. See Jim Casey, "Dwight Yoakam, Larry Gatlin, Marcus Hummon & More Get Inducted into Nashville Songwriters Hall of Fame," October 15, 2019, accessed April 6, 2020, nashcountry-daily.com.
2. Don McLean, email interview with Brian T. Atkinson, July 2, 2019.

INTRODUCTION

1. Rodney Crowell, interview with Brian T. Atkinson, June 29, 2019; Steve Earle, interview with Brian T. Atkinson, June 18, 2019.
2. William Michael Smith, "Mickey Newbury: Houston's Forgotten Son Is Perhaps the Greatest Songwriter Ever—and the Outlaw Movement's Real Father," *Texas Music* magazine, Spring 2011, 31–32.
3. Smith, "Mickey Newbury," 79.
4. Smith, 31.
5 Peter Rowan, email interview with Brian T. Atkinson, July 28, 2019.
5. Ben Fong-Torres, interview with Ron Lyons, *Mickey Newbury: An American Treasure*, Mountain Retreat Records, 2002, compact disc.
6. Kurt Wolff, "Guy Clark & Mickey Newbury: Old Friends," *No Depression*, March 1, 1997, accessed August 5, 2019, https: //www.nodepression.com/guy-clark-mickey-newbury-old-friends/.
7. Smith, "Mickey Newbury," 31.
8. Waylon Jennings, "Luckenbach, Texas (Back to the Basics of Love)," *Ol' Waylon* (RCA Victor Records, 1977), written by Chips Moman and Bobby Emmons.
9. Joe Ziemer, *Mickey Newbury: Crystal & Stone* (Bloomington, IN: AuthorHouse, 2004), 175.
10. Ziemer, *Mickey Newbury*, 108.
11. Lyons, *Mickey Newbury*.

PRELUDE

1. Kris Kristofferson, interview with Brian T. Atkinson, September 26, 2009.
2. Kris Kristofferson, interview with Brian T. Atkinson, February 2, 2006.
3. Lyons, *Mickey Newbury*.
4. Scott Carrier, "What I've Learned," *Esquire* magazine, May 1, 1999.
5. Ziemer, *Mickey Newbury*, 82.

VERSE: JUST DROPPED IN

1. Eric Taylor, email interview with Brian T. Atkinson, August 18, 2019.
2. Jerry Newbury, interview with Brian T. Atkinson, April 6, 2019.
3. George Ensle, interview with Brian T. Atkinson, July 9, 2019.
4. John Carrick, interview with Brian T. Atkinson, April 8, 2019; for more on Larry Schacht and Jonestown, see Craig Malisow, "Cover Story: Larry Schacht, the Doctor of Jonestown," *Houston Press*, January 30, 2013.
5. John Nova Lomax, interview with Brian T. Atkinson, July 5, 2019.
6. Ray Wylie Hubbard, interview with Brian T. Atkinson, May 8, 2019.
7. Sam Baker, interview with Brian T. Atkinson, March 20, 2019.
8. Harold Eggers, interview with Brian T. Atkinson, July 29, 2019.
9. Peter Cooper, "Guy Clark: Scenes from a Songwriting Legend," *USA Today*, July 28, 2013.

VERSE: LOOKS LIKE RAIN

1. Bobby Bare, interview with Brian T. Atkinson, July 3, 2018.
2. Wayne Moss, interview with Brian T. Atkinson, August 7, 2018.
3. Charlie McCoy, interview with Brian T. Atkinson, March 15, 2019.
4. Norbert Putnam, interview with Brian T. Atkinson, July 3, 2018.
5. Donnie Fritts, interview with Brian T. Atkinson, August 29, 2018.
6. Billy Edd Wheeler, interview with Brian T. Atkinson, May 23, 2019.
7. Chris Gantry, interview with Brian T. Atkinson, July 3, 2018.
8. Billy Swan, interview with Brian T. Atkinson, September 25, 2018.
9. Bucky Wilkin, interview with Brian T. Atkinson, March 21, 2018.
10. Buffy Sainte-Marie, interview with Brian T. Atkinson, July 24, 2018.
11. Ramblin' Jack Elliott, interview with Brian T. Atkinson, June 29, 2018.

Chorus: Heaven Help the Child

1. Larry Gatlin, interview with Brian T. Atkinson, July 18, 2019.
2. Allen Frizzell, interview with Brian T. Atkinson, September 20, 2018.
3. Ed Bruce, interview with Brian T. Atkinson, July 15, 2018.
4. Dallas Frazier, interview with Brian T. Atkinson, September 5, 2018.
5. Pat Alger, interview with Brian T. Atkinson, September 8, 2018.
6. Johnny Lee, interview with Brian T. Atkinson, July 13, 2018.
7. Mickey Gilley, interview with Brian T. Atkinson, June 27, 2018.
8. Joe Henry, interview with Brian T. Atkinson, October 22, 2018.
9. Mark Germino, postal correspondence with Brian T. Atkinson, October 15, 2018.
10. Richard Leigh, interview with Brian T. Atkinson, May 21, 2019.
11. Jay Bolotin, interview with Brian T. Atkinson, April 4, 2019.
12. David Shepherd Grossman, interview with Brian T. Atkinson, August 8, 2018.
13. Fred Kohler, interview with Brian T. Atkinson, September 7, 2018.

Interlude: A Song for Susan

1. Susan Newbury Oakley, interview with Brian T. Atkinson, May 31, 2019.
2. Chris Newbury, interview with Brian T. Atkinson, April 21, 2019.
3. Jack Williams, interview with Brian T. Atkinson, March 27, 2019.

Verse: I Came to Hear the Music

1. Juan Contreras, interview with Brian T. Atkinson, July 23, 2019.
2. Troy Tomlinson, interview with Brian T. Atkinson, September 13, 2018.
3. John Lomax III, interview with Brian T. Atkinson, July 2, 2019.
4. Owsley Manier, interview with Brian T. Atkinson, March 22, 2019.
5. Larry Murray, interview with Brian T. Atkinson, August 2, 2018.
6. Randy Dodds, interview with Brian T. Atkinson, July 11, 2018.
7. Marty Hall, email interview with Brian T. Atkinson, June 19, 2019.
8. Jonmark Stone, interview with Brian T. Atkinson, June 21, 2019.
9. Bob Rosemurgy, interview with Brian T. Atkinson, June 21, 2019.
10. Chris Campion, interview with Brian T. Atkinson, September 20, 2018.
11. Joe Gilchrist, interview with Brian T. Atkinson, July 28, 2019.

VERSE: SWEET MEMORIES

1. Chris Smither, interview with Brian T. Atkinson, October 3, 2018.
2. Rodney Crowell, interview with Brian T. Atkinson, July 29, 2018.
3. Steve Earle, interview with Brian T. Atkinson, June 18, 2018.
4. Buddy Miller, interview with Brian T. Atkinson, July 31, 2018.
5. Matraca Berg, interview with Brian T. Atkinson, August 10, 2018.
6. Leslie Satcher, interview with Brian T. Atkinson, August 30, 2018.
7. Jennifer Warnes, interview with Brian T. Atkinson, July 12, 2018.
8. Gretchen Peters, interview with Brian T. Atkinson, June 16, 2018.
9. Will Kimbrough, interview with Brian T. Atkinson, May 13, 2019.
10. Bob DiPiero, interview with Brian T. Atkinson, June 4, 2019.
11. Darrell Scott, interview with Brian T. Atkinson, June 27, 2018.
12. Walt Wilkins, interview with Brian T. Atkinson, July 17, 2018.
13. Fred Eaglesmith, interview with Brian T. Atkinson, October 20, 2018.
14. Tom Russell, email interview with Brian T. Atkinson, February 8, 2019.

CHORUS: A LONG ROAD HOME

1. Chuck Prophet, interview with Brian T. Atkinson, August 17, 2018.
2. Charlie Worsham, interview with Brian T. Atkinson, June 19, 2018.
3. Andrew Combs, interview with Brian T. Atkinson, June 28, 2018.
4. Jonny Fritz, interview with Brian T. Atkinson, July 2, 2018.
5. Joshua Hedley, interview with Brian T. Atkinson, August 21, 2018.
6. Will Oldham, interview with Brian T. Atkinson, March 27, 2019.
7. Bill Callahan, email interview with Brian T. Atkinson, May 20, 2019.
8. Robert Ellis, interview with Brian T. Atkinson, July 19, 2019.
9. Joe Pug, interview with Brian T. Atkinson, July 29, 2019.

CODA

1. Matt Harlan, interview with Brian T. Atkinson, November 12, 2019.

A SELECTED DISCOGRAPHY FOR MICKEY NEWBURY

1. Smith, *Texas Music*, Spring 2011, 31.

A Selected Discography
for Mickey Newbury

ALBUMS

1. *Harlequin Melodies*, RCA Victor Records, 1968
2. *Looks Like Rain*, Mercury Records, 1969
3. *Frisco Mabel Joy*, Elektra Records, 1971
4. *Sings His Own*, RCA Victor Records, 1972
5. *Heaven Help the Child*, Elektra Records, 1973
6. *Live at Montezuma Hall*, Elektra Records, 1973
7. *I Came to Hear the Music*, Elektra Records, 1974
8. *Lovers*, Elektra Records, 1975
9. *Rusty Tracks*, Hickory Records, 1977
10. *His Eye Is on the Sparrow*, Hickory Records, 1978
11. *The Sailor*, Hickory Records, 1979
12. *After All These Years*, Mercury Records, 1981
13. *Sweet Memories*, Airborne Records, 1985
14. *In a New Age*, Airborne Records, 1988
15. *The Best of Mickey Newbury*, Curb Records, 1991
16. *Nights When I Am Sane*, Winter Harvest Records, 1994
17. *Lulled by the Moonlight*, Mountain Retreat Records, 1996
18. *Live in England*, Mountain Retreat Records, 1998
19. *It Might as Well Be the Moon*, Mountain Retreat Records, 1999
20. *Stories from the Silver Moon Cafe*, Mountain Retreat Records, 2000
21. *A Long Road Home*, Mountain Retreat Records, 2002
22. *Winter Winds*, Mountain Retreat Records, 2002
23. *The Mickey Newbury Collection*, Mountain Retreat Records, 2002
24. *Blue to This Day*, Mountain Retreat Records, 2003
25. *An American Trilogy*, Saint Cecilia Knows Records/Mountain Retreat Records, 2011

DOCUMENTARY ALBUMS

Mickey Newbury: An American Treasure, Ron Lyons Productions, 2004

TRIBUTE ALBUMS

Frisco Mabel Joy Revisited, Appleseed Records, 2000

In fond memory of David Olney

"Mickey Newbury [was] probably the best songwriter ever."
—John Prine[1]

Index